Jack Dempsey isn't just a man; he's a collection of contradictions stitched together with the sharp wit of Sheffield and the grit of Sydney. A Ten-Pound Pom who landed Down Under aged seven, he navigates Sydney High and UNSW like a shark in murky water – swift, driven, always hungry. But it's not enough. Back in London, with the Winter of Discontent nipping at his heels, Jack dives headlong into a life of raw, unscripted chaos.

He spots a busker at London Bridge. A flicker of desperation – or maybe rebellion – whispers in his ear. He jumps the turnstile, throws his guitar case down, and lets his fingers coax out a quiet tune. The first coin drops like salvation. Soon enough, Jack can afford milk for his tea, and a hippie bard with a devil-may-care grin is born.

Jack's memoir, *Tip Me, You Wanker!*, spins these gritty tales into a riotous guide to London's underbelly. His pen doesn't stop there. Next comes a tale of magic realism – an amorphous spirit battling the sinister Dr Mesmer – and a dark story of prison, repression, and the liberation of the mind's twisted corners. Jack lives enough lives to fill a dozen lifetimes: busker, real estate mogul, saint, sinner, and everything in between.

This latest work, *Shadows Beneath the Surface*, is a bruising exploration of fear, guilt, and the toll of ruthless governance – a deep dive into humanity's shadowy depths. Jack's life is a patchwork quilt of stories, each one more unforgettable than the last.

Shadows

Beneath the Surface

Jack Dempsey

ALKIRA
PUBLISHING

Shadows Beneath the Surface
Jack Dempsey
Copyright © 2025
Published by Alkira Publishing, Australia
ABN: 32736122056
http://www.alkirapublishing.com

ISBN: 978-1-922329-81-3

This literary dalliance is dedicated to Tamar Goldstein, my better half in life and work

'The great illusion is that I am over here and you are over there.' – Aristotle.

PROLOGUE

The Year 2003

The body was heavier than expected. He dragged her along the tunnel, and the flimsy party dress caught on the rocks and tore. It would be the perfect hiding place. The tunnel would be sealed off tomorrow. No one would find the body for years, long after everyone was dead and gone.

He stopped, breathed out slowly and wiped the dry concrete grime across his sweaty, dusty mouth. He caught a whiff of the girl's perfume and his mind went back to the party. He hadn't meant to kill her. It was a game.

He looked at the beautiful crumpled body on the ground, twisted into unholy shapes. She was the first girl he'd managed to have sex with. Well, aside from his mother. He'd quivered with life. He'd been free and powerful at last. He belonged somewhere. And it was fun. It was such fun and he'd wanted more. And after he drugged her, she was so compliant. She didn't do anything. She couldn't accuse him of anything. He sniffled as he dragged her along. He was grateful to her, grateful that her dead body accepted him, sad that it could never happen again.

If only her neck was not so small and his hands were so big. It had been so easy; it wasn't his fault her neck cracked. There must have been something wrong with her.

Yesterday, he'd been a normal private in the army, lugging equipment through these abandoned tunnels from the secret laboratories at Victoria Barracks where he worked. While the other privates found the tunnels cold and eerie, he had found them reassuring. Down here, you were protected from everything. You were safe.

But he'd had no idea that he would be needing that safety quite so soon.

Up ahead, he could see it now, the *Crucifixion of Civilisation* – a statue of a naked female Christ. At her feet was all the destruction and horror of the scientific mechanised warfare of the Great War – *The War to End All Wars*. The statue had been too controversial to erect on the memorial above ground in Hyde Park, so it was banished down here way back in the 1930s.

Looking up at it now, he couldn't see what all the fuss was about. It was a naked woman. You see naked statues all over the place. She loomed out of the murky air up ahead and gazed down on him – accusing. He shivered. She had no right. It wasn't his fault. It could happen to anyone. He deserved to have sex, didn't he? Everyone else had sex. The statue said nothing.

Last week, he had been down here in this abandoned tunnel on a work detail, shifting the gigantic clay original from the nearby East Sydney Tech where it had been crafted.

The finished bronze statue had never been cast because of the decision by the Roman Catholic Church down the road – no blasphemy near St Mary's Cathedral. The Christ image was holy and belonged to the Church, so the army had been told to get rid of it. The thought made him pause. Maybe they would send more men down here and the body would be discovered.

He looked back along the tunnel where he had come from, then down at the crumpled package of corpse, already being collected by the earth. No, discovery was unlikely; the tunnel would be sealed off tomorrow. Where else could he put the body anyway? He couldn't leave it in the park. What if someone had already seen him and then a body turned up? They would come for him for sure. No, down here was the best place, even under the gaze of that silent, accusing statue.

A lock of hair sprang into place on the girl's forehead. It was golden and innocent. And alive! A horror coursed through him, making his knees collapse. He had killed someone. A single tear trickled down his cheek, and he rubbed his nose with the back of his wrist. He arranged the tress of hair across her cheek and sobbed.

One last look, and he left her dumped there and stumbled back out of the tunnel. It would be sealed off tomorrow, and he would go back to normal life in the army and forget everything about this night. He scrambled away. At least she was safely locked away now.

But he had the strangest feeling that she would pursue him for the rest of his life, seeking her revenge.

CHAPTER 1

The Year 2030

Frank Bargen woke to the buzzing alarm and wondered what had happened to the streetlights. Total darkness. He fluttered his eyelids to make sure they were open. Yes, they were, but it was still dark. He felt a rising panic, like he was locked in a dream where all light had been extinguished.

Gradually, the room began to glow green from the giant numbers on the retro alarm clock and his unease subsided. The clock wasn't in its usual place but further away from the bed and lower down. It buzzed again.

Frank's childhood friend, Jimmy Budabuda, emerged in his mind. He was painted in the traditional splendour of *Songdance*, which Frank had seen only once before; clapsticks rattled out the rhythm to his singing in time with light soles on country.

'Welcome home,' whispered the disembodied head of

Jimmy Budabuda.

Frank smiled to himself, feeling his body relax. He had spent many happy hours with Jimmy beside the Hawkesbury River at Gunderman when he was growing up, and marvelled at all the blackfella songlines. But why was Jimmy here? He hadn't thought of him in years. Something was wrong. What was Jimmy's dreamtime doing in Woollahra?

The sounds of the gentle river came to him. The morning cicadas. The sharp eucalyptus burst into his nostrils and woke him up. Then in the darkness, Frank realised. The family had moved house yesterday, away from leafy Woollahra and back to his childhood home on the Hawkesbury. Frank's father had died a month ago, and the chance to pay no more rent was too good an opportunity. They'd moved in as soon as probate settled.

His eyes had adjusted to the dark, and he reached to kill the alarm, leaned back and fought the urge to go back to sleep. It was strange waking up in the old house. Even stranger to know that it was now his. Frank had been surprised at the inheritance. Not that there had been any other relatives, but he and his father hadn't been close.

Lieutenant Commander Bulwer Bargen was a cruel man and had spent his final couple of decades alone on this river while Frank barely saw him and tried very hard to forget his father had ever existed. But with no other heirs, the old weatherboard shack came to Frank. It would be home now.

He heard the habitual bang-bang-banging of Mercury hitting his wooden train against the wall. The familiarity calmed him, and he threw the blankets off the bed. It was crisper out here on the river than in Woollahra. Frank sucked in the revitalising freshness, but he knew it would likely be another thing for Marta to complain about.

Frank looked around at the unemptied boxes and felt safer than he'd felt for years. Marta was way out of his league. Out here at Gunderman, maybe they were finally on common ground. She didn't want to hear that they couldn't afford their old home and the lavish artsy lifestyle she had grown up with.

They had never been able to afford it. Neither could her parents, who had gone bankrupt after her father's bad business decisions. Marta took it hard. She was attending the National Art School in Darlinghurst but had to drop out. Marta's father had been an admiral, and while the good times were rolling, there was nothing he wouldn't give his wife and only daughter, meaning both women accumulated many bad spending habits. Frank's meagre wages as a bookkeeper at Victoria Barracks couldn't keep up. And once Daddy's money was gone, and then their daughter Palace got sick, the crash into poverty had sent Marta into even more destructive spending. Frank hoped that here on the Hawkesbury, there were not only fewer things to spend money on, but that the peace of the river might even smooth his wife's nerves.

After ten years of marriage, it was dawning on Frank that Marta had a burning desire for something, an unfulfilled hollow inside her, even though she had always pretended that she didn't care about anything at all. That's what he found attractive about her, that sultry indifference. Like she was always hiding something. He didn't know what it was, and he was sure she didn't either.

He pulled his dressing gown and slippers out of the still-packed suitcase and threaded his arms through the sleeves. Mercury's toy train banged against some furniture in the bedroom again, and Frank wondered if his daughter Palace was awake as well. Hard to sleep through that racket. Poor Palace, not enough to battle cancer, but she had to put up with her thoughtless, manic brother in the same bedroom too.

The twins were like fire and ice. Mercury was completely self-obsessed and had to have everything right now. *A bit like his mother*, thought Frank. While Palace was quiet and observant and would look at you with those big eyes that seemed to know the deepest parts of your soul.

Frank pulled on his slippers and started down the short hallway. The train crashed again. Why hadn't Mercury grown out of his self-obsession by now? He had Attention Deficit Disorder. Did that mean he'd be crashing toy trains for the rest of his life? He was ten years old, for God's sake. Maybe he was retarded as well as manic.

'Mercs! Stop!'

There was a sudden silence. The old house creaked in the wind. Peace.

Then, as if Mercury realised he'd got somebody's attention, the banging started up again.

Enough! Frank marched to the kids' room. The toll their son had put them through over the years with his mania; Frank wondered how he and Marta would cope if Mercury developed some second condition.

'Mercury, quiet!'

The banging stopped again. Frank went to the kids' bedroom and turned on the light. Mercury was sitting on the floor under the table, innocent. He frowned, sensing his father's disapproval, and started up shoving his little wooden train backwards and forwards again, frantically trying to crash it through the wall.

Palace slept peacefully. She had her oxygen pipe over her nose and was the picture of serenity. Her body gently rose and fell under her favourite cotton blanket, made by Moroccan Berbers with pom-poms lined up at both ends, golden and brown. Frank held his finger to his lips and pointed to Palace. Mercury looked over at Palace, seemed satisfied with the idea that he should be quiet and let go of the toy train. He slumped down deliberately and looked around the room for something else to soak up that burning inquisitiveness.

'Come and help me make some coffee for your mother.'

Mercury jumped up and banged his head on the table, and crayons spilled all over the floor. He rubbed his head and wondered how to react. Frank watched to see whether Mercury would be angry, his usual response to pain, but he rubbed his head and gave a silly grin. Frank smiled with relief. They held hands and padded off to the kitchen together.

Frank banged his toes on several bits of furniture on the journey to the kitchen. He was surprised how much of the layout of the house he'd forgotten. In the kitchen, Frank turned to look at Mercury as if he was going to show him a big secret. He pointed to the coffee machine in the corner.

'Coffee!' Frank spoke sharp and loud, and the machine sprang to life, automatically starting to grind the beans.

Mercury jumped with delight. He rushed over and held his hands towards the machine in reverence.

'Coffee!' Mercury yelled, and the grinding stopped. He squealed with joy. 'Coffee, coffee.' The machine started up again and stopped again.

'Okay, Mercs, one more time.'

Mercury steadied himself in front of the machine, reverently looked at it and said the magic word once again, 'Coffee.' The grinding started up again. Mercury watched with infinite curiosity. Frank smiled; a new toy for his son.

He looked out the window down to the still, dark river, and a compelling weariness came over him. He needed some quiet away from Mercury for a few moments, and he knew how to get it. Look at something still; take Mercury's attention into stillness and he would run a mile. Sure enough, Mercury glanced at the river, shuddered and ran back to his train in the bedroom. The banging started up again. Surely, it would wake Marta up. Frank needed a few more minutes of quiet before she got up and started her demands.

The first dim light was glancing off the leaves across the other bank and the shape of the old derelict wharf loomed out of the darkness. The flowing river brought back more memories of Jimmy Budabuda – this time, the two of them jumping from the wharf into the cloudy water. They'd see who could hold their breath the longest – it was always Jimmy.

'Coffee!' yelled Marta from the bedroom. Her Highness was waiting.

Frank snapped out of his musings. Time to start the day.

'Coffee, coffee, tea, tea,' mocked Mercury from the bedroom. Frank smiled at Mercury's new game. He knew his son was going to love it here by the river as much as he had as a kid.

~

Marta's slippers padded through the hallway, and Frank was glad he had the coffee underway. Maybe if her first morning went well, she'd find something favourable about the house.

'So, this is where you grew up? Bit of a shack. Where's the coffee?'

The house was weatherboard and was up on high stilts to avoid the floods. Everything needed a coat of paint, but the place was still basically sound. Twenty worn-looking wooden steps took you high above the waters of the Hawkesbury to the front door. A swarm of tiny and stingless native bees always clustered around near the door. Inside, the sturdy Australian hardwood floorboards gave an air of stability despite the shabby and neglected appearance of the house. Each room was a wildly different colour, the result of Frank's father's dabbling in later life.

Frank spun round to Marta, dismayed. She stood there in that flesh-coloured nightie, arms crossed against the cold, just under her breasts.

Don't take the bait.

'Coffee's coming.' He gave her a smile and couldn't help glancing at her nipples; they were erect and begging for attention. She folded her arms a little higher to cover them and leaned a shoulder against the wall. Marta put out tough sex when she felt unsure. She looked out the window and yawned, flashing the large canines that made her look a little vampirish. She'd always been resentful that her teeth had put an end to her modelling career.

'I guess you won't like it much at first, but at least it's ours. No rent to pay, and that means we can get back on track and then start fixing up the house. We can repaint it if you want.'

Marta looked around at all the colours, and she seemed to think that it had been inhabited by a madman. She shrugged. She pushed herself off the wall and closed her mouth over her teeth. There were little bulges underneath her upper canines. Her ample lips pouted. 'I've never paid rent.'

You've never had a job!

He put the coffee cup on the bright yellow Laminex benchtop. That hadn't changed since the 1960s.

'Well, you'll only have to get used to slumming it for a little while.'

She shrugged again.

They'd first met at the officers' ball back in '20, just before the Covid lockdown. She was a swinging eastern suburbs socialite, all glitter and smiles and aiming for a modelling career. But comments about her teeth had given her such a complex that she gave up in resentment and lived off her parents instead, carried along in life by party after party. Frank had sensed a vulnerability and was swept away. He couldn't figure out why she wanted him, but she did, and she always got what she wanted. Ten years later, her interest was waning. Frank hadn't lived up to her expectations; she'd been very vocal about that. Frank tried to not mind about her luxurious tastes and whining about having to leave Woollahra; after all, she'd been an only child, spoilt and needing to be saved from herself. She was alluring.

She sat on the rickety high stool and looked out at the river and sipped from her cup.

'Coffee's not bad though, I guess.'

Palace stood at the door of the kitchen, all bald head and big, dark-rimmed, dreamy eyes. She went to her mother, who guided her away and towards Frank.

Palace came to Frank and looked up into his eyes with a mournfulness that said, *Okay, you're second best after Mum.* They hugged.

Mercury's wooden train banged away in the bedroom. Marta winced. 'Shut up, Mercury,' she yelled.

Mercury's obedience to his mother was total. Silence descended, and a faint morning breeze rustled the leaves outside.

Frank looked at Marta meaningfully.

'What?'

Frank nodded towards Palace, and thankfully, she got the message.

'Oh, come on, Palace, let me give you a cuddle.'

They hugged, Marta still holding her coffee. She looked at Frank and sighed. 'This is going to be great, this godforsaken shack.' She swung her arms into the air in mock exhilaration and spilled her coffee across the kitchen wall. She slumped on the chair and put her hand to her head. Palace put her hand around her mother's shoulders. Frank felt relieved and went across to the sink to get a cloth to clean up the coffee. Marta's pride kicked in and she composed herself and gave Palace another slight thank-you hug.

'Go on then,' she said to Frank. 'Off you go to work. I'll stay here and keep guard over your little hut.'

~

Frank started up the car, still smarting from Marta's sarcasm, but excited about the long drive to work through the bush. He'd always liked morning time to himself, time to think. Back in Woollahra, it only took him twenty minutes between the chaos at home and the boredom and tension at work.

But today he scooted the half hour along the river to Wisemans Ferry. There was a queue at the ferry. Only the smaller punt was operational. *Maintenance*, said the sign. When Frank pulled up, the ferry had cast off with its cargo of twelve cars for the four-minute journey across the river.

That'll add fifteen minutes. Great – he would be late. What a start to his new life in the country. He pulled up in the queue on the wharf and opened the car door. The laughing sound of the kookaburras flooded his ears. The tall eucalypts swayed in the morning twilight breeze, and the cable pulling the punt away splashed invisibly in the dark river. The lights on the gradually receding punt reflected and shimmered.

He resigned himself to the wait for its return. There was a peacefulness here.

He stretched his arms, then got back into the warmth of the car. Eighty-five kilometres to Paddington. Had he really thought this through? A two-hour drive every morning and then back again. It had seemed doable when they made the decision, but now that he was here, the long drive was daunting. He was barely even awake. What if he had an accident in this state? What if he died? How would Marta cope without him? How much superannuation did they have? A familiar feeling of creeping resentment, directed towards her, rose in his mind. A feeling he had to suppress often. He shook his head. Don't be silly. He'd be fine. Even though he was in the army, his bookkeeping job was the safest in the world, well away from any fighting. This relocation was a good move. They needed to settle in, that's all.

At last, the returning punt thumped into the wharf and Frank drove onboard. For the life of him, he didn't know why they hadn't built a bridge over the damn river yet. It was only four hundred metres. He bet they were keeping it quaint for the tourists. He touched the screen for the radio.

> *Good morning, it's seven o'clock on this clear day in Sydney, 28 June, 2030. This is the ABC news brought to you by McDonald's Cornflakes, the best flakes to wake to.*

Frank had never been interested in the news. It was Marta who kept changing the station to ABC. He reached out to change the station to find some light classics, but a news item caught his interest.

The unrest continued in Canberra last night as new Prime Minister Damien Hardcastle, only one week after getting the top job, announced strict new measures against free association in public — his so-called Five-five Safety rule.

Not another one! Seemed like there was a new law every month lately. Frank's bone-dry tedium about politics lifted a little. He couldn't wait to hear what this joke of a rule involved. The punt bumped into the bank of the river. He drove off and onto the concrete slab of the wharf.

Any more than five people within five metres of each other will be guilty of a breach of public order and liable for arrest.

Frank grimaced. That was a bit harsh, even for Hardcastle. Still, nobody could do anything about it. Politics was for the politicians.

Stay clear of other people, the new government warned, for your own good. This is an emergency as serious as Covid was early last decade.

The transgender opposition leader from the LibLab Party shouted from their soapbox outside Parliament.

This new restrictive law from the One Border Party is a joke. They've been separating us from each other since Covid. Their shiny new PM is trying to get in good with their paranoid supporter base. This government won't last until Christmas and they know it. As for their new Minister for Law and Order, Mavis Nations, they'll be gone even before then. Only the LibLab Party can ensure stability in society. Safety, equality and sustainability are what we want. Hardcastle is a mad dog, and Nations is his bitch.

Frank felt a coldness running down his back. This would mean wholesale changes at work. Border Force had finally gotten their man in the top job, and Frank's commanding officer, Major Mike Torus, would be strutting about like a little Napoleon. Frank couldn't bear to think about it. He changed the station to some easy listening and tried to settle in for a moderately agreeable drive to work. But it was nagging him. How would he keep away from Torus? It was going to be a nightmare.

~

In the corridor, on the way to his office, Frank saw Kain Webber leaning against the wall, keeping back and out of the way of the orderlies buzzing about. Definitely more than usual. Something was going on.

Webber was the head of the genetics department of Border Force Bio at Victoria Barracks and had been here forever. He had a thick shock of frizzy black hair and glasses that made his eyes look double size. He saw Frank and pushed himself off the wall and swayed a little on his big, unsteady feet.

'Hey, Frank.' He blinked with his soft, innocent eyes.

'Hey, Webs, what's going on?'

'We can't go in there yet.'

Frank groaned. 'What happened?'

'There's been a spill. Something with the hydrogen.'

Frank's neck itched. 'Not again. Can't you guys keep it together?'

Webber dropped his head. 'Wasn't me. I'm a scientist, not a housekeeper.'

That was for sure. He was pretty hopeless at keeping things in order. Frank had seen his workplace. There'd been three incidents of dangerous animals escaping already this year. Frank saw Webber's embarrassment and softened, slapped him on the shoulder and realised he was happy to be at work.

'Never mind. We'll have to wait.' He slumped back against the wall next to Webber.

'Good about Hardcastle, huh?' said Webber. He was testing the waters. Webber was the last person to be interested in politics, but he was always trying to keep in good with the people they worked with, and politics was the big deal here. Webber wouldn't know whether Hardcastle getting the top job would be welcomed or not, even though he worked in the middle of the most rabid elements of Border Force. He couldn't figure politics out. 'I think they'll like it around here.' Webber nodded to himself, more than half convinced.

Frank didn't care much for politics either, but he could figure it out. It felt as prearranged as the football; the puppet masters were remote and invisible. Hardcastle's promotion would be more than welcomed. It would be revered as the second coming, especially by Torus.

'Maybe we'll get more research money,' Webber muttered again.

'Maybe you will.' Thankfully, Frank's job didn't require constantly asking for grants. Bookkeeping was eternal. He might not be paid a lot, but he'd always have work.

'Hey, Frank, hey, Webs.' It was the voice of Lieutenant

Grantham from Software.

'Hey, Granny,' they both said in unison. Grantham was looking sharp and neat as a pin as usual. He was a dapper dresser and even made the Border Force uniform look like it belonged on a catwalk. He straightened his tie.

'When are we getting out of here?' asked Frank. Granny shrugged, then pulled on his shirtsleeves to straighten them. 'I've got to get into my office before Torus shows up.'

Frank wanted to say Torus was insufferable, a pig of a man. Barely human at all. But you never knew where the ears were in Border Force.

Granny picked an imaginary speck of dirt off his sleeve and stroked the back of his hair. He squinted sympathetically at Frank.

'Did you hear about my spider?' interrupted Webber.

Frank and Granny exchanged a look. *Typical Webber, always wanting to show you his latest crazy invention.*

Sharp footsteps pounded along the corridor. 'Great day, great day,' boomed the voice of Major Mike Torus.

And any hope that the day would improve was gone.

CHAPTER 2

Frank groaned. Too late to escape. They all watched their boss march down the corridor towards them, legs apart, chest out, shoulders looking wider than usual. Did Torus realise that this only made him look even shorter than he was?

He slapped Frank on the back hard enough to make him lurch forwards and fall into Webber. Frank righted himself and wondered how much he should pretend to be more enthusiastic about Border Force's sudden domination. He was working out the precise required enthusiasm while still keeping a fragment of his own thoughts intact. They had finally got their man into power, despite the protests in Canberra. Torus nodded at Lieutenant Grantham and looked him up and down.

'Hi, Granny, looking pretty. As usual.'

Granny said nothing. Frank had always admired his friend's usual devil-may-care attitude, but Torus intimidated even Granny.

Torus smirked. 'Now we can start protecting the

population properly,' he declared, 'against all manner of perversions and disorderly conduct.'

Granny's silence spoke volumes. He was often the first to realise the mood of any moment and when it was best to shut up. Suddenly, society had fundamentally changed and he would need to act differently towards authority. This realisation was dawning on Frank as well. Torus was going to be more than gloating. A clarity was forming in Frank's mind, and the penny dropped that the country had entered a severe stage of government.

Did he care? Suddenly, he did. His body chilled, and he felt a sympathy for Granny. Frank realised he knew plenty about politics and it was clear the puppet masters, who were usually remote and invisible, would now materialise out of the fog. For an instant, the world of politics had come into sharp focus. The One Border Party was running the parliament, and their masters Border Force had finally taken over the country. And they could do what they wanted. And that's all they had ever wanted. Raw power. That's all. And they would exercise it.

Torus's eyes shone. 'We must have order. Without order there is chaos.' His index finger went skywards. 'And with chaos we have nakedness, our secrets exposed, our clothes stripped away, our weaknesses available to be exploited.' He poked Webber in the chest several times as if Webber needed more convincing than the others. 'Without order we live in terror.'

Frank wondered how long they would have to listen to sermons like this, but gave his boss a weak smile. 'Yeah, great.' Torus squinted and Frank could practically hear the yelling in Torus's head.

They weren't being enthusiastic enough. But what was

the right level of fawning response? He looked at the others. Webber was blinking like a nervous animal led to slaughter, and Granny had turned to steel. They were no help. The next few days were definitely going to require some mental gymnastics from all of them.

Torus increased the strength of his finger into Frank's chest. 'You watch, Frank, things are gonna change round here and in the whole country. At last, this is our time.' Torus's shining, bald head seemed to get shinier.

Webber twitched his nose and swayed from side to side. 'Yeah, yeah.'

He too could never quite get the right amount of suck-up to Torus, so he generally overdid it. Webber suddenly realised that he wasn't getting it right, and his chin began a slow sink into his left shoulder. Frank felt sorry for him, for all of them.

Torus sneered at Webber as if a waiter had brought in a cold dinner. 'Those weird animals of yours are finally going to become useful in the service of the country. That's what we pay you for, Webber. What's the point of that mixed-up spider anyway? What is it, half this and half that?'

Webber slowly pulled his chin up from his left shoulder. Frank had seen this before. Webber was a completely passive individual until someone criticised his work. Mocking his creations was perilous territory. Webber stood up to his full height.

'It's a hybrid spider connecting the *Latrodectus hasselti* or garden variety redback spider with the *Atrax robustus* or garden variety funnel-web spider, two of the deadliest in Australia. Anyone with a brain would know that. Naturally, we've called it a funnelback.'

Granny's eyebrows went up in surprise, and he slid a low glance to Frank, who was just as astounded.

Wow, that reply was way more aggressive than Frank had ever seen from Webber. He was really missing the mark on his deference to the new regime. Torus was going to give him hell for that kind of insubordination.

But Torus's eyes widened, and he smiled. He looked like he'd decided to be amused. He really was having a great day.

Webber's voice hissed like a snake. 'It can kill inside a second. It could kill a horse immediately.'

Frank wondered how he knew that.

Torus seemed even more amused now and looked at Frank as if to say, *Can you believe this guy?*

Webber's voice was a whisper. 'You stole my dog.'

Torus shuddered and his hands clinched into fists, his amusement dropping away like a heavy black curtain pulled across a comedy stage. That's it, the show's over.

Frank put his hand on Webber's shoulder, silently begging him to calm down. Torus was heaving now and mute, as though waiting for his thoughts to catch up before he spoke. Webber was in serious trouble if he continued.

'Hardcastle, huh?' Frank blurted out. It was all he could think of as a distraction.

Torus smiled, suddenly finding Frank more interesting than Webber. 'Yes, yes. Great day.'

'Yeah,' said Frank. 'Great day, yeah.'

Torus banged Webber on the back as if he expected a good thump would increase Webber's enthusiasm. Webber's weak feet lost their footing, and he clutched at Frank. Torus grunted satisfaction as he watched his two underlings struggle to regain their balance. He laughed overdramatically and turned to Grantham, whom he poked in the chest.

'You!' said Torus, as if that was enough of a threat. Grantham was again unmoved except for the smallest sneer on his lip, unnoticed by Torus, who turned and marched down the corridor. Was he almost whistling?

Webber was shaking, and Frank let go of him.

A giant Alsatian, big as a pony, came bounding along the corridor. Volf. The dog leapt up onto Frank, pushed him against the wall, licked his face, then rolled onto the floor on his back. Webber smiled, and Frank bent down to rub the dog's belly.

'Don't know why he likes you so much,' said Webber. 'It was *me* who made him.'

At the sound of the dog, Torus spun on his heel and stalked back towards them. 'Volf, come!'

Webber cringed, and Frank knew what he was thinking – his beautiful creation stolen. The dog was the only thing Torus had any affection for, probably because he could torture it at will and Volf could never fight back. When Torus saw weakness, he salivated more than any dog, natural or genetically amended.

Frank watched the dog jump up on Torus, licking his face like his life depended on it. Torus lapped up the greeting for a moment and then grabbed Volf by the neck and squeezed, looking back at Webber for his reaction. The dog squealed but didn't retaliate. Any normal dog would bite his hand off, but Volf had been genetically bred to protect his master, no matter what. He took the violence like it was a generous pat. It was sickening.

Torus looked at Frank and Webber to see if they were impressed by his show of power, juddering the dog's neck. He suddenly let go, and Volf shook his head and half held a paw out to Frank. Torus grunted, and the dog bounded down the corridor into Torus's office. You won't be safe in there, thought Frank, but if you keep him occupied, maybe *we* will be.

Frank looked into the laboratory, wondering how long they were going to be out here in the corridor. A guy in a PPE hazmat suit with mop and bucket came out with a thumbs-up sign.

'All clear.'

Thank God. Both he and Webber were practically tripping over each other to get inside.

'Not today, Frank,' panted Torus, his face red from the exertion of his performance with Volf. 'I want you in the bunker. Be there in fifteen minutes.'

Frank's face fell. 'You can't order me down there, not without written notice.'

'This facility is now under the direct authority of the One Border Party. You'll do exactly as I tell you.'

He then stepped towards Grantham, and the two men looked at each other a moment before Torus poked Grantham's chest. 'And I want you down there as well.'

Grantham barely moved except for a slight quivering in his hands, but Frank could feel his rage beneath the surface. Violence was second nature for Torus.

Frank suddenly had the depressing feeling that all humanity was savage. Some of us repress it for a while. Torus stalked off, probably to do some more dog tormenting. Rip the poor creature's ears off. Grantham abruptly turned and marched off in the opposite direction. Frank wanted to say at least they'd be working together, but Granny didn't want to hear anything. Maybe Grantham hated Torus even more than Frank did.

Webber was still shaking when he slumped into a chair, muttering to himself. 'One day, one day.'

Frank made a move to go back to his office.

Webber jumped up. 'Frank, I was going to tell you about the spider.'

Frank groaned.

'We've been cross-breeding this spider, just at the experimental stage, but it's looking good, the funnelback. It's got a ferocious appetite for biting, which can be turned on and off by the application of some ointment.' Webber moved from one foot to the other.

Frank could never tell if his feet hurt or if he was excited. 'Listen, Webs …'

'A single bite causes immediate death in a human.' Webber did a quick peek out the door towards where Torus had gone. His eyes were now dancing with delight, as if this was his proudest creation.

'Look, Webs, I've got to go upstairs and get some stuff done, then get down to the bunker.'

'Sorry, it's just …' Webber looked contrite. 'How's things in the bunker these days anyway?'

'Apparently, they're monitoring some experimental mines down there that have been put underground on Narus – you know, where the refugees are.'

Webber flinched.

'The top brass think some of those refugees are plants and they're getting ready for a takeover of the island. If they try it, we want to be ready for them.'

Webber grunted and shivered.

Frank smiled at Webber's innocence. 'We can blow up the mines from here.'

Webber was afraid of all that noise and chaos. Just destruction, no sophistication, no finesse. Sound and fury.

The lift opened to take Frank to the lower levels, down to the bunker. It was too late to go back to his office.

'Have fun with the monsters,' he said as the lift door closed.

'Yeah, sure. Why don't you come and have a look at the spider when you've finished down there? It's a beauty.'

'No worries. I will, mate.'

CHAPTER 3

Hassan despaired at the thought of another long day. His third without food. He sat by the chainmail fence on this never-ending morning in the Pacific heat and tried to remember his sister Aleema's face. He was becoming weak and delirious from lack of food.

It had been six years since leaving Afghanistan. First to Jakarta and a three-year detention in a United Nations centre, where he learnt that the wait for an Australian visa was twelve years. He reeled at the memory. Twelve years! That was the first time he'd regretted fleeing Afghanistan.

His delirium took his thoughts back to Afghanistan and Friday prayers, rising up from the carpet. Prayers over, now it was time for the boys' meeting with Mori. He took one last look at the carpet, his favourite, where little aeroplanes had been woven into the fabric by his uncle, to warn children to look out for Russian bombers. There were also Taliban fighters woven in as well, fighting the Russians. The Taliban were their friends then, when his uncle was a boy. Hassan loved the after-prayers meeting with the other boys and Mori, the pious policeman.

'Never forget the madness of the Taliban,' Mori was always saying. 'They were created by the Americans to fight the Russians, but now the mullahs crush Hazaras into their narrow thinking. The Taliban have been beaten back once, and they will be again.'

The Taliban had always been in charge since Hassan could remember, but if Mori said they could be overthrown, it must be true.

After Hassan had fled Afghanistan, in Jakarta, he had heard about Christmas Island, where you were fed and could shower. It was worth the chance. He handed over all the small coins he had earned in three years and boarded the smuggler's boat with his hope renewed, like he'd felt when he'd boarded that first bus for Pakistan.

Every week after prayers, Hassan and the boys had collected in the decrepit hall to play games and learn of Mohammad (peace be upon him) and the teachings of the prophet. This day Hassan would get Mori's answer to his question – what to do with the money Hassan's cousin had sent from Australia. His cousin had encouraged Hassan to make the journey. There was enough money for a fake passport and a bus ticket to the Pakistan border. Hassan could work in Australia and send money to his mother and sister. They would be happy again. The boys gathered on their carpets as Mori spoke.

'Today, we have a special occasion. The cousin of young Hassan has sent money from Australia. Hassan is now sixteen and the head of his family, so it is his decision how to spend this money.' Mori looked over at Hassan. 'Will he spend it on good services, on food for the poor? Or will he abandon his family and go to Australia?'

Hassan was jolted back to his present predicament. A refugee in Narus. His fingers clutched tightly at the chainmail fence for support. How long could he last on this hunger strike?

Abandon his family? Hassan felt himself grow hot with the memory of Mori's reprimand. It had been wrong to try to go to Australia.

On the third dawn out of Java, on the way to Christmas Island, the boat's engine had stopped, and the pumps became silent. The old, doomed fishing boat rotated helplessly in the ocean. Everyone realised they were sinking, and the boat would not last until sunset. At first, the people had knelt to pray for salvation, then as the afternoon wore on and the sea leaked in, they crowded towards the back of the boat and awaited their fate.

Hassan's mind again went back to Friday prayers in Afghanistan.

'Ha!' Al Asag's voice had sneered from the back of the prayer room. 'That's piety. Let Hassan do what he likes with his money.'

Hassan gripped the chainmail fence and smiled at the memory.

Al Asag was always sneering at authority, and Hassan was drawn to his rebelliousness. Al Asag was tall and the leader of a group of boys whom he treated with kindness. They had fun, and Hassan thought Al Asag was the most intelligent person he had ever known, even more than Mori. Mori also knew this and let the jibe go. Al Asag's scorn was driven by compassion and not hatred. Hassan was comforted by Al Asag's words.

On the way home, they walked in silence.

'They are all hypocrites,' said Al Asag. 'All of them. They

are all looking for power, even Mori.'

Hassan's eyes lowered. He really wasn't prepared to think of Mori as a power seeker.

'Even though he's not as bad as the rest,' the rebel anarchist quickly added. He put a hand around Hassan's shoulder.

Hassan wanted to tell Al Asag about his plans to go to Australia and work hard and send money back to his mother and sister but was worried that his friend would scorn him.

Suddenly, a searing pain shot through Hassan's face, and dizziness surrounded him. He would have fallen if Al Asag hadn't been holding him. A flying rock had scudded through the air and blasted into Hassan's cheek.

'Scurvy Hazara,' yelled a yellow-banded boy, keeping a cagey distance, surrounded by a little gang. Hassan's head cleared, and he recognised Nafi, his tormentor. But Al Asag pulled Hassan back, picked up the rock, weighed it in his hand and took time with his aim. The stone flew gracefully through the sky, hypnotising everyone as they watched. It hit Nafi square on the face, and the boy collapsed to the ground. His friends fled.

'Cowards,' yelled Al Asag. He turned to Hassan. 'Even Hazaras like you are people.' Hassan looked up at Al Asag in gratitude, not deserving his protection. He was still dizzy from the rock and reeled about, stumbling along. He fell into the dirt and took a mouthful of dust. The voice of the Jinni resounded in Hassan's head. Go to Australia; they will welcome you. You must cross into Pakistan. From there, you will travel overland and board a boat to Australia. Hassan wilted at the thought of leaving everything – his mother, his sister, Mori, Al Asag. The Jinni spoke again. *Your cousin has successfully made the journey to Australia. He will help you.*

He was suddenly sitting in a café chair with a glass

of water.

Al Asag looked concerned. 'You fainted.' Hassan drank water. 'What will you do with your cousin's money?'

Hassan never understood why Nafi always harassed him. He wanted to approach him, to make peace with him. If he went to Australia, he could send money back to Nafi's family as well. That would make him happy.

Hassan rubbed his head. 'I saw a Jinni in my dream. It was large with golden earrings and a red Hazara scarf. It told me to buy false papers and go to Australia.' He wobbled to his feet. 'I must go and tell my mother.'

Al Asag raised an eyebrow. 'You are crazy.' He smiled. 'A Hazara will never make it even as far as Pakistan.'

'No, I have heard there are Azras in Pakistan.' Hassan's mind calmed. 'I saw a vision. The Jinni told me.'

'Ha! Jinni! You are as mad as the mullahs!' Al Asag marched off, then looked back, shaking his head. He pointed eastwards towards Pakistan. 'It's a long and dangerous journey.'

They walked past the killing post, where the latest stoning had occurred. A bloodied corpse was slumped there, with birds pecking at the remains. The crime was unknown to Hassan, but the carcass wore the red scarf of the Hazara. That could be him one day if Nafi got his way.

Suddenly, he understood Nafi. It was brutal in its simplicity. *Nafi was told to hate Hazaras, and he did what he was told. He would kill me because of that. Australia would be better.*

It was all Hassan could do to hold himself up against the detention centre fence. Images skittered through his mind. He remembered his sister's sad face when he left. The long, despairing wait in Java, the joyful news of the smuggler's boat able to take them to Christmas Island. Then the terrifying water on the sinking boat lapping at his knees. He would drown at sea and never see his family again.

Carried across the still waters came the sound of a motor boat. One or two exhausted refugees craned to see. It pulled up alongside, and the smuggler's captain caught the thrown rope and pulled the small craft to the side of the sinking fishing boat. The captain leapt across onto the motorboat, and it pulled away. He pointed southwards towards Australia. Most of the indolent passengers had hardly registered his departure. The news that the boat's captain had abandoned them was whispered around the deck and they gradually rose and watched the receding motorboat. They crowded to one side of the boat, which listed under the weight.

The terror of drowning made his mind shoot back to the present on Narus Island. He grabbed the chainmail fence and shook it. How was his family coping with the Taliban? They may be dead by now. He stared out into the frightening sea and fell to the solid ground, comforted by the solidity.

'Hassan, my friend, good morning.' It was the voice of Gaspar, the cheerful giant from Iran.

Easy for you to be merry, thought Hassan. You've only been here a year. Hassan struggled to his feet.

'God willing, we will be released from this waiting Jahannam soon. Truly, the Quran is right that there is Hell on earth.' He gave Hassan a hearty slap on the back.

Hassan fell forward into the fence with the force of the blow but couldn't resist a smile. He had learnt the meaning of irony from this dangerous school inside the barbed wire, but he had no energy to speak. He wiped his face with the blood red scarf he'd been given by the Hazara hunger striker in Jakarta before he died. He had promised to take the scarf to freedom in Australia, but now that pledge seemed a lifetime ago. He and the scarf would surely end up in the dusty ground of Narus.

At least the scarf had survived the shipwreck. Hassan shivered at the memory as his mind drifted back again to the last moments of the decrepit, sinking fishing boat six years ago.

'Ha! Ha!' Hassan pointed at the horizon to a big, strong, steel boat. Three hundred refugees yelled and waved.

'The Australian Navy!' The deck was a sea of waving, yelling refugees. They scrambled to one side of the boat. Hassan was filled with euphoria and then just as quickly with horror as the boat, already laden with water, creaked and rolled and tipped its deck deep under the surface. Hassan lost his footing and surged across the deck. The boat scooped up more water, too much water, cascading across the deck. It lurched back upright, but the weight of the gushing water pulled it too far over to the other side. Hassan scrambled to his feet and floundered along in the onrush. Down under the sea went the other side of the boat, but this time it did not right itself. The boat keeled over and Hassan slid into the boiling foam.

He swallowed a mouthful and his lungs stung like Jahannam. His arms grabbed onto a piece of flotsam. He heard the screams of three hundred sufferers tipped into the cruel waters, scrambling for anything to hold on to. He clutched his piece of floating salvation. The Jinni came to him and smiled. He felt the salvation and peace of his coming death. After an age, an arm pulled him up from the sea.

'C'mon, mate, c'mon,' was all he heard.

Back on Narus, Hassan's hands gripped the fence and throbbed. Fewer than a hundred people had survived. He felt Gaspar's hand on his shoulder and released his grip on the fence.

He looked up. Gaspar's wife Jazmin appeared from the hut with Minu, their two-year-old. Jazmin smiled; it amazed Hassan how she could still be beautiful in this wretched place. She had no veil, her modesty preserved by her actions, not her coverings.

Minu dragged behind her a fluffy rabbit with one ear. She had the biggest brown eyes. Perhaps his sister Aleema had brown eyes like that. Oh, how he missed his sister. How cruel the world was. He should never have gotten on that bus and left Afghanistan. The rabbit fell from Minu's grip into the dust. A tear came to his eye.

He had failed his family. If only he could rip these fences away. He should have been in Australia by now, working and sending money home. Instead, he was wasting away. The red scarf his only strength. Hassan felt no ground beneath his feet and began to shake in fear.

Jazmin came towards him. 'Are you thinking about that boat again? Let it fade, Hassan, let it fade. It will always be with you, it is part of you now, but let it fade away. You must have hope here. That's all we have. There are bigger things to worry about just now. The showers have stopped working.'

The giant Gaspar picked up his tiny daughter out of the dust and waved her gently around. Jazmin brought out some breakfast in the takeaway containers and began to eat.

Hassan looked at the food. He was not made for the endurance of a hunger strike. He had seen hunger strikers in Java, the wracking pain, despair and weakness when the body starts to eat itself. Hassan saw that three days was his limit. Jazmin offered him food, and he snatched at it greedily, all the while self-disgusted at his weakness.

'Eat,' said Gaspar. 'Surely, it is Allah's will.'

Nobody wants me to go to Australia except the Jinni. Hassan felt a crushing loneliness. It will be done, he thought. For my mother, for my cousin, for the proud Azras, descendants of Genghis. The great Khan would never have allowed the persecutions by the Taliban.

Jazmin looked at her husband. Her voice was flat and cold. 'God has abandoned him.' She stood up. 'Allah has left this place. That's why I will no longer wear coverings. It is not the tradition on this island, in this camp. When we get out of here, I will become a Muslim woman again, but in this place, no. It defiles.'

Hassan looked at Gaspar, whose eyes dimmed a little. He slowed in his swaying of Minu, not sure what to do. Hassan had seen Gaspar diminish bit by bit every time his wife spoke harshly. But he recovered quickly. He held Minu up to the sky to make her laugh, and they all smiled in relief as she giggled.

The food strengthened Hassan. His fingers curled into the chainmail fence again. Everyone at home was surely dead by now after nearly ten years. Ten years – almost half his life. What was he doing? What *could* he do? He shook the fence. It gave him strength. He shook more. And more.

'Stop,' said Gaspar. 'The guards.' But Hassan was gaining strength and his anger felt like it could defeat any foe, deliver any wish. He shook and shook the chainmail fence. He would shake it down and pull this world apart.

CHAPTER 4

The industrial lift shuddered open, and Frank stepped into the control room. It was white and quiet, just a few techos hunched in front of monitors, fingers tapping keyboards and swiping screens, looking busy, with the occasional bit of football talk flying across the room. He looked around and wondered what he was supposed to be doing down here. It had been months since he'd been in the bunker. They'd added a few more bits of machinery and electronic gadgets, and there was a smell of burnt plastic and a hum of transformers in the air. That was new, but it hadn't improved the chill of the place. Frank shivered.

What did all this stuff do? He saw Torus over in the corner, muscling in for a look at Granny's monitor. He was almost pushing him off his chair, Torus at it again. One look at the room and Frank wanted to get back upstairs to his quiet, comfortable life in Accounts, where every little number had its proper place, every little cell in his spreadsheet had an assigned purpose, and Frank also had an assigned purpose. It was neat up there. Even though the creeping AI accounting algorithms were getting closer to replacing him.

Torus had obviously heard Frank come out of the lift because, without looking, he pointed to a chair, desk and monitor on the far side of the room.

Huh? What did it matter where he sat? All the workstations were the same. He knew he should do just as he was told, but he didn't see why he couldn't take the seat next to Grantham.

'Hey Granny,' said Frank. Granny looked up, surprised, looking like he'd woken from a deep sulk, and glad to have been jolted out of his own thoughts. Frank hadn't got his equilibrium back after his encounter with Torus upstairs, and here was Torus continuing the intimidation. Granny shot a glance at Torus and raised a quizzical eyebrow at Frank. Disobedience would have serious consequences. Frank smiled, keen to help get his friend out of his funk. Frank slid into the chair next to Granny. Granny smirked. They were on the same page.

'What's this all about?' said Frank.

Torus turned around and gave Frank a thunderous look. His hands started to flex like he was about to choke something, and he took a step towards Frank. Just one step, elbows out wide, feet spread. He pointed to the desk again on the far side of the room.

'*I said, sit there!*' Frank was about to object, but the look of malevolence on Torus's face changed his mind.

'Okay, okay.' Frank and Granny exchanged a look – *mad bloody Torus!* The sooner he got this over with, whatever it was, the better.

He trudged over to the other workstation and stopped next to the chair. It was bigger and more comfortable than the other chairs in the room, some kind of driving seat, as if sitting there would be a long job. Frank felt his whole day slipping away. Bloody jocks down here, fighting wars, causing mayhem. They were all deranged, especially Torus.

He looked at the monitor and saw a chainmail fence that stretched away into the far distance. It was sunny and dusty, probably out in the Pacific somewhere if the feed was live, allowing for the time zone. He looked around the room. A dozen people were tapping away. Now what?

He wondered if Torus had permission to drag him down here. Torus wasn't supposed to have absolute control of everyone's work life, surely. Maybe it had something to do with the new government. The facility, and especially Torus, had sparked up since the news. Frank took a closer look at the monitor and realised that he was looking at some kind of outdoor jail. His curiosity overcame his irritation for a moment.

'Is that Narus?' Frank definitely did not want to have anything to do with sitting down in that chair.

'Sit down, Lieutenant Bargen.' Torus's voice halted the small patter of mumblings, and the room dropped into a humming silence. Torus grabbed Frank's shoulder in a tight grip and forced him down into the chair. He squirmed but pretended not to mind. Torus gave him a final little shove. Torus was itching for something.

'Now, listen up.'

The crew swivelled round, and Torus pointed to the big monitor. At the bottom of the screen was a single word: Narus. It was the refugee processing camp out in the Pacific. Frank felt the weight of Torus's hand still on his shoulder and itched to flick it off.

'These reffos are going to be causing trouble. They'll hear about our new prime minister and realise they've got

Buckley's of ever coming to Australia.'

Torus laughed into the monitor and released his grasp on Frank's shoulder, only to slap him on the back as if they were old mates. He leaned forward and muttered into Frank's ear. 'Now we'll get 'em.'

Frank didn't get why they were monitoring the refugees on Narus. The camp had been shut for ten years and had been reopened a year ago by the LibLab government. Frank didn't give politics too much time – too many lies – but he knew that demonising refugees was the path to power. Splitting the population weakens your opposition. That had been made clear over the last few decades. Split people into groups, set one group against the other, manipulate and control the mental space. He didn't want any part of it. Frank always tried to live in a politics-free bubble.

Frank remembered when Narus was first re-opened by old Prime Minister Shortbull and the LibLab party.

'The reality is, we must hold back these growing flames of authoritarian nationalism fanned by the One Border Party,' he'd said at the time. 'That's why we have no choice but to open Narus so illegal refugees don't get to the mainland. That will mollify the right-wing elements in our political system.'

Shortbull's plan hadn't worked. The One Border Party had been elected anyway. Frank shrugged. More of the same – made no difference. But he did know that Border Force had been lusting after government for years, and now here they were. Their man was in power.

Frank looked round the room to see if anyone else had heard Torus's remark. Everyone was deliberately looking at monitors. They must have heard. What was Torus up to?

'They'll be ready to riot, but we'll be prepared for anything. We've got the outer fences electrified and mines buried over there to quieten them down. This is our chance to show what we can do. Keep an eye out for trouble.' Torus strode across to the other end of the room, chest out, like some kind of try-hard Napoleon.

God, how he hated him. Frank recognised that feeling he always got when he thought about confronting anyone. Boiling anger versus trying to control himself. He imagined smashing Torus in the face. He suddenly smiled at his own absurdity and took a deep breath. He remembered the breathing exercise he'd been prescribed; what was it called? Anuloma viloma pranayama. They said it would help with his stress in dealing with Mercury. His hand went to his nose. Block the right nostril, breathe in through the left nostril, count to five, breathe out through the right nostril, count to five, breathe in through the right nostril, count to five, breathe out through the left nostril, count to five, repeat. His mind started to calm, and his hatred for Torus subsided. His heart rate was going back to normal. He felt some satisfaction that Torus's grip on him was lessening.

He looked at the Narus monitor. Nothing happening there. *Ready to riot?* Just some refugees milling around. One guy hanging onto the fence with his fingers, his head leaning forward, looking like he could hardly walk, let alone riot. Behind him, a big guy holding a child with a fluffy toy. Also a Muslim woman there handing out food packages – and without a face covering. *Unusual.*

He looked over at the guys across the room, heads down, staring at their monitors. Granny wasn't really looking at anything but keeping away from Torus's attention.

'Okay, everything looks calm … sir.'

Torus glared. 'Shut up, Bargen. Sit there. We're making sure there's no fucking trouble. If you see any trouble, speak up.'

Frank and Granny looked at each other across the room and rolled their eyes. Trouble? The man had gone insane with pretend power. Maybe he'd calm down if they all kept quiet. He gazed into the Pacific – still nothing happening. He wished he could put his head down and take a nap.

The morning stretched on. Frank needed to pee, but didn't dare ask. A couple of times, the men had tried to talk, but Torus had erupted into a screeching tirade, and so now there was a suffocating silence in the room. It was like being a child trapped in a classroom. He tried to distract his mind from his full bladder.

His twins were ten years old next week, and Marta wanted to take them for a day out at Luna Park. Could be fun. He caught sight of a child's fluffy toy rabbit in the dust, one ear missing. Frank yawned. He would rather be anywhere else right now except here. Even visiting the hospital with his sick kid would be more fun.

He looked at the clock on the edge of the monitor screen. He'd been sitting there for three hours. Torus had no right to do this. And yet they all sat there like idiots, taking it, acting like schoolkids. He should go and have a pee, for Christ's sake.

Torus circled the room, staring at each monitor. When was he going to accept there was nothing to see here, stop this manic hustle so they could all have a tea break, at least? If something didn't happen soon, he was going to get up and leave and take the consequences. He was busting for a leak now. He needed to take a shit as well now.

He squirmed and his surveillance went idly back to the chainmail fence. It moved a little – was he imagining that, getting delirious from the boredom? He looked closer.

The guy holding the fence swayed sideways, then

backwards and forwards. His head swung from side to side and the fence began to sway. He got more vigorous and the big guy behind him came over and put his hand on his shoulder to calm him down or something. But he shoved him away and carried on pushing and pulling at the fence.

The two men started arguing, and the woman without the headscarf stepped forward. What was she doing without any kind of head covering? He didn't know much about Muslim women, but he knew about that, especially ones that had arrived from the Middle East. She pushed between the two men, and they backed away from each other. Were they fighting over her? Watching, Frank felt tense. *Is Torus right? Will there be a problem here?*

The big guy threw his head back, let out a huge grin, and slapped the smaller man on the back. He stumbled to the ground. The big guy picked him up and propped him against the chainmail fence, and he held it tightly, panting. The woman gently put a hand on the smaller man's shoulder. He leaned his head on the fence, then looked at her and smiled. He looked at the big guy and nodded.

He pushed and pulled at the fence again. Frank looked over at another screen. It had a wider angle, pulled back, that showed the whole corner of the facility. A group of raggedy people had taken up the fence pushing. Frank had that feeling that something terrible was about to happen.

For fuck's sake, stop it. This is what Torus wants, what he'd been waiting for. Maybe he'd been manipulating the refugee camp from here. He could have ordered the toilets to be shut down, done something to wind them up.

A guard came into the picture and waved his arms, trying to stop the crowd, but they kept on. More people gathered. There was no sound, but you could see them yelling and jeering.

Frank looked around the room. Everyone was riveted to the monitors. Frank leaned over towards Granny. They exchanged a look of incomprehension. Frank opened his mouth to speak.

'Shut up, Bargen.' Torus was jumping from one screen to another with a gleam in his eye and a small smile. He opened and closed his fists.

He leaned into a monitor. 'Yes,' he whispered.

Frank looked round. Everyone sat stock still. Was he the only one here onto this craziness? He had a bad feeling he knew where this was going, and he didn't want to know about it.

Suddenly, Torus leapt into the middle of the room and pointed at the door. 'Out!'

Frank jumped to his feet. The roomful of technicians looked around at each other, muttering and pointing at screens. Frank wondered if they were thinking what he was; that Torus was engineering something or other.

'Everybody out!'

Frank didn't need to be asked again. He shuffled towards the door with the other technicians.

'Get the fuck out!' Torus bellowed. Frank followed. At least he would get to have a shit now. Torus pointed at him.

'Not you, Bargen. Stay there.'

What?

Granny was leaving when Frank caught his eye, and they both shrugged. The last of the crew left the room, and the quiet came down, leaving only the humming.

~

Frank took a hesitant step back towards the monitor. The fence was waving crazily now, the guard pressed into a corner. There were even women, children and babies in the crowd. Bargen saw a grubby toddler with no pants on, a small one-eared rabbit clutched in its hand.

Get out of there, get back inside.

Torus lurched across to a plastic-covered box on the floor, about waist high, and then pointed to an identical box near Frank.

'Hang on. Why did you send everyone away?'

'Get over there.'

Frank didn't move. He had a bad feeling about this.

Torus marched up and got right in his face, his voice a coarse whisper. 'Just you and me, Frankie boy. Better that way, not so complicated.'

He ripped open the plastic cases, revealing identical red buttons about four metres apart. 'Needs two people, Bargen, and you're the lucky one. You'll have to hit your button within two seconds or the mine won't go off.'

Torus wanted HIM to set off the mine?

Frank's guts fell out of his belly, his cheeks shivered, and his shoulders shook. Nausea filled him like a giant balloon, bursting his stomach. He couldn't speak.

Torus grabbed him by the shoulders and marched him to the red button and forced his hand down. Frank saw his own arm, but it wasn't his. It wouldn't move. His hand sat there like a foreign object, resting on the button, ready to obey some other command, but not Frank's. His eyes watered.

You can't go round killing people. And Torus had all his trigger-happy buddies down here in the bunker and sent them away, only to keep me. It doesn't make sense.

Torus hiked back to the other button. 'On my mark,

Lieutenant Bargen.'

Frank's elbows shook, and he stiffened. He couldn't – he wouldn't – do it.

'N-no.'

'Bargen, I am your superior, and this is a direct order.'

Frank shook violently. He couldn't stop his shaking. It was as if his whole body had been taken over by ants and they were crawling all over his insides. 'I … I can't, I …' No way could he make his hand press that button, even if he wanted to. His stomach felt sickened.

Torus reared up over him. 'As the commanding officer in this bunker under the authority of the new prime minister and the One Border Party, I am giving you an order. I will have you court-martialled if you disobey. Do you understand? This will be the end of your career.'

Frank imagined crashing out of the military, a failure like his father always said, never living up to Marta's father. No pension, no income. Marta would take the kids. He'd end up on a park bench.

'And I will break your fucking fingers.'

A cold slime slithered down Frank's spine. His face was a swamp of sweat. His fingers twitched.

Maybe nothing will happen anyway. Maybe it's a warning.

Frank took a breath. He looked at the monitor and saw the guard was being overrun by the rioters.

Time to be a hero.

He looked into the face of Torus. It was scrunched up tight and his eyes blazed. Frank gave a limp nod. Torus's face smoothed out, and he looked smug.

'Remember – two seconds.' Torus pressed his big red button. 'Go!'

Frank saw his own hand move, and he watched as his

fingers pressed it.

The ground swelled up like he'd never seen. Dust and shards burst out of the earth, and the screen clouded over. Frank looked at the other monitor, the one with the wider view, farther away, and the image was mostly still clear. He breathed again. *That's not too bad, a bunch of dust.*

Torus had a grim, satisfied look on his face. Frank cringed; he'd seen that look before, and then he knew it wasn't just a cloud of dust.

A detainee, wearing a red scarf on his head and holding on to the chainmail fence looked around like he was trying to figure out what was going on.

'Look out!' Frank yelled, then bit his lip. *How useless.*

The earth rose up under the man and hurled him into the air towards the camera. Frank couldn't look away.

He landed in three pieces, each piece throwing up a little cloud of dust. Thud, thud, thud. The red scarf floated to earth while a severed head landed next to the toddler's crumpled one-eared rabbit. Frank slumped on the chair and felt the oozing warmth of his bowels emptying.

'Fuck!' Torus grinned. 'There was only supposed to be one explosion.' He leaned closer to the screen. 'Maybe it was some kind of chain reaction.'

The man was the devil.

Torus straightened back up, looked over and shrugged. 'Don't worry, we'll say collateral damage. It's you and me, Frankie boy.' Torus sniffed. 'Have you shit yourself?'

You and me.

Frank stared back at the screen in numb fascination. His thoughts couldn't comprehend what he had just seen. His throat was full of dust and his head was screaming.

CHAPTER 5

Torus looked around at the empty control room and nodded to himself. A good thing he'd decided to clear the room. It was bad enough seeing Bargen crash into a panic; he'd never seen any action and completely lost it. He was screaming, really screaming. And he shat his pants! Imagine if all of them acted like a bunch of snowflakes screaming their heads off and shitting everywhere.

Okay, so bits of body parts had come thudding down, but that was war and they were in the middle of one. It was a good decision setting off those explosions – made an impact. The newly promoted Colonel Bradsleap had only authorised one explosion, but the man had no clue. It was all going well, but Bargen going off like that had made him a little unsure. He should have picked somebody with more guts, but he needed someone he knew would press that button, and Bargen was the easiest one to intimidate at short notice.

Torus leaned back in his chair; he could feel his mind going into that place where everything became calm and clear.

There was no indecision, no fear, no guilt. Just uncomplicated truth. It was the best feeling. Life should be like that all the time instead of all that stress and tension he usually carried around, trying to keep people out of his business. *All the time, all the fucking time!*

He seriously had to keep this quiet.

Bargen was breathing in small gasps now, and Torus almost felt sorry for him, poor sod. He grimaced at the memory of Bargen covering his eyes. *What would covering your eyes do anyway? It wouldn't change anything; what was done, was done.* But he'd toughen up. He'd been working at that little desk upstairs for too long. Torus could turn him into a soldier who would look at dead enemies, shrug, and keep going.

He put his hand on Frank's shoulder.

'It's a mission, Frank, remember that. Okay, these explosions were bigger than expected, but we have the authority for that detonation. We are doing a public service.' He smiled to himself. 'It's too bad we didn't know all the explosives were connected; that was a bit of a surprise, but if you're going to make a statement, then why not make a bloody statement, hey, Frank?' Bargen's only response was to begin sobbing. 'Don't be so fucking irritating, Bargen. Get out of here! Get to a toilet.'

Bargen lifted his face out of his hands. Torus had seen this before with rookies. They freak out, then scream, then cry, then look back at what they've done on the battlefield to make sure it's real.

Sure enough, Bargen was struggling to look at the screen. Only for a second though. Then he pushed his chair back, turned around and glared at Torus.

Actually, he had the audacity to eye him with something

close to horror. Like he was somehow above what they had done.

What the fuck? He can't look at me like that.

As though realising what he was doing, Bargen's eyes shot to the ground, and he stumbled over his feet towards the door. When he got there, he held himself up by the doorframe and took one last look at Torus. What was Bargen thinking? A cross between defiance and anger. Not if he was smart.

'Keep your mouth shut, Bargen,' shouted Torus. 'Listen, if you get any trouble – you know, mental trouble – there's a place down in Palmer Street that Border Force approves of where soldiers can get some sympathy. Oregon Ranch, it's called, and they have women there who will do anything for you, clear up any problems. They are professional amenders. They know what they're doing.'

Frank appeared to hardly take in what Torus was saying, as if thinking Torus was telling him to go to a brothel. He nodded.

'Oh well, Frank, do what you want. I can't babysit you. There are bigger fish to fry.'

The operation had been approved by Bradsleap, but the higher-ups might get the willies if the full story got out. He couldn't let Bargen stir up trouble.

Suddenly, Frank was gone, and there was only the humming of the equipment in the room and Bargen's leftover stench. Torus looked at a monitor and saw the dust was settling. Images of the building started to appear in the smoky gloom. A mangled fence lay crumpled on the ground. He saw several bodies and body parts, looking like rags strewn about. *That was too much.* But boy, was it satisfying when you knew you'd taken the correct course of action. But because it had gone over the top, he would need to clean up the mess.

He needed to make sure Colonel Bradsleap didn't lose his nerve. Torus had managed to convince Bradsleap that a small explosion on the island would deter any troublemakers after they learnt about the new, more legitimate government. Torus had other ideas. He got the sappers to wire up a string of extra explosives just in case they were needed later on. But the sappers were obviously fools, and they had strung all the explosives together. Everything had gone up at once. Now that the whole thing had gone to shit, he had to make sure the blame fell in the right place. Bradsleap had to keep quiet for a while until the top brass was able to cover it up. They would happily throw Torus under the bus, but not a colonel, even one that had only just been promoted. That would be too hard to keep quiet. So, Torus needed to make sure that Bradsleap was directly in the firing line for the blame. Torus would be in the clear because the top brass wouldn't dare let it out.

Despite Bargen's tantrum, Torus wasn't worried about him. The man was a mouse. Torus slipped out the door and was headed to the elevator when he spied Bargen and Grantham at the end of the corridor.

Ahh, the faggot!

The pair of them had their heads together, and Grantham was trying to get something out of Bargen.

'Nothing,' insisted Bargen, squirming his shoulders. 'Nothing happened.'

Good, thought Torus, smart man. No spilling the beans. But Grantham would need to be pushed aside. Couldn't have him talking, making trouble. That deviant pervert could be a real pest if he got it into his screechy little mind.

'Then why did we get sent out?' Grantham pushed.

Bargen pulled away. 'I don't know. Leave me alone.' He scurried off into the toilets.

Run, little mouse.

'Frank, talk to me!' Grantham shouted after him. Then, seeing Torus in the corridor, he rounded on him. 'What happened in there?'

Grantham stood out in the middle of the corridor shaking, full-on shaking. He'd actually raised his voice, pussy-liver Grantham of all people!

'Stand down, Lieutenant!' Torus pushed past.

Grantham grabbed hold of Torus's arm, who looked at his hand and waited for Grantham to let go. He didn't. Torus's mouth widened in a snarling grimace.

'What happened, Granny? Take your courage pills this morning?' he spat. Granny pulled back. Torus jerked his arm away, settled his shoulders, screwed up his fists, and stared Grantham down until he dropped his head.

'Grantham!' Torus yelled into his face. 'Watch this.' Grantham lifted his head, and Torus walloped him straight on the nose. Grantham's eyes burst open in surprise.

No more trouble from you.

Torus kept walking, and when he looked back, Grantham's hand was covering his nose, blood oozing between his fingers. Torus flexed his bruised fist; maybe he shouldn't have done that. Normally, Grantham would shut up after a few words. Still, strange times.

Torus hightailed it up to Bradsleap's office. According to army seniority, Bradsleap was the guy running the place, but they both knew he did nothing without Torus's say so. He'd have to straighten him out as well, but punching a colonel wasn't on.

He pushed straight into Bradsleap's office, no knocking, and found his superior red-faced and blustery. He had obviously heard already.

'What the fuck happened?'

What was it with people today? Had everyone forgotten who they were talking to?

Higher rank or not, this newly promoted bumbling fool wouldn't know how to run a chicken farm, let alone a squad of elite soldiers ready to take over and bolster up the new government. Nevertheless, he did have the rank now.

Resigned to play the game for a moment, Torus stood formally at ease, hands clasped behind his back. 'It was necessary, *sir.*'

Bradsleap's face cooled down a little. He'd asserted his dominance, and now he wanted what he always wanted – Torus to take control.

'But what happened, Mike?'

'It was an act of war.'

Bradsleap went bright red and his cheeks puffed out. 'War? We're not at war!'

'We are now. You authorised the explosive … *sir.*'

'You told me to! You said it was to be a little experiment, that's all. How did those extra explosives get underground? Who authorised that?'

Bradsleap had that strange look on his face that Torus had seen on Bargen. Hard to tell if he was defiant or angry or what. 'You've gone too far, Mike.'

Why couldn't these so-called commanding officers support their soldiers when they did the right thing in the heat of battle? Bunch of pussies.

Torus's hands clenched behind his back, and he started shaking. It might be anger. Yes, he was angry. Bradsleap would need watching as well. Everything was going to shit.

'You authorised it … *sir.*'

Bradsleap slumped into his chair. 'I don't know what we're going to do.'

God, he was hopeless. Dare he say it? Torus released his hands from the *at ease* position behind his back and walked slowly up to Bradsleap. He looked into Bradsleap's rattled face and was filled with contempt. He couldn't help himself and spoke in a lowered voice. 'You'll take the blame. They'll quietly retire you with a promotion, and that will be the end of it. You're not cut out for the army anyway.'

Bradsleap's mouth opened, and he was about to say something, but Torus went on.

'If you blame me, the whole thing will come out into the open, and we'll all be drummed out in disgrace. No pension.'

Bradsleap pulled at his collar. He didn't know what to do. Maybe he really would leave the army.

Torus, still up close in Bradsleap's face, looked into his eyes. 'The best thing you can do is keep quiet.'

'I can't do that. What about Bargen? Wasn't he down there as well?'

'Leave Bargen to me. He pushed the final button. I'll keep him quiet.'

Torus went back to his office to think. He normally knew what to do, but his mind was fuzzy and his hands were trembling. Things certainly weren't shaping up like he wanted. First Bargen loses his shit, then he had to hit Grantham, and now Bradsleap was losing his nerve. Bradsleap been over-promoted. He poured himself a whisky and knocked it back.

His hands trembled more on the second one, and he spilled more than went in the shot glass.

He leaned back and looked up at the ceiling. Images of his dead mother's smooth white skin drifted across his mind. He felt an erection coming. He poured himself a third whisky, this time with calmer hands, and picked up his phone.

'Phone, wake,' he said to the phone. 'Call Lila.' The phone began dialling noises.

The Year 1990

Michael Torus was nine years old when his mother died. It had an exhilarating effect on him. Michael had always been big for his age. At his difficult birth, he weighed in at seven kilos and nearly killed his mother. Neither was expected to survive when the breach birth got stuck for hours.

Michael's mother never really recovered. There were no lasting physical problems, but over the years, the miracle birth developed into a cloying bond between mother and child. Some said the bond was *too* close. Michael breastfed for many more years than seemed healthy. His mother had more children, weaker than Michael, and talk got around that the main reason for having children was really to create more breast milk for her miracle child, Michael. He grew and grew and became huge and healthy. The rumour that he was still breastfeeding at nine years old got round the playground. He was strong and became a bully.

Every Sunday afternoon for several hours, mother and child lay down together, and she suckled him, the mutual pleasure so satisfying that the admonishments of the world could not stop them.

Michael was so overdeveloped from his mother's nourishing breast milk that he hit puberty at an early age. He began to notice changes in himself. Hair was growing. Girls became interesting. The gang of boys at school boasted about imaginary girlfriends. They discussed how to lie on top of them. The Sunday afternoons with his mother became even more pleasurable. But eventually it became too much for the mother, who finally succumbed to the traumas of Michael's birth. She died with Michael's nine-year-old lips around her nipple.

Michael continued to feed for several more hours, thinking of his imaginary girlfriends, the pleasure in his body and how he was the biggest, toughest boy in the playground. He loved his dead mother even more than the live one. He deserved everything.

~

Crowley sat at the cramped desk in the reception room of Oregon Ranch Amending Service, nestled in a back lane off Palmer Street, surrounded by East Sydney brothels. The Amending Service was confidentially funded by Border force to provide *Counselling, Psychiatric and Amending* services to soldiers. Crowley shivered at the word *brothel*. How low he'd come! He used to be a distinguished teacher of tantra, but his guru said he'd fallen prey to hubris, sloth and carnal greed. So Crowley was now consigned to manning the desk at his little back street establishment. One day soon, he would get back to the light.

The light of teaching the healing power of human

sexuality in a more salubrious environment. Pre-orgasmic bliss had the power to make the mind so blown away that it becomes impossible for the practitioner to tell the difference between their own ego and the outside world. The mind becomes so clear in its vision that the ego is transcended and the practitioner is left with an orgasmic oneness like the Sages of Old had described. The techniques of tantra had proved useful in bringing damaged soldiers back to a normalised form of sanity – amending them.

Crowley himself had been singed by the gods, and permanent Nirvana had eluded him. He had been dogged by the negative emotion of despair and needed to regroup, so he dismantled his school in India and became a recluse for a year in the Himalayas. Then his guru said it was now time to atone for his hubris and work amongst the anguished in society. So Crowley rented a house in the red-light district and set up the sexual healing clinic, Oregon Ranch. At the start, business was bad until he managed to get a contract with Border Force Army to treat the mangled minds of soldiers. He only had another few months of this purgatory to go before he could go back to his guru.

The phone rang. Crowley recognised the voice. He felt immediately wary and stroked his neck where the man had choked him that time. Torus was a regular client – not a desirable one, but Crowley knew how to handle him. Torus had peculiar needs.

Crowley was at first reluctant to provide these services, but who was he to judge? He had been wrong about many things, and he could be wrong about this as well.

'Do you have Lila?' Torus asked.

'We can have her prepared for you in an hour.'

Torus hung up the phone. He never said much. Crowley

mused that Torus was fundamentally an embarrassed person. One of these days, he would come good after he'd had enough of his perversions, after he'd satisfied his grief that his mother wasn't coming back – after he was amended. Oregon Ranch supplied many needs, and it didn't judge. This would assist Crowley's return to his guru.

The terrace house on Palmer Street was not far from Victoria Barracks and had a back entrance from the dunny lane. When Torus had first gone there after hearing they took exotic requests, he told them he needed a woman with pale skin to lie there very still. So still, she could be a corpse. The proprietor was okay with that. If he'd smirked, Torus would have hit him.

The first woman he tried did lie very still, but her skin was too hot. The whole experience was unconvincing. In frustration, he'd got her to lie in an ice bath for a while. After that she was nice and cold, but she had goose bumps, and so that was no good either. He needed smooth skin.

Then they managed to find this woman who had a medical condition that meant she didn't get goose bumps. After half an hour in an ice bath, her skin was cool and smooth like marble. Torus had been so excited he could barely wait to get her to the bed, but the stupid bitch wouldn't stop shivering and shaking. It was frustrating. They were supposed to be able to supply special needs. Torus had grabbed the fat little proprietor in the orange clothes by the scruff of the neck and demanded his money back, but the guy assured him he could come up with the goods.

At last, they found Lila. Lila didn't get goose bumps, and

she didn't shake. They gave her some drug or other. Her skin was like his dead mother's: smooth, white and cold, burnished with the lustrous gloss of silk, comforting, hairless, polished.

Torus climbed up the grubby stairs at Oregon Ranch. The only incorrect thing about Lila was that she didn't lactate, but they were working on that for him. Maybe this time they'd got that figured out.

Lila was getting out of the ice bath, towelling off when he arrived. She was under strict orders not to speak. He waited inside the door. His mind twitched with anticipation at the profound relaxation to come. She walked across to the bed, and he glared at the shape of her body. She was having no effect on him except a slight revulsion in his stomach and a turbulent bile in his throat. His fingers started to squeeze. Was it going to work? Nothing was happening, until she settled herself on the bed, as instructed, in the pose that his mother was in after she died. Then he relaxed, looking at her. He breathed deeply. It was happening! His sphincter tightened, his erection started. His hands relaxed, and he felt the slight tickle of saliva drooling from the corner of his mouth. He went to her. He stroked her belly, and his fingertips tingled as he brushed them across her frigid nipple. It was going to be good. He undressed.

Lila opened her eyes from time to time when she was bored. His mother had died with her eyes closed in ecstasy, and that's what Torus wanted from Lila. But she was being still, and he didn't mind too much, so long as she closed her eyes again. He couldn't allow himself to be curious about how she felt inside. He needed her to be dead. Who cared what she felt? She was getting good money for this. And she was good, very good, at being dead.

His nerves settled, and electric fire went through the back

of his hands like they were defrosting after being cast into ice. The warmth spread up his arms, and the trembling calmed a little, but it was going to take a few hours. Lila was able to lie in the same position for an hour at a stretch and not move, not move at all. That's how she charged, by the hour. An hour of blessed arctic stillness. After an hour, she opened her eyes and stretched. Her bones cracked from stiffness, and she moved to take her break. She needed a five-minute break between each hour, and he granted her that little kindness. His mother used to do that as well, take a break after an hour. He swelled with pride at his own magnanimity. This was a gift to Lila, even though he suffered as soon as she'd left the bed.

He lay back, and images of his childhood swirled through his mind. The taunts from his schoolmates about his breastfeeding at nine years old. A tear came to his eye. His hands began to tremble again, but not as strong as before. Lila's magic was working. She turned the light out because he didn't like to see her walking about during her break. She had it all down pat. After a few minutes, he heard her plunge into the ice bath again for a top-up.

The next hour was even better. That skin, that skin, hardly breathing, and his fingertips were tingling in ecstasy, his hands and arms and shoulders smoothing out into that familiar feeling of power. His chest stretched out, and he realised it had been shrunken in by the day's events. He expanded his breath. This was what he needed to be himself. He put his lips over her nipple and sucked. Nothing came out though, and that was disappointing. He reminded himself to talk to the proprietor.

Towards the end of the second hour, his hands were almost normal again, not trembling. Then she moved, ready to take her second break. He was angry about the nonlactating nipple, and now she wanted to stop again. The cheeky cow insisted.

But soon it became blissful again in a few minutes. She really was very good, and he wanted her forever and ever. At the end of the third hour, her skin was tinging blue, she didn't move at all, and his hands were now satisfied.

CHAPTER 6

Marta sat opposite Palace on the old wooden bench in the kitchen and nursed her almost-cold coffee. The last couple of hours had been frantic getting the kids ready. Frank had gone to work long ago, happy as a lark. *He* got to drink hot coffee, while managing the children was completely left to her. Whenever she asked for some help, he pointed out how he worked and she didn't. Bah! She'd like to see him get Mercury off to his first day at Wisemans Ferry Primary School.

She watched her son sit on the opposite chair and wave his feet in the air like he was doing a dance to music only he could hear. That was going to be crazy enough, let alone the fact that afterwards Marta would have to troop all the way to Westmead Hospital with Palace.

'Mercury! Put those shoes on the right feet!'

Palace and Marta had a little smile together at Mercury's antics.

'He does that to be funny,' said Palace. 'He knows which

foot is which. He's trying to get attention.'

'I know, sweetie.'

Marta touched Palace's cheek. Despite the oxygen pipe being a constant reminder of her daughter's illness, she looked okay today – brighter. Maybe it was the country air. Whatever it was, Marta would take it. She loved both her children, but Palace was a walking angel. She didn't deserve anything that she suffered, and yet she took it all with a smile. Marta wished she had half of her daughter's strength and endurance.

~

Frank sat mute in the car as he drove northwest out of Sydney, barely registering the journey, shocked when more than an hour later, he suddenly arrived at the ferry terminal at Wisemans. His fingers unlocked their grip from the steering wheel. They'd gone numb, he'd been gripping so tight. He flexed his hands. He needed to be back home, resting in his chair, gazing at his river. Then the horror would fade.

The punt slid across the water, the river eerily quiet today. Why weren't the kookas laughing? He could see them, but they didn't make any sound, even though their beaks were going. A kookaburra perched on the car in front of Frank's. Its mouth was open wide in full squawk, but there was only silence. Frank felt the cable tugging at the punt and saw the water swishing past. That didn't make a sound either. It was like the car had become soundproof.

The punt bumped into the bank on the other side and, suddenly, the world of sound opened up in a cacophony. Squawking cockatoos, the screeching of the cicadas, the humming of the ferry motor, the rushing river. It was all abruptly deafening. Was his brain playing tricks on him? Did that explosion really happen? Did he imagine it? Hope lifted him for a moment. But the dismembered arm flying through the air – that was definitely real. He drove off the ferry and onto the tarmac towards home. The drive along the river to Gunderman drifted by in an endless forever.

~

Marta heard the approach of a car on the gravel. Odd. Why would anyone come out here? She gave Palace's cheek another pat and got up to go to the window in the lounge room. Mercury leapt into action and ran to the window to get there first. She paused to let him past; this was his thing. He did it all the time. But today, he'd forgotten that he'd tied his shoelaces together, just for fun. She'd forgotten too, otherwise she would have warned him.

Over he went, sprawling face first on the ratty ancient carpet. Marta flinched, but it meant nothing to him. Didn't slow him down at all. Off came one shoe, and he was at the window in a flash.

'It's Dad!' he shrieked.

Frank?

Marta moved to Mercury's side and saw Frank sitting in the front seat, hands on the wheel, not moving.

He must have forgotten something. Typical.

But he left hours ago. Normally, he would have called her if he needed something brought to work. She waited for him to get out, but he sat there.

Mercury looked at his mother. 'What's Dad doing?'

Marta had no idea.

Finally, Frank laboured to open the door and get out of the car. He didn't look well. A fissure of anxiety opened up in Marta's stomach. She didn't need another sick person in the house.

Frank left the car door wide open and slouched towards the house. Mercury ran for the front door but tumbled over again, trailing a shoe dangling on a shoelace. This was ridiculous.

Marta quickly untied his knotted shoelaces and pointed to his feet. 'Put them on the right feet, or else.'

What was Frank doing home?

She met him at the front door. He was half in and half out of the house, seeming to be stuck there. 'What's going on?'

He leaned his head against the doorframe. 'Trouble at work.'

On Mercury's first day at school and when she and Palace had to trek into the hospital, was Frank seriously going to disturb her day because of some accounting problem!

Instant sarcasm rose in her mind until she noticed he really did seem sallow and sickly and his manner was positively grave. Maybe it was serious. He seemed incapable of moving from the door, so she bundled him inside and sat him down at the bench.

'What happened?'

He looked up and seemed to be trying to focus, with that annoying *try to understand me* look. 'Classified.'

The number of times she'd heard that word – *classified!* Her father had said it all the time when she was growing up. It drove her mother insane.

Marta had a long, hard look at Frank's face. He seemed completely muddled. Was he being a drama queen, or had something terrible really happened? Whatever it was, she wouldn't be getting much of an explanation out of him anytime soon.

Frank suddenly got up and pushed past and headed for the back veranda and the swinging chair overlooking the river. She followed him and watched.

Maybe it wasn't such a bad idea, Frank coming home. He could help with the children. She would let him calm down for a while and then get him to help her with delivering the children to school and hospital. No way was he going to sit there all day while she did all the work.

'Since you're here, you can take Mercury to school in Wisemans. I have to get Palace to the clinic in Westmead.'

Frank's head jerked up as if he'd been sleeping. 'No!' His face was vexed. The sharpness was fierce.

'What?'

'Need to sit. Rest.'

Frank really didn't look well. She sat down next to him. 'What happened?'

He shook his head and held his ears.

'Couldn't hear, then loud. Body parts.'

She took his chin and lifted his head. He looked like a stranger, his face contorted with some kind of boiling pain.

'I can't …'

'I know, I know, classified.' How could she help if he wouldn't talk? 'But are you okay?'

He struggled to get some words out. 'Nothing happened. Need to relax.'

He stood up, walked back into the house and over to one of the unopened cardboard boxes that hadn't been unpacked yet and ripped it open. He pulled out a half-empty flask of whisky and slugged it straight from the bottle.

A bubble of resentment exploded inside her. She'd tried being patient and understanding, but this was too much. 'Bit early for that, isn't it?'

He shrugged, stumbled out the back door and slumped into the swinging chair and took another swig.

A vivid image ran through Marta's mind. An image of life without Frank, just her and the kids. How would she survive? Where would she live? She blew the image away frantically.

Inside the house Mercury was running about, banging that wooden train against the walls. The school were not going to know what hit them after today. She sighed.

'Mercs, stop!' yelled Frank.

Mercury carried on.

'Mercury, fucking stop!'

The house dropped into silence. Marta had never heard Frank talk to Mercury with such venom. 'Frank!'

He held his head. 'Jesus, fuck. Sorry.'

Something had changed today. Classified or not, she didn't like it. Something dark seemed to have settled on the house. Better that she take the kids and leave Frank be.

'Mercury?' she called. 'Come out here, sweetie.'

The fly screen door squeaked on its hinges as Mercury pushed through it. His shoes were tied up neatly on the correct feet. He nuzzled into her, and she put her arm around him. Frank gulped his whisky, and Marta stared at the ground, feeling a grinding loneliness.

The screen door squeaked open again, and Marta snapped out of it. It was Palace peeking around the door, taking it all in. Marta's heart ached at the thought of Palace having to endure more grief.

'It's okay, sweetheart.'

But after a quick look around at the scene, Palace went over and sat next to Frank. Maybe she could pull Frank out of it.

'Why don't you take Palace to Westmead, and I'll take

Mercury to school?'

Palace sidled up to her father and touched his hand. Frank looked at her and pulled his hand away.

'No, can't drive, can't hear.'

Palace did a quick intake of breath and also snatched her hand back.

The bastard. Marta had had enough. She banged her fist on the table. 'I'm trying here, Frank. Everyone is except you. What the fuck happened at work?'

'Can't talk.'

'Oh, for God's sake!'

Frank emptied the bottle. She felt like slapping it out of his hand and throwing the bottle at the wall, but it was bad enough that the kids were seeing their father acting like a spoilt brat. She would not join him. Instead, she wrenched open the back door.

'I haven't got time for this. Come on, kids. Move it.'

She slammed the screen door on the way out to the car and looked back. The bastard was still out the back. Palace looked up at her, eyes wide, wanting answers.

'There's something wrong with Dad, isn't there?'

Marta crouched down and looked into her sweet little face. 'Never mind, dear. It will all be okay.'

'Something's wrong with him. I don't think it's because Mercs put his shoes on the wrong feet. He does that sort of stuff all the time. Usually, it's just funny.'

Marta opened the car door. 'Let's take Mercs to school, and then we'll go to the hospital.'

Palace's forehead crinkled like she wasn't satisfied with the answer, but Marta gave her a prod. 'Come on, sweetie.'

A slow and distracted Palace climbed into the front seat of the car while Mercury jumped into the back. At least he seemed to have forgotten his father's antics.

Damn you, Frank.

~

From miles away Frank heard the front door slam and then the beautiful silence. The house descended back into the forest, as it always did when it was empty. Only the screeching cicadas and the river, trying to get the naked bush back.

Growing up, the river had always soothed him, taken his troubles from him and floated them away. Jimmy Budabuda said the river was coming from everywhere and going to everywhere, feeding everyone and protecting them. The river was home.

Home. What did that even mean after what he'd seen? His memory blurred. Torus killed all those people, and Frank was the only witness. Why had Torus emptied the room? Like he deliberately only wanted Frank to see what he'd done. He thought about the explosion on the monitor. He couldn't remember everything. What was missing? It couldn't be legal, what Torus had done. How did he think he could get away with it? An explosion would be all over the news. Questions would be asked. What if they thought it was all Frank's fault? He felt sick. He needed to report it to Colonel Bradsleap.

No. First, he had to get his thoughts together. Yes, that was what he would do. He put his head back against the easy chair, and gradually, his hearing returned to normal. He was aware of a dreamlike state in himself. Like the river was taking him away from his problems. A flying, dismembered head streaked across his imagination, but the river did its magic, and he drifted into a fitful unconsciousness.

~

He woke to the sound of the gravel driveway and Marta arriving home. At first, he sat up, happy to be in their new home, on the water, his childhood home. Mercury barrelled in the door, Marta and Palace behind, holding hands. Then the memory descended like a black cloud, and he held his hands to his face.

'Still asleep? Good. Relaxing day?' Marta's sarcasm stabbed through him like the barbed spears that Jimmy Budabuda had told him the old blackfellas made.

'Won't come out, you die,' Jimmy Budabuda used to say, 'but bullets better, make bigger hole, die quick. Body in pain, mind in worry. Spear take many days to die, much time to think and take last breath peacefully.'

Frank clutched his side as if he'd been speared and wondered what Jimmy would have thought of Marta. He knew she would have been afraid of him. Marta didn't like anyone different from her.

He pulled himself out of his chair and went to the kitchen to put the kettle on. His hands shook. No more whisky. He would have tea.

'Doctors said Palace is holding steady, if you're interested.'

He spun around. *She thinks I don't care.*

'I love you, honey,' Frank said to Palace. She gave a small proud smile, and Frank cupped her cheek. So soft.

Marta sighed and sat in the chair where Frank had been and looked out at the river. 'What did you do out here when you were growing up? I would have gone crazy.'

'Go for walkabout with Jimmy sometimes. Camp out, look for signs. Look after the country, the forest.'

'Who is Jimmy?'

'Jimmy was my old aboriginal mate. Taught me about the country. Told me songs about the first white settlers around here. Pretty gruesome stories. I haven't thought of Jimmy for years.'

'I went to La Perouse once,' said Marta. 'There were aborigines there. The kids used to entertain the tourists by getting them to throw a coin in the water. The little aboriginal kids would dive in and come up with the coin between their teeth. I didn't like it much. I thought it was a pretty stupid game, especially when they came up with a copper coin between their teeth and said copper was too hard to see, silver coins only, please. Cheeky.'

Frank grunted.

'No parties when you were growing up?' she said.

He put a cup of tea in front of her. 'Not many. Went to Windsor a few times, but that's about it. I was happy, I think.'

A great heave of sadness overwhelmed him. His mind went back to the last moments before the explosion. His thoughts cleared out of their cloud. His sharp memory, clear as day, was this: *that he had pressed the final button that had killed those people on Narus.*

He held the wall for support. He had a great urge to tell Marta, but Torus's unstated threats coursed through his mind. He'd better keep quiet, keep schtum.

'So, are you ready to tell me what happened at work?'

No, came the voice of Torus in his mind.

His head waved about. 'I can't.'

Marta didn't look surprised. 'Fine.' She stood up. 'Well, you're not going to mooch around here all day. We've got to unpack these boxes.'

'Boxes, boxes,' sang Mercury. He jumped up and tore at one of the boxes, bits of cardboard flying around.

'Mercury! Take it easy. Palace, take him out into the back yard,' said Marta, pointing. 'If you're not going to tell me, let's at least try to be normal today and get these boxes unpacked.'

Normal, thought Frank, *that would be nice.* He felt bad about being crazed before and wanted to make it up to his family. He shrugged and pulled at the box Mercury had started on.

'C'mon, Mercs, let's open these boxes.'

Mercury eagerly snatched at the boxes. He pulled out bits of paper, throwing it about. He scrunched it into a ball and threw it at Palace. She batted it away and looked at her mother as if to say, *how childish.* Frank threw a paper ball back at Mercury, who hooted with glee and took this as a signal of freedom. He pulled out huge bits of packing paper and pulled them all together into a basketball-sized clump.

Frank undid a bit of crockery, and Mercury threw the massive paper basketball straight at his dad's head. The thing bounced off Frank's skull and surprisingly stung. *Little shit.* He picked it up and flung it back with a little too much force. It hit Mercury square in the face. Startled, he fell backwards onto the floor.

The room went quiet for a moment. He shouldn't have done that. Frank looked at Marta, but she burst out laughing. Then Palace joined in. Frank exhaled, relieved. Then he started laughing too.

Mercury was flummoxed for a moment, looked confused, unsure what to do with everyone laughing at him. The gang's laughter reduced a little to a murmuring giggle. They waited. Mercury could be violently unpredictable, but he jumped up, grabbed the ball of paper and weakly threw it back towards his mother and Palace. They laughed at the feeble attempt. He tried again, this time pulling at a new carton, collecting paper and throwing it everywhere.

Frank knew he was going to have to step in. Mercury's antics were only making him frustrated. But the silliness was just what he needed.

Then Mercury grabbed a small metal teapot and launched it across the room. It crashed into the wall with a clatter.

'Okay, okay, Mercs, that's enough.'

But he dived for more objects to throw and launched a dinner plate across the room. It spun over and over, and Frank thought of the dismembered arm.

'Mercs,' he yelled as the plate hit the wall. 'Enough!' But Mercury was deep into it. He pulled out a cup and raised it to throw.

Frank grabbed both his wrists and held him fast.

'No!' Mercury struggled and kicked at Frank.

'Mercury, stop!' Marta yelled.

Somehow, his mother's voice cut through, and he gave up the struggle. Great, not even his own son listened to him.

'You all good now?' Frank demanded. Frank wasn't sure that Mercury's storm was over. Mercury wriggled to be free, just enough to make Frank relent and let go. Mercury slumped to the floor. They all smiled in relief, but Mercury used his freedom to grab a saucer and launch it up at Frank. It hit Frank on the forehead and smashed.

'Little bastard!' Frank grabbed Mercury's shoulders and shook him hard. 'What the hell are you doing?'

'Frank, stop, stop,' shouted Marta. But Frank was frenzied. He shook and shook and Mercury's head wobbled crazily. He made a sickening gurgling sound, and Frank halted, panting. He let go, and Mercury ran to his mother.

What had come over him? His mind went to Torus. It was all his fault. He had made him a killer. He'd made him assault his own son. He had no choice.

Must report Torus.

He thought back to Torus's face after the explosion. He hadn't just been satisfied, he'd been excited. What would he do if Frank revealed what they'd done?

Torus will kill me.

There was no way out. He slumped to the floor and sat there amongst the boxes and sobbed.

Marta knelt next to him. 'Jesus, what's going on? Tell me, Frank!'

He couldn't. Even thinking about it brought Torus's threatening face to mind. He pushed her away, stood up and wiped away a tear. 'Let's get these fucking boxes done.'

He tore the box apart, spilling contents on the floor. Like the guts of the refugees.

He had to get away. He gave the spilled goods a mighty kick and stormed across the room and out to the car. There was only one place he could go.

He drove out to the tree with the signs that Jimmy had shown him years ago. Immediately, his heart slowed underneath the eucalypts. Rushes of childhood memories came back to him, flushing out the horrors of the present. He slept the sleep of the dead.

CHAPTER 7

Frank dreamt he was a British soldier in the NSW Corps, sent to the Hawkesbury to 'destroy as many as they could of the wood tribe and to erect gibbets whereupon the bodies of all they might kill were to be hung.' A dozen Darug had been killed already, and the losses to the NSW Corp were one soldier. Frank looked down at his speared companion, not yet dead, but with a spear through his chest. The spear could not be removed, and he would take several days to die. Frank was dreaming – he knew he was dreaming and yet he was still dreaming. He checked again – was he still dreaming? Yes, he was! He had never experienced this before, dreaming and at the same time knowing that he was dreaming. He decided to prove it, to prove there was no pain in dreaming. He got Jimmy Budabuda to spear him through the ribs. The spear entered his left side painlessly, and the tip poked out of the right side of his chest. The weight of the spear pulled him down to the side, but still there was no pain. He was still asleep! He was ecstatic, and the shock of the delight woke him up.

Immediately, a severe discomfort, fast and sharp, shot up the left side of his ribs. He felt for Jimmy's spear, then realised he was in the front seat of his car, frozen stiff and couldn't move. The gearstick was sticking into his ribs. He checked again to see if he was still asleep. He wasn't. He was definitely awake now and amazed that he could *know* that he was awake. He had two great sensations. One, he was elated that he had had a lucid dream, and two, he was in agony as he could now feel the pain of Jimmy's spear in his side.

The forest was arctic in the night this time of year. He must have collapsed over onto the gearstick and fallen asleep. The cold had stiffened his body solid. He groaned and loosened up a little and eventually managed to get himself into a sitting position. The sun was up, and he looked around at the gum trees. He was in the spot where Jimmy used to take him as a child. He could almost see Jimmy waving his spears in his solemn dance. Frank rubbed his ribs.

He needed to get back to the house and explain things to Marta. He started the car and drove the few kilometres back to the house. When he arrived, Marta's car wasn't there. He didn't know if he was relieved or not. He wasn't in the mood for a fight, but he didn't want her to leave him either. If she knew what he had done …

Where had she gone? She had nowhere to go. A tide of fear rose and slid through his body. He was alone, eternally alone.

He stumbled into the house, still clutching his side. He smelt the faint smell of breakfast and then heard the sound of the gravel driveway. He looked out the window and saw Marta get out, look at his car and run towards the house.

The fear left him, and he was relieved that the argument to come would sustain him, hold him still, make him real again. Here we go. He slumped onto the couch and prepared for the onslaught.

She ran inside and the screen door banged. 'Frank, Frank! Where the fuck are you?'

She came running into the room and stopped when she saw him, hands on hips, looking relieved and furious in equal measure.

'Where have you been all night? I've taken the kids to school.'

He felt strangely glad that she was yelling at him. Oh God, he needed this. He stood up, the pain stabbed at him to remind him it was still there, to punish him for what he had done. He grimaced and grabbed his side, then sagged back down.

'What's wrong with your ribs?'

'Slept on the gearstick.'

'You idiot!' Her eyes softened a little then, and she came towards him. 'Why didn't you tell me where you'd gone?'

'Couldn't.'

She sat next to him and took his cheeks in her hands and squeezed till it hurt.

'Oww!'

'I know … classified.'

He dropped his head. Could he tell her? What Torus had done was extraordinary, but it was still military information.

'I need you to call into work and tell them I'm not coming in. They'll know why.'

'Not till you tell me what's going on. Why don't you call them yourself?'

'Can't. Need to sleep. Sleep and forget.' He lurched towards the bedroom.

'Forget what?' she called.

He ignored her and crawled under the covers.

A moment later, he heard the sound of Marta throwing off her shoes and getting into bed next to him. Her hand was on his shoulder. It was soft and comforting and he wanted to turn to her and tell her everything, but his body wouldn't move, and he began to shake. She moved closer to him and put her arm around his waist and onto his stomach.

She shuffled closer, and he knew what she was trying to do – get him to talk. He wanted to, really wanted to, but what about Torus? Everyone at the base knew Torus was crazy, but after the explosion, Bargen had to wonder what the man was truly capable of. After killing all those people, he might do anything. Frank didn't know who was in on it. Did Colonel Bradsleap know about it? Maybe the whole of Border Force knew. Maybe there was nothing to be done.

'Remember your father?' Marta whispered. 'Before he went completely nuts and you got him locked up in the nuthouse?'

Frank shuddered at the thought of his father's cruelty.

'I don't want you to turn out like him. You have to get some help. Someone you can talk to before you go completely insane.'

Frank stiffened.

'I won't stick around if you go crazy. I can't … the kids, it's not right …'

Frank remembered his father locking him and his mother in a cupboard, screaming from outside that he was protecting them from germs, from aliens and from the worldwide lizard conspiracy. He reeled at the memory. He almost prayed. *Please don't let me be like that.*

'C'mon, I'll call work if you agree to go to see an amender. They provide them, don't they?'

Frank was relenting. If they'd caught his father's illness early, things might have been different. But Frank's body wouldn't move except for the shaking. Marta moved her hand down towards his loins as she always did when she wanted something. But her hand felt like dead cold clay. But at least he stopped shaking. He knew she wouldn't let up. She would be like a dog with a bone. Anyway, he would get some time off work.

'Okay, I'll go to see an amender.' Predictably, she squeezed his penis, happy to have got her way. 'Can I sleep now?' He pulled away from her, burrowed into his pillow and immediately sank into unconsciousness.

~

Several untidy plastic chairs congregated along the wall of the empty waiting room at Oregon Ranch. Frank hesitantly moved forward and sat down. He caught a sideways glance of a painting on the wall – red splatters strewn across a green field. He expected to see dead horses, but a second look showed it was a relaxing hillside with poppies. So much red splashed across the grass. His neck was sweaty, and he fidgeted. It had been three days since he'd been to work, and the violent images raced constantly through his mind. Frank still had no clue what to do about going over Torus's head or not. This amender would surely be able to tell him. You can talk with them. You don't have to have sex.

It shouldn't take too long. Amenders are supposed to be pretty good. I'll be out of here in no time, all fixed up.

Finally, the door opened, and Frank lifted his head. A little girl stepped out of the room. No, not a child, a dwarf! A black dwarf.

Poor sod, must be terrible being a dwarf. No wonder she needs an amender. He didn't move from his chair, expecting the amender to walk out next, but the dwarf looked at him square in the face, waiting for a reaction. Her face was dark, and a small glimmer of a smile danced round the edges of her lips, which were the colour of poppies. Jet-black curly hair fell onto her dress, also the colour of poppies. She waddled towards him, and when she spoke, she had a New Orleans drawl.

'Frank? I'm Darcta Tarmsun, an amender here at Oregon Ranch.'

She's the amender? Frank did a double take, then stood up quickly.

'Oh,' he said. 'Doctor Thompson? Okay.'

'Pleased to meet you, Frank.' She held out her short arm with stubby brown fingers to shake his hand. Her fingernails were poppy coloured too. 'Call me Yo-Knee.'

She looked at him steadily with dancing in her eyes and a trace of amusement at the edges of her poppy-coloured lips. She waited a moment while Frank's mind whirled. How could a New Orleans black woman dwarf be an amender in Sydney? Maybe this isn't such a good idea after all.

What did a dwarf know about acts of war?

She waited more. And more. Holding the pose. Her dancing eyes started to freeze over a little. She cleared her throat.

Is this a joke from Torus? Is he spying on me?

Frank felt like backing off into the wall behind him. It couldn't be Torus, because Frank had arranged this appointment through Colonel Bradsleap. Or maybe Bradsleap had told Torus. He still didn't know who was in on it. It was all so confusing. His head hurt.

'Frank?'

He leaned down to shake her hand. It was small and soft. 'How do you do?'

'Would y'all like to come in?' She withdrew her hand at exactly the right speed.

Huh, she's studying me.

He felt some resistance fall away, and he followed her into the office. His eyes went to her behind. Was she wiggling it? Maybe that was the way dwarves walked. She turned, caught him staring, and he knew he'd been nabbed. His cheeks heated up. She put her hands on her hips and raised an eyebrow.

'An itty bit o' housekeepin' first. You git farve free visits; after thaat, you will be charged at the standard rate. The military figures if you cain't be fixed in five visits, you ain't no use to them.'

She talked and watched at the same time. Her lips smiled a little, and her arm gestured for him to sit down. She sat opposite, crossed her legs and pulled her skirt down, almost covering her pudgy little knees. Her skin was the colour of moody caramel. Her lips pouted a little. Frank sneaked a quick look at her breasts. Then longer. They looked … normal. Frank felt a tingling in his groin. His eyes were resting on her breasts. She slid off the chair and stood with hands on hips.

'Honey, from this height, I could look straight across and see what *you* got for sale.'

He was stunned. *Are amenders allowed to talk like that?* She seemed to be enjoying herself. He gave out a smile. She watched him intently.

'I'm married,' he blurted.

She raised an eyebrow.

'You're a dwarf.' *What have I said? Oh God.*

'Nicely observed.'

He felt like a fool, but he liked it.

She allowed him to sit in silence as his thoughts raced. It must have been hard, growing up as a dwarf. It must have been terrible. *I wonder why she's an amender? Does she do it to keep people away or to help them?*

'Both,' she said.

'Huh?'

'You're wondering if I do amending for myself or for other people. The answer is both.'

He didn't care that she'd penetrated into his thoughts. It was a relief, and he exhaled some tension. He leaned back on the couch and looked around at where he was.

A shaft of sunlight streamed in through the large window. The walls were beige and undecorated. There was no desk, but there were a couple of white armchairs and a small set of wooden steps. They reminded Frank of the steps in his school library to reach the higher books, the ones that no one read. A large purple-coloured glass globe sat on a little table in the corner, with bubbling water. A steady plume of steam came out of it, and a faint smell of lavender.

She let him study the room, waiting till he was ready. 'So, how can I help?'

Frank looked around. He'd never been in an amender's office before. He didn't know what he'd be in for, and his collar chafed. He was suddenly overcome by the shakes again. He straightened himself up in the chair, swallowed and said, 'I've been advised to come here because of various incidents that have recently happened.'

She waited in the silence and then said, 'That's a long sentence, honey.' She lingered, that questioning eyebrow raised again.

He looked at her aggressively. Was she trustworthy?

'I killed people.' He didn't know where the words came from. He didn't choose to say them. They were just there. Out. Free. He felt guilt and relief wash through him in equal measure.

She took the pencil from her mouth and wrote something down. 'Tell me what happened, honey.'

Frank tensed as the image of the dismembered arm flying through the air came into his mind. 'I was ordered to blow up innocent people.' He waited. Let her ask the questions, and that would make it easier to talk.

She watched him, her eyes sympathetic. Finally, she said, 'Go on.'

'This won't get back to Torus, will it?'

'Of course not, it's amender/client confidentiality.' He looked into her big, brown eyes, soft as a kitten's fur, and he relaxed a little. She was seducing words out of him, and he liked it.

'It was a normal day. Torus was being a dickhead as usual.' The moment he started talking, he felt uncomfortable again. He looked around the room for some escape. 'He's the one with the problems. He's the one who should be in here getting this grilling.' The walls seemed to close in.

'It's not a grilling, Frank. We're having a conversation. Let's talk about you.'

He nodded quickly and swallowed. 'Yes, okay. Anyway, we were monitoring the detainees, and they started to swing on the fence. The loudspeaker bellowed out they were to stop, but they didn't and it got worse. They were up to something. It looked like they were about to attack the guard. I don't know if they were really or ...' He looked up at Yo-Knee again. 'Do you think they were trying to attack the guard?'

'Go on.'

'Torus said it was because of the election. The refugees were testing us out, see what they could get away with. We had to teach them a lesson, otherwise all the families in Australia would be in danger.'

Yo-Knee picked up a notebook and scribbled. 'Do you think all the families in Australia are in danger, Frank?'

But he hardly heard her. He was reliving body parts flying through the dust. That dismembered arm again. It looked so alive.

'Torus said we had to blow up the land mine as a warning.' Frank was talking to himself. 'It needed two people to press the buttons. He made everyone leave the room except me. He screamed at everyone to get out. Granny and me didn't know what was going on. I didn't know what I was doing. I don't even remember pressing it. But it caused all the other land mines to go off as well.'

He shook. 'It was terrible. Everything went into slow motion. I saw a man's arm flying through the air. An arm! Like at the butcher's. It landed in the dust. The hand looked real, like it could move.' Frank's body was tense as a statue, and he realised he was gripping the edge of his chair like a steel vice. He released his fingers. 'That's it.' He sat back. 'I went home after that.'

Yo-Knee stirred, and her chair creaked. She didn't speak.

Frank suddenly began to shiver. 'I bet you think I'm a monster.' He wiped a tear off his cheek. 'I didn't want to do it. I feel guilty. I deserve to be the one getting blown up.' He put his face in his palms. He didn't want to cry in front of her, but he wasn't sure he could stop it.

He felt her hand on his shoulder. It was surprisingly firm and soothing for one so small.

'What should I do?'

'It's not up to me to tell you what to do.'

What the hell!

He pulled his shoulder away from her hand and glared at her. 'What am I doing here then?'

'You're the one who has to decide what to do. I'm here to ask questions and listen to throw some light on things so you can decide.'

He studied her face. She didn't look like she was fobbing him off or thinking he was crazy.

'Okay.'

She nodded. 'You obeyed an order, right?'

'Yes.'

'So first off, you have to take in that simple fact. You obeyed an order.'

He couldn't be let off the hook that easily. He shook his head, feeling the pressure rise. 'It's not that simple. It may have been an illegal order.'

'Tell me about that.'

'It was horrible. I know it wasn't my fault.'

Yo-Knee leaned back, and her chair creaked again. 'People are ordered to kill – that's what happens in war.'

How could she say that? She thinks killing is okay? 'It's not a war, not a real one. I could have refused. Soldiers have disobeyed bad orders. It's legal to do that. I'm not really a soldier anyway, just a bookkeeper. I've never seen any action.' He remembered the pathetic ragdoll in the dust. 'Until now.' He shuddered.

The room went silent as if it was waiting for him. Steam issued from the lavender fumare. The blue sky filled the window.

He grunted and shifted uncomfortably in his chair. There, he'd told her. Shouldn't that be enough? He didn't feel any better. Maybe this amending stuff was no good.

'You'll have to tell somebody in authority the whole story someday.'

He looked up into her eyes. She was waiting, looking over the top of her glasses, eyebrows raised. He bent forward and ruffled his hair.

'War is war, Frank, terrible as it is. You were given an order.'

'But I could have disobeyed,' he yowled. 'They would still be alive. It wasn't even a war.' Frank looked into her soft face. Her eyes had a slight glisten to them. Her eyelashes were prominent. Her brown eyes were like pools of deep water, safe to dive into and drown in.

'You have to tell someone. Find out if the order was above board.'

He shivered. She was making it sound so easy, too easy. Killing people wasn't supposed to be easy. The thought of going back to work and seeing Torus made him want to run away. Away like Jimmy did. Away where he would never have to deal with this again.

'It's okay, Frank. You're safe.'

Frank's heart moved into her eyes, and against his will, his spirit dived right in there. A deep satisfaction filled him. He was released from all anxiety, and his body relaxed. She was right. Here, he was safe. 'I can't go out,' he blurted. 'I want to stay here. I can't go outside. I want to stay here with you forever.'

He jolted back at what he had just said and the complete weirdness of it. What had she done to him? The blue sky in the window felt harsh, and he closed his eyes. The tears were going to come whether he liked it or not.

'It's okay, Frank, sit there quietly for a while. It's a big thing you've done. The images will subside over time, and you'll start to feel normal again. Give the mind time to process them and get back into conventional habits.'

She looked up into his face, but he couldn't look at her. His body tensed up again. He was crying now. Actually crying in front of this woman.

'I don't know what's happening,' he blubbered. 'I don't even know you.'

'It's completely normal.' She stood up and put her hand on his shoulder again and looked up into his face. 'Can I hug you?'

His body gave a huge sob, and he nodded. She put her small arms around him, just reaching past his shoulders. He relaxed.

A part of his mind was completely sharp. *I'm crying in the arms of a black dwarf.* The thought was hilarious, and he burst out laughing and crying at the same time. She softly let go and then everything went quiet. Right then, Frank felt that he was being dragged towards a cliff. He knew that he would have to go over Torus's head, but he fought against it, dreaded it.

'Tell me what to do.'

She sighed and thought for a moment. Her brow crinkled as if she was not sure about what she was about to say. Frank waited. At last, she breathed out as if she'd made a decision.

'I normally don't tell people what to do, but here goes. I would speak to Bradsleap. If the order was illegal, then Bradsleap will take over the investigation. If the order was legitimate, then you need to deal with it, and I will help you do that.' She smiled. 'We'll be seeing a bit of each other.'

'I can't. Tell me something else to do.' He put his face in his hands. He could feel that cliff coming closer.

'Tell me this, Frank – what do you need that would make you feel better?'

He shrugged. 'I wish it had never happened.'

She shook her head. 'We cain't undo what's bin done, Frank.'

Frank breathed, nodded and got up to leave. He was walking along the edge of a precipice, close to the edge, but his steps were steady. 'Okay.' They both smiled.

'Y'all come back now.'

CHAPTER 8

Frank went straight to work. If he didn't report to Colonel Bradsleap now, it wouldn't happen. He strode through the car park to the lift, every nerve twitching, his courage seeping out with every step.

The lift took ages. Maybe he should take the lift on the other side of the car park. He paused, watching the numbers barely moving. This was taking too long. Yes, he'd better get the lift on the other side of the carpark. He made it across to the other side just in time to hear the ding of the lift he'd just left, announcing its arrival. *Jesus Christ.* He hurried back, but he wasn't fast enough. The lift doors closed before he got there. He snorted, took half a step back towards the stairs, but then thought he'd be better off waiting. Was somebody doing this on purpose to stop him from getting to Bradsleap? How could he get past this elevator trickery? He thrummed his fingers on the lift doors. A flying, exploded body seared through his mind. Frank rested his head on the elevator door. It suddenly opened, and he jumped back. Several privates piled out, looking important, on some kind of mission. He waited for their salute, but they did not even acknowledge him, not even a nod. He was a lieutenant, goddammit. They couldn't ignore him.

The rage steamed away in his head and around his shoulders as he forced himself into the lift. His hands shook as he urgently pressed the button for the fifth floor before anything fizzed out of him. From inside the lift, he watched the doors close, and he pictured the newly promoted Colonel Bradsleap in his office. What would he say when Frank told him? What kind of trouble would it cause with Torus? Anyway, whatever. It would be over soon. He would tell Bradsleap and that would be that.

But when the lift doors opened, it was the second floor and Kain Webber stood there with his woolly eyes. The last person Frank wanted to see. Webber took a step towards the lift, then saw Frank and stopped. Frank didn't want to lie to his friend, but *don't tell anyone, even Webber,* swirled round in his head. Webber wasn't ready when the lift doors started to close on him. Frank was relieved that he wouldn't have to talk to Webber, but suddenly Webber stuck his arm out to stop the lift from closing.

'What happened, Frank?'

No, don't tell him.

Frank jammed the close button again, wishing the doors would close faster. But they slid open instead.

Webber had that confused, curious look on his face. 'You know, the other day. You took off after going down into the bunker. There were explosions on Narus.'

A rumour must have started about the bunker. Frank shrugged and looked away. Thankfully, the lift doors started to close again. Until again, they touched Webber's arm and sprang open. Webber still had his arm jammed between the lift doors. This time the doors didn't open but instead made a raucous buzzing sound, insisting that they be able to close. Webber was tenacious; he wouldn't give up when he had a bee in his bonnet. Frank sighed, surrendered and pulled the doors apart and walked out of the lift into the corridor. He'd give Webber five minutes. Webber looked at him, seeming to say a thousand words without speaking. Trying to spook him out, make him talk. But Frank would not give in. Webber changed tack.

'I was going to show you my hybrid spider. It's a dandy.'

'Okay, look, I'm sorry,' Frank said instead, wishing he could say more.

Webber waited, but there was nothing else Frank could say. Finally, Webber shrugged and said, 'Come into the lab.'

Frank could feel his own determination weakening. He really didn't want to talk to Bradsleap. It would be much nicer sharing a cup of tea with Webs than going upstairs to report Torus.

'I've only got five minutes.'

Webber pulled at his elbow, and Frank followed into Webber's laboratory. Frank sat down on one of Webber's high stools.

'You don't look good, Frank. You haven't shaved. You look like you've been camping out.'

Camping out was almost the truth. He'd slept all night in the car, woke up stiff and couldn't move. Frank rubbed and stretched his neck and relaxed onto the stool.

'I'll put the kettle on.' Webber's voice seemed far away. The 'kettle' was a small flask suspended over a Bunsen burner. Webber had another try. 'What happened down there, Frank?'

Frank's determination to see Bradsleap was leaking out of

him. 'Got to get upstairs,' he said feebly. *But a cup of tea can't hurt. I'll rest for a moment.*

Webber gave up with the inquisition and sat down on another high stool at his bench. Frank looked up at him, surrounded by his toys. Test tubes, Bunsen burners, all kinds of measuring instruments, books and documents falling all over each other, wires and cables everywhere. How in the world did he keep it all together? Frank felt an envy that Webber's life was so disorderly and comfortable. Webber noticed Frank's interest. He leaned in as though ready to share his greatest secret.

'Did I tell you we've created the world's biggest cockroach, big as a mouse?'

A mouse? Frank latched onto the opportunity to be distracted from his own thoughts. 'Oh yeah?' He had to admit that was funny. 'What're you gonna do with it?'

That seemed to stump Webber for a moment. He shrugged. 'Dunno. Somethin'.'

Frank had to admit, Webber could always lift his mood. He was a strange one, with his little family of inventions. What had he bred so far? Giant cockroaches, an Alsatian as big as a donkey that would defend you to the death – but it was stolen by Torus. And that killer spider he was talking about.

'Let me show you the spider.' Webber pulled away a little curtain from in front of a see-through Perspex box. In the bottom corner of the box was a little curled-up black piece of fluff. Webber knocked on the side of the box, and the little piece of fluff sprouted legs and stretched them out. It became the distinct shape of a spider. Frank clenched his fists, trying to get his resolve back. What was he doing here? This wasn't going to solve his problem. He had to see Bradsleap.

'It's a cross between a redback and a funnelweb.'

'I know, I know.'

'It kills immediately.'

'You said that.' Frank had to get to the colonel. He shot upright. 'Listen, Webs, I can't see your spider right now.' But Webber's eyes twinkled.

'Watch this,' he said and opened a tiny hole at the top of the box. He poked a little plunger into the hole and squeezed a mist into the box. The spider immediately sprang into life, running around the cage, banging into the walls, fangs out, snapping at the sides of the box like a mad thing.

'Bloody hell!' Frank jumped back, startled at the ferocity of the little beast. Torus would love something like that. It made Frank wonder about Webber sometimes.

'You go do your important stuff,' Webber said with a twinkle.

'Bye,' Frank mumbled as he scurried out of the lab and back to the lift. He felt even more nervous about talking to Bradsleap, but he forced himself to press the button for the fifth floor.

Frank lowered his head and wished he was going to his own office as the lift lumbered up to Bradsleap's office. At his own office he would wander in, swivel his chair right and left, nudge the mouse, and the screen would come alight, showing the spreadsheet he'd been working on. He would become calm. Numbers, little boxes all in order, doing what they were told. His fingers would click on the keyboard, calming him as he worked. All his yesterdays would recede. Maybe it would all fade away if he ignored it. The lift door pinged, and Frank jolted up his head, startled to see Colonel Bradsleap standing there, just outside the lift.

'Frank, I was coming to see you.' Bradsleap looked a little ridiculous with his big handlebar moustache; he should have been in the air force rather than the army.

Why is he coming to see me?

Frank stepped out of the lift, expecting to follow Bradsleap to his office, but Bradsleap ushered him back inside the lift.

'No, Frank, let's go down to your office,' he said brightly. He was a genial character, well liked as a major, but generally ineffectual. Not usually this secretive though. Frank's nerves tightened a notch.

In the lift down, Frank stood formally at ease, dry mouth, hands behind his back, while Bradsleap fidgeted with the points of his moustache, clearing his throat regularly. Did this change anything? Why did Bradsleap want them to go to Frank's office? Frank thought he must be in more trouble. What did Bradsleap have on his mind? What did he want?

Outside Frank's office, Bradsleap threw a conspiratorial glance along the corridor, then bustled enthusiastically inside. He grabbed Frank's hand to shake it.

'I need to tell you something,' said Frank.

'Shut the door for a moment.'

'About Torus.'

'Come inside, Frank.'

'About what happened in the bunker… I don't know what Torus has told you, but …'

'Frank, will you come inside, for God's sake?' Bradsleap's enthusiasm seemed to have turned to irritation. He sat down in Frank's chair, then twiddled the left end of his moustache, even stiffer than usual. Bradsleap cleared his throat.

'Major Torus told me about your heroic actions down in the bunker. I thought I'd come down here and see you myself. I know it's a great strain, what you had to do, but I have told Torus that you will be getting a citation for your work.' Despite his words, there was a nervous edge in Bradsleap's voice, and he twiddled the other end of his moustache.

'You spoke with Torus already?' asked Frank.

'We have to keep things in order, Frank. I've been advised that we need to keep this quiet.'

Advised? But he was the Colonel, supposed to be in charge. 'By General Praxis?' Frank was unable to sit down. He paced over to the filing cabinet.

Bradsleap cleared his throat again. 'Never mind about that.' Frank had a nauseous feeling that Torus was behind the decision to keep things quiet.

'You'll be getting a citation for bravery, and also, we'll bring your promotion to captain forward a few years.'

A promotion? *It must really be a big deal.*

Bradsleap leaned forward and whispered, 'I can see you're sceptical. Don't worry, I can arrange these things.' He chuckled, leaned back, and tapped his finger on the side of his nose. 'Good for you, Frank, Captain of Bookkeeping. Funny, huh?'

Frank screwed his eyes shut. *Torus must have more power around here than I thought. What's he got over Bradsleap?* Maybe it's because Bradsleap is a lazy, over-promoted buffoon who has no interest in Border Force protocol.

'I was going to tell you about what happened in the bunker. Have you ever been in a war, sir? Have you ever seen a dead body, half a dead body flying through the air?'

Bradsleap didn't seem to hear a word.

'And captains make more money than lieutenants,' Bradsleap sailed on. 'Quite a bit more. It's all arranged. We'll rush the promotion through so there's no messing about.' He tapped both his index fingers on the points of his shiny, waxed facial hair. 'And don't worry about the repercussions.'

'Repercussions?' Frank imagined himself hauled up

before an enquiry, taking all the blame, and Torus innocently sitting in the back of the room, smirking.

'Yes, all that dreadful psychological stuff.' Bradsleap shuddered. 'Some fellows can get very disturbed after an incident like this. The amenders will take care of all that.'

'I know about the amenders.'

'You get five free visits, courtesy of Border Force.'

'I know about the five free visits.'

Frank's intercom buzzed.

'You better get that.'

It was Torus. 'Bargen, get up here.' Torus snarled.

Frank looked at Bradsleap, wondering what to do.

'Yes, yes. Don't keep him waiting. He's a busy man. Great assistance to a colonel like myself. Well, I'm off. Make sure everything's okay with the major.' Bradsleap cleared his throat again and hastily left.

Why did Frank even think it would be any good talking to Bradsleap? Torus was obviously running things and could do whatever he wanted. Bradsleap was following his orders, not the other way around. But why? It was a reversal of the proper way to do things, the way all armies operated and the way every recruit was trained. Colonels do not take orders from majors. Bradsleap was as scared of Torus as the rest of them.

~

Frank stood in the waiting room outside Torus's office, next to the desk where the adjutant would normally sit. He was relieved the desk was empty. The adjutant, Corporal Carnley, was creepy, a complete suck-up to Torus. Frank never really came up here to Torus's office. He usually spent his working life locked away in his office, which gave him some respite from his crumbling home life. But now, even his workplace was turning on him.

A picture on the wall caught his eye, a battle scene from about two hundred years ago in an expensive-looking, gold Baroque frame. The painting was crammed with horses screaming, their nostrils flared, mouths wide open and teeth bared, eyes bulging as they lay dying in the soil. Some were already dead, and some were rotting carcasses, puss oozing from wounds and decay starting. Frank could almost hear the thundering hooves and cacophony of the battle. How could such pain and distress be allowed to exist in the world? If there was a God, He must be criminally insane!

Frank's mind went back to Sunday School as a child. They said Jesus would wipe away your sins. Little Frankie's contribution was that life must be like a long toilet roll where you write down all the things you have done wrong, and Jesus comes along with a big eraser and rubs out all the bad bits. The other kids in the class laughed. Frankie went home humiliated and figured that Sunday School wasn't for him.

Frank wilted, his knees dropped, and the throbbing screams in his mind came back. No way could he confront Torus.

Carnley appeared with his bald head and crooked smirk. He'd never got past corporal, having spent his army life sidled up against Torus to give himself some pride. He took a long, suspicious look at Frank, then sat down at his desk, leaning back with his hands behind his head.

'I'm expected,' Frank said.

Carnley did not reply. He continued to silently study Frank as if he was soaking up his discomfort. He was trying to be a copy of Torus, chest thrust out, buttons straining to keep his shirt closed. Frank got nervous, then angry at

Carnley's impudent staring. Frank's mind raced, trying to think of some cutting remark to make Carnley back off, but he couldn't focus. A leering smile started to spread across Carnley's face, revealing his missing front teeth. Rumour had it that he lost them in a bar fight over in the Cross. Frank slowly opened his mouth to speak.

'Frank, come in!' Torus suddenly bellowed from inside the closed office.

Carnley flicked his head towards Torus's door and smiled as if Frank was in for a mauling. What did Carnley know anyway? He was Torus's stooge, didn't have a brain of his own. Frank wiped the sweat off his brow, creaked opened the door and sidled inside. There were more pictures on the walls of horses dying in battle. Frank shuddered.

Torus looked out the window over the parade ground with his back to Frank. Cigar smoke floated around. Frank waited inside the door, standing *at ease*, hands clasped behind him. Torus turned and blew out a cone of cigar smoke.

Did Torus have special permission to smoke inside, or did he just not care? He recalled Bradsleap telling him not to keep Torus waiting and thought the latter was more likely.

He can probably do exactly what he wants.

'Go ahead, Frank, sit down.' He waved an arm at the easy chair, and Frank sat stiffly, ambushed.

Torus pulled out from his desk drawer two glasses and a half bottle of whisky. 'I want to congratulate you on your great dedication to duty.'

Frank watched the whisky slosh into the glasses, spilling a little. Was Torus already drunk?

'I know it wasn't easy obeying that order, never having seen action.' Torus offered the glass and glugged his own back quickly. Frank took his glass and held it with both hands, cradled in his lap. He had picked up the veiled accusation of cowardice. What did Torus want now? Bradsleap had already told Frank to shut up, so Torus was definitely in the driver's seat.

'Drink up, Frank. It's a great day for you.' Torus sat down behind his desk. Frank was a deer in the headlights, and Bradsleap was going to be no help. Frank had to think of something to do, but his mind was a whirlwind of confusion, refusing even to bring the whisky to his mouth. The glass sat there in his lap, quivering slightly.

Torus swivelled his chair back towards the parade ground. A drill sergeant was shouting orders to the practicing platoon.

'What you did down there was… dutiful,' Torus said to the window. 'Dutiful… and even heroic.'

Frank didn't feel heroic. He felt scummy.

'Maybe it doesn't feel like that yet, but it will.' Torus spun his chair directly towards Frank and fixed him with a stare. 'You're an experienced officer, Frank, one of the best, looking after the home front. Bookkeeping is an important function in the army. You understand that we can't let this little episode get out, so you will have to be an unsung hero.'

Torus took a puff on his cigar. 'Keeping secrets is heroic too. We all have our little secrets. Of course, there's a promotion coming up for you. *Captain Bargen.* Sounds good, doesn't it?'

Frank looked down at his scotch and quivered.

I was following your orders. He waited. Should he say it? He watched the scotch swirl in the glass and took a quick slug for courage and wiped the back of his hand across his mouth and growled. 'Maybe it wasn't the right thing to do.'

Torus snapped the cigar in his mouth and snarled through his teeth, doing his best Jack Nicholson impression.

'Indeed, it was, Frank. Never forget that following orders is always the right thing to do. Leave the morality to the higher-ups.'

Frank recoiled. He couldn't say he had ever thought much about morality before. He assumed it was obvious what was right. 'And killing refugees is the right thing to do?'

'They were illegals, causing trouble. We had to test the ground. It's a war zone out there. Now we'll know how far we can go. If it all blows over, we can consolidate.' Torus sucked in on his cigar and shrugged. 'I'm following orders too.'

Frank was starting to doubt Torus followed any orders against his will. He was a cruel *Salivator*, an animal. Like an attack dog let loose to eliminate the enemies no one wanted to acknowledge.

'We're on the same page, aren't we, Frank?' Torus watched him like he was an ant ready to be stomped on.

Frank shifted uncomfortably, and the chair creaked so loud it was like an alarm. What would Torus say if he told him how he really felt?

He saw the screaming horses with their guts splattered on the battlefield and shivered. It didn't bear thinking about.

He nodded.

'I knew you were a smart man, Frank.' Torus sipped more whisky and blew a perfect smoke ring.

A promotion, and he wouldn't even have to do anything, just shut up. They could move back to the Eastern Suburbs. Marta would be happy spending all day with the officers' wives. All those medical bills for the kids – he could pay them with ease. Maybe he could even get better health insurance if he pushed Bradsleap a bit. There were definite benefits to keeping quiet, and it's not like he even really had a choice. It wasn't as though Bradsleap was going to back him over Torus.

This morning had made that clear.

He took a small sip of whisky and forced a weak smile. 'I guess they were just illegals.'

Torus eyed Frank cautiously. He did not quite look convinced.

'So, you see what has to be done here.' Torus opened a drawer and quickly grabbed at something and grinned. 'Let me show you what I've got here.'

Torus stalked round to the front of the desk, fist closed. Something weird was about to happen. Frank's shiver turned into a chill. Torus came close, closer than was comfortable, and snatched the cigar out of his mouth and threw it out the window. He spat out some tobacco dregs.

'Have you heard about the latest little monsters those boffins down in the genetics lab have been creating?'

Frank was startled by this sudden change in the conversation. What was going on?

Torus lifted his closed fist in front of Frank's face. He slowly unrolled his fingers, and a huge cockroach as big as a mouse was crawling there. 'This is Kain Webber's latest.'

Frank shuddered.

'It could be bad for everyone if too much of this story got out, don't you think?'

Torus snapped the cockroach into his mouth and chewed slowly, deliberately, his eyes never leaving Frank's, as its legs waved about.

Frank stared horrified at the insect's legs flickering about on Torus's lips. Disgust swarmed up through his belly. The man was an animal. Frank jumped up, dropped the whisky glass and ran, collided with the wall, righted himself and somehow made it through the door, clutching at his stomach.

He barely registered the smirk on Carnley's face outside

the office as he groped past.

Got to get out of here. Don't care, got to get out. Go home.
He staggered his way towards the lift, bouncing off the walls, the hallway spinning as Torus's maniacal laughter echoed behind him.

CHAPTER 9

Torus nearly gagged as he spat out most of the cockroach. It tasted like crunchy chicken, but was disgusting, floating round his tongue. Just one of the things you have to do to get people to do the right thing. Carnley was in hysterics. Torus couldn't tell if he was laughing or dying of repulsion. Carnley couldn't tell either, by the look of it. He was pretty dumb, but he did what he was told. He looked pretty funny with his missing teeth. But Torus had had enough.

'Shut up. Shut the fuck up, let me think!'

Carnley slammed his hand over his mouth, but he couldn't stop the hysteria. He snorted and gushes of snot came out of his nose.

Now that was funny.

'Get out of here, you fool,' laughed Torus. Carnley nodded and staggered out the door. *What a moron!*

'Get back in here.' Torus heaved a huge breath. 'I can't believe you actually walked out. Carnley, come here and stand in front of me.'

Carnley slithered back in the door, trying to stop laughing or crying or something, in a state of one hundred percent attempted obedience. *Poor little fool!*

'When I said *get out,* I didn't mean *get out.* It was a joke.' Torus waited for Carnley to stop sniggering. He was taking his time with it.

'Stop it, you're irritating me. Just shut up!' Torus felt a twinge of unease that Carnley wasn't immediately obeying the order. Torus screwed a tight look at Carnley. *Is he laughing at me?*

Torus's mind flashed back to 1999 and his first time at that party. He remembered himself creeping out of the bedroom after that stupid girl got away from him. From across the room, that kid from school was smirking at him. Micky knew that the kid was trying to make him look like a fool who couldn't get laid. Micky Torus had felt that familiar feeling in his hands – that crazy burning fire. He'd raced across the room, knocked over a table and grabbed the kid by the throat and squeezed. His hands abruptly cooled off, pleased. The intolerable fire subsided, and the others dragged him away. That kid never smirked again.

Torus looked at Carnley. His missing teeth and oozing snot made Torus step back, disgusted. His hands were burning with the desire to choke something. Torus looked at Carnley's neck, exposed and inviting, his hands drawn towards it. He reached over and cupped his palm under Carnley's chin and slowly put the other hand around Carnley's neck and gave it a little shake.

'Do you think Frank will be a problem, Carnley?'

Carnley was smart enough not to back away, but his eyes were bright with terror. Carnley's extreme fear calmed Torus.

'So, no laughing now?' Torus pushed Carnley's chin and

slapped his face, just for fun. 'Watch Bargen. I don't trust him. I want his emails checked and his phone bugged. Tail him. Now you get out of here, you idiot.'

Carnley bolted.

CHAPTER 10

Frank had only the vaguest recollection of leaving the barracks. Blurred images of the elevator, through the car park, his lungs screaming for air.

As those burning refugees would have screamed.

The drive to Gunderman was a complete haze. Marta stood by the door when he got home. His mind had closed down so much that he hardly knew where he was.

'Getting promoted,' he mumbled, pushing past her.

'Oh.' Marta looked confused. 'How was the shrink?'

Frank vaguely remembered visiting Yo-Knee earlier that morning. It seemed like ages ago. He dipped his head, feeling guilty somehow.

'Good, good. She was good. She's an amender, not a shrink.'

Marta looked him up and down. 'She?'

He nodded, then turned away. Surely, she couldn't be jealous. There were lots of women psychiatrists around. It's normal. He had to try harder.

'I'm getting promoted,' he beamed. Or at least he tried to. He had no idea how he appeared; he felt drunk.

'What do you mean?'

That vague tiredness came over him again. The words stuck in his mouth. Why couldn't he tell her? She'd be thrilled. He would definitely tell her, but not until he could get his head around everything that was going on.

'Not now.' He pushed past her and out the back door. He needed the river.

'But Frank, what—'

'I said, not now!' he yelled. Why did no one listen to him?

He trudged out to Jimmy Budabuda's tree round the back of the house, where the flowing river used to soothe him as a child. He lay on the hammock and tried to calm his furtive breath. If only Jimmy was here with his wisdom. He tried to focus on the river, listen for its gentle song, but it wasn't properly there. He closed his aching eyes and jerked as the rope weavings of the hammock irritated his cheek. He rolled sideways and his fingers caught in the netting. The river was too silent. Or too loud, or just too … something.

He opened his eyes and stared mournfully at the bush around him. Maybe if he went for a swim. Maybe the river would calm him then. Looking down, a cockroach crawled beneath him on the ground, and his mind filled with the image of Torus's mouth chewing it. No! Not here, in his place. Torus wasn't allowed here. River, river, you've abandoned me!

He scrambled back inside, grabbed a handful of Xanax, lay down in his old childhood bedroom, and fell asleep.

⁓

Next morning, he woke in a raging fever. All that day, the fever flamed through his body. The next day, he awoke shivering in a cold sweat. Even blankets couldn't get him warm.

'I'm cold, Marta. I'm getting promoted.'

'Never mind, Frank. Go back to sleep.'

'You're going to be happy.'

In the middle of the next night, the fever started up again. And on it went for a week. Hot, cold, hot, cold.

One morning, he opened his eyes and the morning sun streamed through the window. The tempest was gone, and Marta was merrily vacuuming the house. She came into the room and felt his forehead.

'Fever's gone.' She smiled at him. Was she really happy? He could hardly remember the events of the last week. Just flashes of her shooing away the kids' curiosity. He vaguely remembered telling her about his promotion and plans to move back to Woollahra. How much did he tell her?

'You said something about getting promoted. What's that about?'

'Something I did down in the bunker.'

'The bunker? What's that?'

'It's a secret facility underground – beneath Victoria Barracks.'

'What did you do?'

'Classif—'

'I know, I know.' She gave him a quizzical look. 'Whatever it was, it must have freaked you out. You've been crazy lately. And now they're promoting you. Are you being paid off for something?'

Suddenly, Frank knew that's exactly what was going on. He was being silenced. 'No, no, nothing like that. It's a promotion.'

Marta went quiet and then looked up directly at Frank.

She was waiting for the penny to drop, but Frank became uncomfortable. She continued looking. Frank still tried to keep things from her. At last she spoke. 'Frank, they're trying to keep you quiet about something. My father was in the navy. I grew up surrounded by the military. I can smell it.'

'Keep me quiet?'

'Whatever that thing is that you won't tell me about. That *classified* secret, that thing that freaked you out so much that you spent the night in the bush. You had that look about you. I saw that look in my father's eyes once. My mother never found out what had happened.' She shrugged. 'He was more attached to his country than his family. My father got a medal.'

'It's classified,' Frank said weakly, mutely confirming all she'd said.

She raised her eyebrows. *See?*

'What's the promotion for again? Bookkeeping bravery?'

Part of him crumpled inside. She was right; his life was a hopeless mess. He was a bookkeeper, not a soldier.

'It's for following my duty as a loyal soldier.'

'Whatever you say, Frank.'

The kids stood at the end of the bed, watching. Even Mercury was quiet, hanging onto a broken toy and standing mute next to Palace. He held her hand, looking forlorn. But suddenly he ran towards the bed, pushed past his mother and hugged his father like he'd found a lost toy. His dad was back. Frank held his son tightly and caressed the back of his head. Soon Mercury was excited about something else, let go, and raced from the room. Frank watched him go and felt an immense urge to protect his son and his family.

Palace slowly walked towards him, her head down. Frank put his hand under her chin and lifted it up. He looked into her soulful eyes. She breathed in and let out a big sigh and smiled. They hugged. Frank looked at Marta, and she had a tear welling in her eye. She smiled at her husband and looked relieved that he was back from his craziness. Behind her, he noticed the shabby walls. *This isn't the place for them. We'll go back to Woollahra.*

Mercury darted into the room with a football, ready to play. Palace let go of her hug, and Frank felt a tsunami of exhaustion hit him. He fell back onto the pillow.

'Why are you getting promoted, Dad?' asked Palace.

Frank wearily opened his eyes and looked at Marta. Had she put the kids up to questioning him?

'For something I did at work.'

'Something good?'

Getting promoted and moving to Woollahra was the right thing to do. 'Yes, something good, sweetheart.'

~

Mercury bounced about in the car as they drove along Oxford Street. They passed the barracks where Frank worked, and he shivered as the memories came up. He sped up and shot through Paddington.

'Turn right here,' said Marta. Frank wheeled into Centennial Park, not far from where they used to live. 'Let's have a nice picnic like we used to, and I'm sure you'll feel better about moving back here.'

'We're going to Sentil Park, we're going to Sentil Park,' sang Mercury.

Palace sighed. 'It's Centennial Park, dummy, not Sentil.'

Mercury dropped his head, and Frank could feel his disappointment.

'Centennial, Centennial. See, I can say it.' Mercury poked his tongue out at Palace.

She huffed. 'It takes you so long to learn things because you're too impatient. I'm not impatient and I learn things quickly.'

'I don't care. Centennial, Centennial,' he chanted proudly.

Frank pulled the car up alongside the narrow horse track that circled the park.

Marta gazed across to the lake. 'I used to ride round here all day long when I was a kid.'

Frank smiled as he carried the Esky out of the car boot.

'Can we eat now?' moaned Mercury.

'You were always fast, Mercs,' Frank said with a coy glance at Marta. 'When you were born, you were in such a hurry, you chased your newborn sister right out of your mum's belly half a minute later.'

Marta smiled. 'We didn't have a name for you,' she joked, 'We didn't even want to know what sex our new baby was going to be, and suddenly there you were, Twin Number Two.' Frank and Marta looked at each other, sharing the memory. Mercury stared at the ground.

'I've got a real name now though.' He dragged the picnic table across the grass and over the horse track.

'The nurse thought of your name,' Frank went on. 'She said that was the quickest second twin birth she had ever seen and reckoned we should call you Mercury, the fastest planet in the sky.'

Palace listened intently. 'I was first,' she said.

'But I'm the fastest star in the sky.' A horse galloped by, too close, throwing up clouds of dust, and Mercury spluttered.

'No, the fastest planet, Mercs. Stars are the ones that don't move, but planets move past the stars. Remember, I showed you the planet Mercury, and then a few weeks later it had moved?'

'I move faster than that.' And he took off towards the horse track, then halted. 'That horse smells like poo,' he frowned. 'We used to live here, didn't we? I liked it better when we lived here.'

Frank looked at Marta, and she stretched her arms out and did a little twirl. Her dress flared out, and she had that *home at last* smile.

She leaned down to Mercury. 'Do you like it here, honey?' He nodded furiously. 'Maybe we'll move back here then.'

Frank bustled with the picnic table. He looked darkly towards Oxford Street. Woollahra reminded him of the events in the bunker, and he felt the familiar knot in his stomach.

'Can we move back here?' Mercury implored.

Frank was having serious doubts about that. 'Let's have a picnic first, then we'll see.'

Afterwards, when the picnic was cleared up, Frank said, 'Let's go and look at the labyrinth.'

Mercury jumped up. 'Lab-rinse, lab-rinse!'

Palace looked at him with that look she reserved for special looks at Mercury when he was being particularly annoying. It was a look so strong she seemed to be talking. 'You idiot,' she said. 'It's not lab-rinse, it's labyrinth.'

'I know, I know, lab-a-rinth. We came here before, and I got to the middle first,' Mercury yelled back at her.

'Yes, but you're not supposed to go straight to the middle in a straight line. You're supposed to go round and round the pathway, like a snake.'

'I know, I know, I can do it now.' He ran to the entrance to the labyrinth and waited impatiently while everybody else caught up.

Frank cast his eyes over the labyrinth, a giant concrete platter with a sinuous pathway leading to the centre. A sign said, *Begin Here.* Frank started reading. *The Labyrinth is a journey to the centre of your adversity – walk calmly and feel the happiness of being. Let your light be a lantern, not a spotlight.*

Mercury fidgeted.

Marta yawned. 'I'll give it a miss, I think. See you back at the car.' She put her arm around Palace's shoulders. 'You should walk to the centre, Frank. Get some of that distress out of your system.' Palace frowned at her mother and Marta bit her lip, sighed, and led Palace back to the car. 'C'mon, baby, let the boys do their thing.'

Frank recoiled at Marta's jibe. He was trying, wasn't he? Trying to be normal. 'C'mon, Mercs, let's walk it together.'

Mercury stood to attention and concentrated as Frank explained the rules.

'You have to walk along this wiggly path that leads to the centre, and you aren't allowed to be tricky and cross over to the next bit of the path. You could easily pull a fast one if you wanted to and get to the centre quickly, but that would be trickery, and we don't want that.'

Mercury stood more erect. 'I'm not tricky!'

'No, mate, no. Everything's good, okay?'

Mercury took up his position at the front and proudly stepped into the labyrinth. Marta and Palace watched from over near the car. Mercury walked forward to the first turning and went round the bend, then another bend, then a third. He was itching to dart straight for the centre, never mind all the turning backwards and forwards along the pathway.

'Be patient, Mercs.'

'I'll pretend these are high walls,' said Mercury, 'and you can't cross them.'

'That's right, mate.' Frank's thoughts went back to his own childhood. No way would his father have done anything like walk through a labyrinth with little Frankie. It would have been absurd and faintly unmanly.

'And there's pretend electricity,' said Mercury. 'If you touch the walls, you get a shock.' He raced ahead with his shoulders scrunched up to avoid the electric walls. He hurtled round the twists and turns and reached the centre. Frank smiled and felt pride.

Mercury wondered what to do next, and Frank watched his confusion. Would he keep going along the meandering path and back out of the labyrinth again, or would he feel that the game was finished and he could now bolt back out in a straight line, never mind the pretend electrified walls?

Mercury jumped up and down a little, waiting for his dad, who was only halfway through the labyrinth.

'I got to the centre, I got to the centre.' He pulled his arms in to his sides, as if he really were trapped in a small space. 'I did it! I got through the lab-rinse without touching the sides.' He looked over towards his mother and Palace.

Palace watched sternly and gave him that look again.

'Lab-a-rinth,' Mercury corrected himself and poked out his tongue towards Palace, who looked at her mother. Frank looked over towards them and saw Palace mouth the words, 'At least he can do *something*.'

Marta smiled.

Mercury's jumping got more and more frenetic, like he was rooted there. His face became more distressed; he couldn't go back, and he couldn't go forward. He couldn't go anywhere, even though there really wasn't any wall. Frank had seen this before. Mercury had conjured up such a fantasy world that he was stuck within it. Frank hurried through the labyrinth and caught up to him at the centre.

The spell was broken, and Mercury suddenly dashed across all the wiggling pathways, breaking all the rules, crashing through the imaginary electrified walls and straight back to his mother and Palace waiting near the car. He was still panting by the time Frank got back there.

'Nearly made it,' said Palace, and she punched him gently on the arm. A tear rolled down his cheek. Frank softly touched Mercury's cheek and felt an overwhelming feeling of protection for his family. He had no further doubts that he would keep quiet, take the promotion, and move back to Woollahra.

CHAPTER 11

The day arrived. Frank stood in front of the mirror in the bedroom and checked himself out. Shoulders back, chin tucked in. He saluted. Then he caught himself. *Seriously? You're saluting yourself?*

He grinned. Well, it was a big deal. First day back at work. They really wanted to get this promotion done quickly. There was some sort of medal coming as well.

Marta came up behind him and put a hand on his shoulder. She smiled. 'You look like my father. Every time he got promoted, he saluted himself in the mirror. My mother thought it was boys playing with toys. I think she died of boredom in the end.'

He adjusted his tie. 'You'll probably die of boredom as well as a captain's wife.'

She laughed. 'Not me, I can't wait to get back to Woollahra.' Marta really was happy. He was making her happy, finally.

Unlike his last journey, Frank's drive to work was sharp

and clear. He was feeling better.

He greeted Webber in the corridor. 'Hi, Webs.'

Webber stared, looking up and down at Frank's neat uniform. Frank waited for Webber to acknowledge in some way that Frank was back to his best. There had been rumours around the base that he was losing it.

'Better that the last time you were here,' Webber grunted. He shrugged and turned away. Frank was unnerved, but Webber could be moody.

At five to ten, Frank strode up to Torus's office, where the promotion ceremony was to take place. Frank knew he had gone off the rails a bit, but that week off had done him a world of good, and he was ready to settle back into work as usual. He was eager to get the whole thing over with, but he didn't want to be too early and have to talk to Carnley. Luckily, Carnley's chair was empty, and Frank sat down in the other chair, relieved. He forced himself not to look up at the painting of the dead horses on the battlefield. He wondered why they picked Torus's office instead of the main hall downstairs, where these ceremonies usually happened. *Were they trying to keep it under wraps as much as possible? Oh, keep quiet, stop thinking too much. Everything will be okay.*

The peace didn't last long. Carnley came round the corner and grinned that grin of his, not saying anything. It was like he was mute; a lurking sneer said everything. He deliberately glared at Frank and then up at the painting, but Frank kept his head down.

'Gunna be a captain, huh?' Without waiting for an answer, Carnley threw his satchel onto the desk and sat down. Frank pulled his feet under his chair. This corporal wouldn't be giving him any more respect as a captain than he'd got as a second lieutenant. But as he was Torus's man, it was to be expected. Things would be different with everyone else. Everyone else round the base would respect his new rank.

Colonel Bradsleap sauntered up, looking nonchalant. Was he whistling?

'Hello, Frank, ready for the big promotion? I remember when I was promoted to captain.' He leaned forward towards both Frank and Carnley as if about to tell a great story. Carnley tried not to look bored.

Bradsleap wistfully pointed out of the window. 'It was in a ceremony with ten others down there on the parade ground. This is exciting. I've never seen a field promotion before, let alone awarded one. I've only been a colonel for a few weeks. Just getting to know the ropes.'

Frank nodded slightly. Bradsleap patted him on the shoulder and disappeared into Torus's office. Carnley gave Frank a look as if to say *that man's an idiot.*

Volf trotted round the corner, followed by Torus. The dog saw Frank and barked. He bounded into Frank and barrelled him into the wall and off his feet, Volf's enormous tongue licking Frank's face. Frank laughed and grabbed Volf by the ears and shook his head, propelling Volf into a storm of licking saturation. Frank was going to be in trouble for this. Volf was Torus's dog, supposedly.

Torus yanked Volf up by the collar, and the dog made a sickening, choking noise. Frank scrambled to his feet, ready to protect the dog, but then remembered where he was. Torus stared him down, and Carnley smirked. From inside Torus's office, Bradsleap coughed quietly. Frank brushed down his uniform, trying not to look at poor Volf. Without a word, Torus let go of the dog collar, and Volf slumped to the ground with a small whimper. Torus strode into his office. Carnley followed, leaving Frank and Volf behind.

'Come inside, Frank,' shouted Bradsleap, and Frank wondered again why his promotion was being done in Torus's office. He followed carefully.

'Stand here.' Bradsleap motioned opposite the picture of the dying horses. 'In front of Major Torus's wonderful reproductions.' Frank looked slightly to the side to avoid looking at the painting.

Bradsleap coughed and stood up straight. 'This promotion ceremony is designated a field advancement because of the secret nature of the events.'

Secret? Is it even a real promotion? Frank rigidly fixed his eyes on the wall to avoid those chilling, dead warhorses.

Bradsleap approached to pin on the medal, then noticed Frank's eyes looking at the wall and shot a quick glance to where Frank was staring. Nothing there, just a blank wall. He continued.

This is definitely a bribe to shut me up. Frank stood stock still and somehow knew that everyone here had caught on to the fact that Frank now *knew*. He sighed and indulged an inner smile. Everyone, including Frank, now wanted it to be over with. He heard Torus's feet shuffling in impatience. Carnley lurked in the far corner, almost out of eyeshot.

'You are hereby promoted to the rank of captain and awarded the Australian Overseas Service Medal,' said Bradsleap.

Frank had never been out of Australia in his life, but Narus Island was considered to be part of Australia's border protection zone, and Frank's button-pressing in the bunker meant that he had technically served overseas. Amazing how far the army could stretch the truth.

Bradsleap pinned the medal on Frank's uniform, handed over the new captain's epaulettes, and shook Frank's hand.

Frank saluted sharply. Bradsleap's salute was more casual. Torus coughed, and Carnley lazily pushed himself off the wall.

'Well ...' said Bradsleap, 'that's that, I suppose, er, good luck, Frank. I suppose I didn't do too badly, my first field promotion, eh?' He twiddled his moustache. No one said anything, and Bradsleap made a quick exit, followed by Carnley. Frank felt empty and disappointed. He had imagined there would be more of a fanfare. They really were keeping this quiet. He felt grubby.

He looked at Torus, who grabbed a handful of Volf's fur and said without looking up, 'Okay, Frank, that's it.'

He was dismissed.

~

Frank was suddenly in the corridor outside and then stopped. There he was with his newly awarded AOSM, full-dress uniform and captain's epaulettes clutched in his fingers. He tried to feel proud, but it was hard to make much of a go of it.

So that's it?

Halfway back to his office, he was distracted looking at his new epaulettes when he bumped into Kain Webber. Frank had never seen such coldness. What was it? Disdain? Betrayal? Kain looked at the medal, shook his head, and walked off.

Frank watched his stiff, hunched shoulders and felt something real disappearing from his life. He had never realised before how much he liked Webber. He may never talk to him again. No more cups of tea in his lab looking at his strange creatures. But why? Was he that bad for doing his job?

No, he had no choice. Fuck it, Webber's attitude was his problem. Everyone only put up with him because he was so brilliant despite his eccentricity.

Frank was nettled and stood erect. He had nothing to be ashamed of. *Captain Frank Bargen. Doesn't sound too bad. New medal as well.*

Frank sauntered back to his office and collapsed into his chair. He loosened his tie, tight after the ceremony, but kept his coat on for a while, the medal pinned there. Everything seemed exactly the same, yet totally different. He tried to feel okay … no, he *was* feeling okay.

He attached the new epaulettes to his shoulders and fingered them. He touched the medal and tried to put everything out of his mind. The extra $30,000 a year would go a long way towards paying for the move back to Woollahra. He had done the right thing, and it would all get better now.

A gale was blowing when Frank drove across the gravel at Gunderman. He was surprised how eager he was to tell Marta about his promotion ceremony. He wouldn't tell her that it was a hidden-away secret, not held out in the open, but never mind. He was a captain now.

And she was so happy to be going back to Woollahra. She'd smiled so much all the time since he told her. Life was better when Marta was happy. Life would be better for all of them.

She was dressed in a ragged t-shirt when he arrived. In the back yard, hanging out the washing, battling a high wind, that southerly buster that blows through Sydney after a hot day. It was strange that she seemed to be settling into life in the country; Frank had never seen her hanging up washing in her life. She looked sexy. He couldn't resist.

He sneaked up and grabbed her bum and squeezed. She got a shock and dropped the sheet she'd been fighting with. The wind caught it, picked it up gracefully, high into the air, billowing across the garden. The air abandoned the sheet, and it dropped its ungainly tangle into a puddle.

'Jesus, Frank,' she muttered, half turning around so he could see she had two pegs between her teeth.

Definitely sexy.

He spun her around to him and kept his arms around her waist, starting to roam his hands downwards. She struggled and tried to push him away.

'What are you doing?' She looked tired, and the pegs in her mouth looked like demented teeth. She didn't look angry though.

Frank smiled and felt a little ease coming over him. Also, his dick tingled. He pulled her in tighter.

'Stop it!'

He felt her wrestling, squirming body against his. He let her go, and she spat out the pegs at him. 'You've brightened up.'

'I got the promotion and medal today.' He puffed out his chest in mock pride.

'Yes, I know, big boy.' She trooped over to the crumpled sheet and held it up for inspection. A huge muddy stain covered half of it. 'Feeling pretty proud of yourself, huh? I should get a medal for this.'

She bundled it up and threw it across the grass towards the house. She opened out a washing bag from the basket, unzipped it and pulled out her red bra and pegged it to the line, then Frank's argyle socks, then another bra. He wanted to take her inside to the bedroom and caress the inside of her clothes. She picked up the muddy sheet and put it in the now empty clothes basket, lifted it up and turned towards the house. Both the kids were at the back door watching, Mercury fiddling with that wooden train again.

Frank followed her across the lawn. His eyes went to her behind. He'd never seen her in an apron before. He imagined her wearing it with a bare arse. Maybe some heels on too. Isn't that one of those fantasies? Little Miss Homemaker.

'Come inside.'

'Where do you think I'm going?' She shooed the kids out of the way, pushed past them and in through the back door. Marta leaned against the washing machine, and her body sinewed like a snake. A strand of hair fell across her face and stuck to her sweat. She brushed it away from her mouth. There were tiny crow's feet at the edges of her eyes, those sparkling blue eyes. Even after ten years together, she could still make him hard.

'Come to the bedroom,' he whispered, coming up behind her again, his hands reaching for her breasts.

'Settle, Romeo.' She punched a couple of buttons on the washing machine and glanced at the control panel, looking for the final *Go* switch. Her fingers hovered over the controls.

The controls.

Frank flashed back to the moment before he pressed that button in the bunker. He felt his neck sweating. Marta pushed, and the washing machine exploded into life. Frank jumped, startled. He touched the wall to steady himself until the memory faded. *Will these flashbacks never stop?* His dick dwindled into a vanishing fizzle.

'Come on, tell me, what happened with the promotion?'

He followed her through to the lounge room. The kids stayed out in the back yard. Mercury was unusually quiet.

Marta flopped on the couch. 'Will you stay working at Victoria Barracks?'

Frank sat next to her. 'Yes. Everything else will be the same. Same building, same office. I will get more money though.'

'That's new. They've improved their bribes.'

Frank flinched.

'Dad didn't get more money, just a medal. You must have done something really special.'

Why was she trying to ruin this for him? 'I'll be getting an extra $30,000 a year,' he reminded her. 'Went straight from second lieutenant to captain in one go.'

Her face went quizzical. 'Well, that's cool!'

'I meant what I said; we will have the money to move back to Woollahra.'

She smiled and rubbed her fingers through her hair. 'But we've only just moved here.'

She couldn't be serious. 'I thought you hated it here. You want to be in Woollahra, don't you? I thought you'd be excited about moving back. You were before.'

'I suppose so. I've always lived there. Moving here was a bit weird, but over the past weeks, I've gotten used to being a country lady.' She leaned back against the couch and looked him over in his uniform and checked out his new medal. 'I remember when I was a little girl, I don't know how old, must have been very tiny. I used to run up to my father whenever he came home from being at sea. I got so excited that I peed my pants. I must have been really young.' She flicked a finger behind his new medal and fingered it lightly. 'So, border protection man.'

He touched her shoulder and tucked the tip of his fingers under the neckline of her loose t-shirt and traced the backs of his knuckles across the front of her neck. His dick started to fizz up.

Her eyes shifted to the back door, but there was no noise

from the children. 'They must be over in the shed.'

'They'll be okay.' Frank took her hand and stood her up off the couch.

She peered at his medal. 'I suppose going back to town would be okay.'

Frank felt better. This was how it was supposed to be. She put her hand on his chest and poked her fingers in between the buttons, undoing one, and pushed her hand further in. Her other hand slid down his chest to his belt buckle. His dick fired up. She grabbed his belt buckle and pulled him towards her. She thrust her hips, put her hand round his back, and her other hand slid down and squeezed his dick.

He groaned, and they looked at each other, then both looked out to the shed. Everything was quiet out in the back yard. She grabbed harder on the belt buckle and pulled at the zipper. It came apart smoothly, like a ripe mango splitting. He grabbed the wall behind him and let her hand probe around inside his open fly. Her hand squeezed harder, his dick straining against his underwear.

Frank's mind drifted back to his appointment with Yo-Knee. He imagined her poppy-coloured lips, the way she crossed her chubby legs and tugged down at her skirt. Marta slid her fingers inside his undies and pulled out his stiffening erection into the outside world. In his mind, Yo-Knee was pulling her dress off and striding towards him. She was tearing at her clothes and leaving a trail strewn across her office floor. She was a naked elf and twirling a little dance. Marta's hands tugged at Frank's dick as she kissed him. He tasted those salted lips. He felt the sharp metal of the zipper tangling in his hairs. Marta's hands dug around inside and pulled out his balls into the cool air; one hand cupped them as the other moved along the shaft. Yo-Knee's hair was flying loose now.

She was thrusting her hips towards him and rubbing herself. Her pubic hair was glistening jet black, and her mane of stygian hair was caressing a large stiff nipple. Yo-Knee was sucking him. He hardened up suddenly in Marta's hand and pushed out of his foreskin and gasped. Marta's finger tapped the end of his dick, and she showed him a little dab of precum on her finger and licked it. She looked down at his dick.

'Did I ever tell you, I saw my father's penis once on a camping trip? He didn't have a foreskin. Until I was older, I thought all dicks looked like that, exposed. That whole generation got circumcised. My first boyfriend got alarmed when I closely examined him. I was fascinated. Yours looks protected, nice and calm until it's ready.'

Frank's fantasy of Yo-Knee had evaporated.

Marta pulled back, one hand on his erection, and the other squeezing his balls, really squeezing.

'What happened at work that you're not telling me about? I need to know. For my mother.'

His head dropped, and his erection shrunk inside her hand. His balls suddenly ached, and his mouth zipped up tight. His lust was gone, and there was no way he would now tell her anything. She recoiled as though she'd surprised herself, then touched his cheek. She looked like she wanted to say something but could not find the words.

Out in the back yard, Mercury banged on the shed wall.

'Never mind.' She fumbled his dick back into his pants and zipped him up. 'You'll keep.' She patted his dick, pulled away, and straightened her clothes.

Mercury burst in through the back door and threw his wooden train against the wall. A wheel broke off and skittered across the room. Palace approached warily from behind, and Marta went over to them. Frank sat stunned on the couch and scattered images of Yo-Knee shot through his mind. Why couldn't he get things right with Marta?

CHAPTER 12

His first full day as a captain, Frank got out of his car at the barracks, straightened his tie and strode to the elevator with extra power in his step. He felt taller. Was this the right elevator? Yes, of course it was, he just felt… taller. Stronger. He touched his new epaulettes; captain's epaulettes. What do captains do? he wondered.

He never really planned to visit Webber; it was just that when the lift stopped at Webber's floor on the way up, he found himself getting out of the lift. He wanted to make some kind of peace, and he was sure Webber would want that too.

Straightening his tie again, he walked into Webber's lab. Webber was peering into a glass cage.

'Hi, Webs.'

Webber barely looked up.

'That the spider?'

Webber turned and took in Frank's bearing, standing to his full height.

'Yup.'

'Okay.' Frank stood there. It looked like Webber was still pissed off. Must be jealous. Surely, he would come round.

Webber slowly turned back to his cage. 'Promoted?'

Frank stood taller, glad that Webber had finally acknowledged it. 'Looks like it.'

'What for?'

Frank tensed. *Why's he asking that? I'm a captain now, and it's not his business.*

'Classified.'

Webber nodded slowly. 'Okay.'

This wasn't going how he had hoped. Frank stepped forward. 'Look, Webs, this doesn't make any difference.'

'Difference to what?'

'To …' Frank suddenly realised that he and Webber had never acknowledged that they were friends, that they had any relationship at all. They treated each other like jokey workmates, but Webber wasn't playing his part today.

'Look, Frank …' Webber looked up, his eyes shining behind his glasses, half burning curiosity, half couldn't care less. 'Not my business.' He turned back to his spider and waved his finger at it through the glass. The spider responded with agitated legs and fangs.

Frank realised Webber was an eccentric nobody, buried away in his lab with his obsessions. He wasn't getting anywhere. 'Okay, see you then.'

'Okay.'

Frank suddenly felt sorry and realised how much his little morning meetings with Webber meant to him. A heavy sadness descended, but then *no*, he would not let that tech geek bring him down.

Who cares what he thinks?

He was Captain Frank Bargen, moving up the success ladder at last. Things would be different, and he would love his promotion more than his friends.

He hurried to be inside the familiarity of his office. He slumped down and looked around, and it seemed unusual. It was strangely familiar, like someone had made a good copy of his office. He tapped on the keyboard, and the last spreadsheet he'd been working on came up. But it seemed a world away from him.

He heard steps behind him. 'Captain?' Frank didn't register at first. 'Captain Bargen?' It was the private delivering the mail. 'Your mail, sir.'

Frank smiled, took the small parcel of letters and, for the first time, felt like a captain. The private half saluted casually and retreated. Frank's cheeks were flushed. It was real. *I'm really a captain.*

He clicked open his to-do list, but something wasn't right – it looked like an index of drudgery. His little obedient spreadsheet cells had always soothed him, but now they looked like tiny enemies, miniature landmines in his mind. He couldn't concentrate. This was work for a second lieutenant, not a captain. Nothing had really changed. Memories of the hidden office promotion screeched through his mind. He felt deeply unsettled.

Maybe he needed a coffee. He would go to the officers' canteen. He could go there now without sneaking in, and it was more comfortable than the junior officers' down the hall. At least the canteen arrangements had changed. He wandered along to the canteen, his nerves screaming that he didn't belong. The junior officers sometimes sneaked in there when it was quiet to take advantage of the better, nice comfortable chairs, but he rarely did. The thought of being reprimanded was too much. But this time was different. *I belong.*

He took a breath, then went in. Lieutenant Grantham was in there pouring himself a coffee. What was he doing there? The two of them looked at each other, neither speaking. Frank was feeling like retreating, but held his ground.

'Granny,' he nodded.

Grantham looked at Frank's epaulettes and huffed, 'Someone got paid.'

Frank flushed with shame. The fact that Granny had been down there that day made it harder to say his *classified* line.

'What happened down there, Frank, after we left? It's going to come out eventually.'

Frank felt Granny's disdain, and it rankled. Granny was jealous he wasn't in on the secret. Frank's shame disappeared.

'Sorry, that's classif—'

Grantham's eyes crinkled. 'I know, I know, classified.'

'They gave me a medal.'

'Ooohh,' mocked Granny, stirring his coffee. 'Must be special then.'

He had no right to speak to him like this. Frank edged over to the coffee machine as if he owned it.

'Should you be in here, in the *senior* officers' canteen?'

Granny's eyebrows shot up in surprise. He waited a moment, looked directly at Frank, then tipped his coffee carefully into the wastebasket and sashayed towards the door without a further word. Frank felt satisfied at last. It felt good to throw his new authority around.

'Stupid bastard,' growled Granny as he left.

Frank started shaking. He was now in a new world, and he wasn't sure if he liked it.

Back in his office, Frank stared at his spreadsheet for hours, couldn't make any sense of it, his mind racing between feeling proud of his promotion and disgusted at the way he got it. He was getting that familiar feeling of boredom. His job was easy, no challenge, and if he couldn't get those little spreadsheet cells to entertain his mind, he would get that nauseous feeling of uselessness. It was no good. He was feeling terrible about Webber and Grantham. There had to be something he could do to fix things.

At lunchtime, he went down to Webber's floor.

Webber was scooting around his lab and didn't notice Frank at first, so he stood in the doorway wondering what to do. The lab had that strange combination of smells – faint animal odours combined with science and antiseptic. Webber seemed to be more animated than usual, carelessly bumping into things. He came right up to Frank without seeing him there, then started and jumped back.

'Jesus, Frank! What are you doing here?'

'Just looking around. Wondered if you'd like to have lunch together.'

'What for?' Webber's head bowed.

Frank bit his lip and felt embarrassed. They'd never talked like this before – never a lunch date. Usually, they just sidled up to each other in the canteen. But this felt like a date, a proper invitation out to a date.

Suddenly, Webber lifted his head and nodded. Frank knew Webber could not resist for long the opportunity to rave about his animals. 'Okay. I'll meet you up in the canteen at one o'clock. Order me a lasagne.'

'No, I mean outside. In Paddington, in a café. At twelve.'

Webber squirmed, and Frank felt like he was making a rude proposition. But Webber nodded carefully.

'Great, looking forward to it.' Frank exited, surprised how relieved he felt.

They walked up the hill, along Oxford Street and past the RSL club, where Frank looked up into a window and distinctly felt he was being watched. Was he imagining it?

'Where's this restaurant then?' asked Webber.

Café Bolly was the only restaurant tucked in between the strip of boutique clothes shops and pharmacies strung along Oxford Street. Bottles of wine were displayed along the back wall behind the bar, and glasses dangled down, ready for quick service. The Bolly was Italian, so Webber could safely get his lasagne. It was owned by a Chinese couple, Franny and her husband, the chef, whose name no one knew. The very camp waiter Benny was on this lunchtime, putting on his usual show.

'Hello, gentlemen.' Benny winked at Frank. 'Won any wars lately?' He gestured with his hand splayed out and his elbow tucked firmly into his ribs. His other hand reached out and almost touched Frank's chest. 'I do like a man in uniform.'

'Hi, Benny,' said Frank, who was relieved how normal the Bolly seemed after the recent chaos in his life.

Webber grunted and sat down in the corner. 'Is this place okay? Never been here.'

'Terrific place,' said Frank, sitting down. 'Marta and I used to come here a lot when we lived in Woollahra.'

Webber was jittery and played with the cutlery.

'This is a bit early for me.' Webber ate lasagne every lunchtime at 1 pm. 'It's only twelve o'clock.'

Frank knew Webber was making a strenuous effort to adjust. He was a man who liked routine. Frank wanted to ask about his spider, to ask about his experiments, make small talk about the football, but no words came out. This never usually felt so hard. He straightened the tablecloth and wiped off some imaginary crumbs.

They both blurted out together: 'Do you think the Roosters will win the comp this year?' ... 'I think the roosters will win the comp this year.' Then silence again. Tense.

Benny came up. 'Gentlemen?' They both breathed out.

'Lasagne,' said Webber.

'Spaghetti,' said Frank.

The waiter raised an eyebrow as he poured water. 'That's all for now?'

'Yup,' said Webber, and Benny retreated.

'Kain?' began Frank. Webber suddenly looked up. He'd never called him Kain before, always Webber or Webs. Frank felt peculiar.

'You remember that day, down in the bunker?'

'Couldn't forget it.' Webber put both hands face down on the table as if to steady himself. He was ready for an explanation.

Frank's head bowed. The ticking clock on the wall got louder. Webber carefully lifted one of his hands and scratched his cheek, then just as carefully, put it back in its place on the table.

'Torus ordered everyone out.'

Webber nodded slowly.

'I heard about that.'

'He blew the place up – Narus.'

Webber leaned in and lowered his voice. 'I heard about that as well. Granny told me he was ordered out of the room and under strict orders not to discuss it.'

'Granny told you?' Thinking about it, Frank wasn't surprised. Granny was never one to keep a secret. Webber waited for Frank to say something, but he lapsed into an awkward silence. How many people knew now? Maybe everyone knew his promotion wasn't real.

They drank water, and the meals arrived. Webber's hands immediately picked up the knife and fork, and he hoed into his food with gusto. Frank wondered if he was simply relieved his hands had something to do, and he had somewhere else to look. Nothing felt normal.

'What else did he say?' Granny really was being a pain, thought Frank.

'He's been making some noises about the place,' Webber mumbled through a mouthful of food.

'Noises?' Anxiety took flight deep in Frank's bowels. 'What sort of noises?' Frank twirled some spaghetti round his fork and lifted it to his mouth, feeling his hand shake.

'He said that you and Torus were the only ones left in the bunker.'

The spaghetti unravelled and fell off Frank's fork. *Damn it. Was Granny blaming him?* Frank felt the heaviness of the secret weighing on him. He ignored the shake of his hands and twisted the fork again through the spaghetti. Again, halfway to his mouth, it fell off. Frank dropped his fork with a clatter and heaved out a sigh.

'Okay, none of my business,' said Webber, watching intently as Frank picked up a spoon and had a little more success. 'I don't know what happened down there, Frank, and I don't want to know. Granny has been told to keep quiet, even though he wasn't there in the room at the end. I can tell you there are lots of rumours going around the base.'

Frank felt a stab of panic go through him, and he snatched up his fork like a fist. 'What sort of rumours?'

'Like I said, not my concern.' Webber wolfed down the last of his lasagna and placed the cutlery neatly back on his plate. 'The official version seems to be holding up – that it was an electrical fault.'

So, that was what they were telling people.

Frank gave up on his spaghetti and held his fork in the air, doing nothing, like he was about to stab something. The fork loosened up in his fist. 'Yes, electrical,' he said quietly.

Webber scratched his cheek. 'I've been down there in the bunker, Frank. It takes two people to set off those explosions.'

He knew! How did he know? Frank felt a rush of denial coming up from his guts. 'Torus did it!' He threw the fork back down on the plate.

'Whatever you say.' Webber seemed to have lost his boyish innocence. 'Nothing to do with me.' He poked his tongue around inside his mouth, searching for bits of leftover food. 'I heard that Granny's getting transferred. He always did want to go out to Pine Gap and dally around with the Americans.' Was Webber being serious or sarcastic? They ate the rest of their lunch in silence, and then Frank paid the bill on their way out.

'Bye-eee,' sang Benny as they left. 'Stay out of trouble now, you two.' As they walked down past the RSL club, Frank looked up at the window, but no one was there.

Back at the barracks, Frank pushed open the glass door and instinctively straightened. The relentless hum of the air conditioning and machinery seemed to get louder as he walked in, and the slight burning plastic smell in the air got more pungent. He semi-marched through the building, feeling a little of both pride and fear. Granny was being transferred, Webber had said. He would not be spreading his nonsense to even more people. Frank was safe.

He looked down at his tie to make sure there were no remnants of his spaghetti lunch spilled there.

The whole afternoon, he couldn't settle down to work. What was he supposed to do now? Just carry on as if nothing had happened? He was beginning to calm down when five o'clock rolled around, and he headed for the elevator. He rounded the corner and was confronted by a couple of military police in full helmet-and-truncheon regalia looking like they were expecting a riot. *What now?* Between them was a soldier carrying a cardboard box. It was Granny.

Granny locked his eyes on Frank with cold, hurt fury. 'See what you've done?'

He hadn't expected the transfer to happen this quick. *Hang on, was it a transfer?* Granny was being escorted from the building.

'I didn't do anything. I got promoted,' said Frank feebly.

'Only blew the whole place up,' Granny sneered. 'Still, it's my own fault, couldn't keep my mouth shut. I'm too dangerous to have around here.'

One of the police tugged on Granny's arm to shuffle him along. Granny's eyes narrowed, and he seemed a little relieved that he'd been able to insult Frank to his face.

'Tell you what, Frank, watch that Torus. He's after you.' He turned to go. 'See you sometime.'

Frank had never felt more isolated in his life, but he touched his captain's epaulettes, and his nerves settled. If Granny wanted to shoot his mouth off and get reassigned, that was his decision. Frank's determination to keep quiet hardened. He looked at one of the policemen and nodded to him.

'Carry on,' he said.

'Swine!' Granny's whispered voice grated into Frank's innards.

The two police tugged at Granny and marched him to the

elevator. Granny was really getting transferred? He thought of Yo-Knee. Maybe he'd be going back there soon.

CHAPTER 13

Outside the train window, the tunnel walls zoomed past in a blur. They were almost at Circular Quay. Mercury had been amusing himself by shuffling at Palace's feet, but he'd stopped now in anticipation that the long journey from Windsor was nearly over.

Over the last few weeks, Frank had been finding it difficult to be near people. Human bodies sickened him. His panic didn't seem to be settling down. He'd assumed everything was going to be okay after his promotion. Marta said he'd embarrassed her and the kids in public. She didn't understand at all – didn't want to. She'd picked up he'd been stressed at work, but his work was always full of secrets, and she'd gradually come to accept that and didn't push too much. Frank figured she'd learnt from her mother how much to push and when to keep silent. He'd wanted to tell her what was going on when they went to the labyrinth.

The events on Narus were still sharp in his mind, but at least he'd managed to section them off into that little niche in his consciousness. Things did feel more orderly now, and he was probably calm enough to face the world again. He'd enjoyed soaking up the quiet out at Gunderman for the last few weeks, and the visit to that labyrinth hadn't been too bad, where they'd made the decision to move back to the eastern suburbs. It was time to start their new life. He would have the money now, and it would make Marta happy.

She had suggested Luna Park would help him get used to the crowds, make him feel better about people. The thought had made his insides squirm, but he'd eventually agreed. Making people happy was why he was here today. Seeing Mercury's joy at the labyrinth had softened him up. Marta had scoffed that Frank was becoming depressingly dull and said the excitement of Luna Park would be nice. He hadn't been there for years, knew it would be good for the kids, so he'd agreed. He felt some peace that he had not known for weeks. The travelling train soothed him. He glanced along the carriage and noticed there was only one other person on their train carriage. At the other end, an old guy looked out the window into the distance. He turned slightly towards them, and Frank thought he saw a pipe in the man's mouth. *You can't smoke on a train.* Then again, maybe the pipe wasn't lit. Frank couldn't really tell from this distance, but it was still peculiar. He also had a patch over his right eye. Frank rarely caught trains, and there was probably a whole world of strange people out there that he never normally came across.

The train pulled up at Circular Quay station, and the doors opened with a hiss. Mercury jumped up and headed for the platform. Palace gazed across at the harbour. Marta took Frank's hand as they stepped off the train. Frank looked back to see the guy with the pipe get off through the doors at the other end. He was definitely puffing smoke from his pipe.

Did he just light it? Is he even allowed to smoke on the platform?

Frank didn't know why he should care. But he did. People should follow the rules.

'Frank, Frank,' Marta shouted. 'What are you doing? Come on.'

Frank turned to see Mercury bolting away along the platform.

'Get him, Frank!'

But Frank was mesmerised by the guy with the pipe who had now disappeared.

Marta dropped her head. 'Not again … not again.'

'I'm coming, take it easy,' yelled Frank.

Marta clenched both fists. 'You're daydreaming again. Mercury's run off while you've been dawdling.'

A stranger from the train glanced at them, and Frank bristled with embarrassment.

'Go and get him, will you?'

'All right, all right.' *Always bitching*, thought Frank. He chased after Mercury and caught up to him at the ferry wharf.

'C'mon, Mercs – always causing trouble.'

Cold, yellow sunlight shot sideways off the water and skimmed across the wharf, drenching the expanse in a too bright, shimmering morning dazzle. Frank squinted, and the chilled wind whipped up his cheeks into a sharp tingle. Marta and Palace caught up with them and led the way to the ferry. Frank followed, holding Mercury's hand.

All round him was the jostling crowd.

'Keep hold of me, Mercs.' Was he saying that to protect Mercury or protect himself? He overheard a cacophony of voices, people talking trivia, their little worries and fixations, their lives.

'… and then I said more off the sides …'

'… and then, you know, that bloody idiot rang me back and …'

'… I thought the big loaf would be enough, but she wouldn't have it …'

'… she told me to get lost, right there in the shop …'

Frank recoiled from the trivia of people's obsessions. What did they know about anything?

His mind filled with the refugees in the camp scrambling about in terror. *No, don't think about that.* He gave his head a violent shake to get rid of the bad images. He needed to forget about it. He had been making reasonable progress and settling into his new life as a Border Force captain. The same as before, really, except for the nightmares. As soon as the bad dreams cleared up, he would be fine. He had been doing his job after all, a soldier following orders.

Despite the crowds, he was determined to have a nice, stable day out at Luna Park for the kids. They needed their father. It would help make things normal again. But God he was tired. The crowd started to move. He sighed and took a determined step forward.

A sharp pain shot into the back of his ankle. He spun around, let go of Mercury's hand and restrained a vicious curse. The axle of a child's pram had smacked into him, and he saw a harassed mother. He was about to rail into her, but Marta, ever-vigilant, squeezed his elbow, and he caught himself. Marta grabbed hold of Mercury. Frank smiled grimly and took a step forward away from the pram. Yes, that little bit of distance felt better.

'Don't worry, Frank.' Marta's voice was soothing but hard too. 'You'll be okay.' She looked across at the sunlight. 'Should be a nice morning.'

'Nice morning, yes,' Frank mumbled.

'Not too cool,' she went on.

'Not too cool, no.'

Mercury couldn't keep himself still. Marta held his hand tightly so he wouldn't run off and disappear into the crowd. He struggled to be free, but his mother yanked him back, winced at the effort and rubbed her shoulder. Frank felt a gnawing guilt that Marta was doing all the children duty.

'Mercs, be still for a minute,' he contributed.

Mercury's condition was forever. He would always be frightened of the quiet and scared of peace. It took hours to get him to sleep. Sleep was boring; nothing was happening. He had a precarious sense of self, the amenders had said. Peace and silence meant oblivion to him. Poor little bugger, he loved being alive. He was a tornado of trouble. Watching him made Frank weary, but Marta was on top of it as always.

She gave up on the small talk and threw away Mercury's hand. 'Keep an eye on him. I'll watch Palace.'

That threat in her voice. Frank swallowed, felt put out that she was treating him like a child, then caught himself and remembered that he had to make up for some pretty weird things that he'd done lately. *Responsible, be responsible. Don't let Marta down.*

Palace looked at Mercury. She used to encourage his escapades, always entertained. He would do anything to make her laugh. One time, he parachuted out of a tree with a tablecloth; it was hilarious until he bruised an anklebone. These days Palace was too ill to do much of anything and was content to watch. It broke Frank's heart when they got that piteous diagnosis. So young, so young. Over the months, his anger had turned into waves of sympathy. His chest tightened, then he sighed.

The ferry approached, turned with an easy majesty and shuddered into the wharf. The water boiled around it. The seagulls squawked, and the passengers shuffled forward. An old lady dressed in black bumped against Frank's arm. Deliberate? Maybe, maybe not. She jostled to find her place, and he saw she had a scowling face and a broken umbrella, probably from a previous encounter at a ferry terminal. She looked like the kind of woman to invite trouble. Definitely aggressive. These people who thought they could take up all the space, who thought they deserved to step on you to get what they wanted. He would not have it. Frank turned, fists clenched to control himself. *Let it go, let it go!*

A ratty little child jostled his other arm, and he flinched, jerked his elbows back into his ribs. *Brat!* His breathing piled up in short, sharp jabs. One breath starting before the last one had finished. He wanted to let fly and scream at the crowd, but the tightness in his chest held him back. His jaw locked, and he remembered his promise to Marta. A fun day out. That was all she wanted. He had to calm down, relax. He grabbed Mercury's hand and decided to make the best of it. She deserved a nice day out with the family and, so far this morning, he'd been coping okay, up until the old lady and the pram.

He felt Marta watching him closely. No vicious paranoia yet, no evil flashback visions, fingers crossed. Yo-Knee never said so explicitly, but she implied that he wouldn't be able to get over whatever was bothering him until he told someone about it. She had a way of saying things without actually saying them. But she must be wrong. The evil was gradually fading away into a little compartment in the corner of his mind.

The old lady with the broken umbrella shuffled off to bother somebody else, and Frank exhaled. He'd stayed in control. Everything was fine. Maybe Luna Park might be fun after all.

The ferry bumped into the wharf, and the crowd shivered in unison. It seemed amusing. We're all in this together, he thought, like a school of fish.

Palace and Marta were just up ahead. Palace's headscarf had come loose and drifted sideways, revealing her bald head. Fatima from the support group had taught the chemo girls how to tie up a hijab. It was way better than beanies. Palace hadn't quite got the hang of it yet. Frank reached over to adjust the scarf, but she shrugged him off, fiercely capable as always. She adjusted the hijab and shrugged up her shoulders, causing the little oxygen tank on her back to settle into place. She took in a big breath, and the pipes in her nostrils steamed up. Frank backed off. He knew she didn't like being fussed over. *The treatment must be working, it must.*

Most of the time, the tank didn't seem to bother her, and Fatima had suggested she decorate it to feel more friendly. Frank looked at the bright butterfly stickers and purple flowers. He felt a flush of pride for her bravery and put out his hand for her. She was weak but had enough strength to pull away and reach for her mother's hand instead. Frank's heart tightened from the rejection, and a harsh intake of breath went down his throat. Such a small thing but so painful.

Mercury scuttled towards the ferry, wanting to be the first in line to jump aboard. The crowd crushed in. Marta and Palace ambled towards the boat, hand in hand. Frank wished they'd walk faster to catch up to Mercury, everyone together. Frank felt trapped in the crowd. He wanted to be at home in his shed, making wooden things, achieving solace.

No, don't think that way. Be cheerful, be cheerful. You promised to not cause a scene.

The passengers shuffled and jostled their way onto the boat. Frank got jumpier with every touch. Only a few more minutes, and he would be able to sit down. Where would the quietest part of the boat be? Maybe on the outside. Yes, he could see a good spot near the rear.

Mercury pushed through the crowd, nudged past the woman with the pram, then shoved into a young couple holding hands. It was definitely time to intervene. Frank let go of Marta's hand and hurried to catch up.

'Mercs,' he shouted. 'Mercury, stop.'

But Mercury was away. Frank got that feeling of dread he'd had when Mercury ran straight across Oxford Street that time, right through the traffic, chasing a ball.

'Mercury!'

But the little bugger pretended not to hear and barged further into the crowd. He was now yards ahead. He blasted through the young couple holding hands and ripped their arms apart. The old woman with the umbrella was further in front, and she would retaliate if shoved. As if on cue, Mercury lost his balance and skittled into her. Horrified, Frank scrambled through the mass of people.

'Excuse me, excuse me.'

The old lady turned on Mercury, her face a mask of irritation and lashed out with her umbrella. She caught him a giant wallop across the head. He toppled over, slipped and headed for the drink. Frank pitched forward and snatched Mercury's coat and catapulted him back onto the wharf. Mercury scrambled to his feet. It had happened so fast that no one really noticed.

Frank put his hands on his hips and breathed heavily. He looked down into the water and a trickle of cold sweat ran down his cheek. He imagined Mercury dead, their home without his crazy running around. The three of them, left morosely sitting around the house. He held his son in a tight grip while the crowd trooped past them onto the boat. He looked at them coldly. They didn't even care.

Frank held him tight, and for a brief moment, Mercury didn't struggle. He'd understood that something really serious had happened.

'I slipped,' he offered, as if that was all that was needed to consign the episode to the past.

'Mercury, that was really dangerous. You could have ended up in the water.'

Mercury's stillness didn't last. Nothing could hold him for long, and he struggled to escape. He was getting stronger, Frank noticed. How would they control him in a couple of years?

Mercury broke free and took off for the ferry, rapidly forgetting what had just happened. He turned back and waved at his mother and sister for being slowcoaches.

Marta rushed up with Palace. 'What happened?'

Frank looked shamefaced. 'He slipped over.'

'But that woman hit him with the umbrella.'

'He slipped. He's okay now.'

Marta sucked in a quick breath, and her hand went to her mouth. 'He nearly fell in!'

'He's okay now. Nothing happened.'

'Nothing happened? What are you talking about? You were supposed to look after him.'

'He ran off.'

'Of course, he ran off, that's what he does.' She looked at Mercury, who was happily looking for more mischief.

Frank's head sank. He was hardly able to summon the energy to defend himself.

Marta was red faced, frantic and bristling. 'You should have been watching him.'

'I thought he was with you.' That's not true, why did I say that?

'Of course, he wasn't with me. I was with Palace and you!'

Mercury tired of waiting for everyone else and charged back towards them. Palace had a worried frown on her face and closed in towards her mother.

Frank grabbed Mercury's hand in an iron grip and dragged him towards the ferry. The crowd boarded. Frank knew he shouldn't have come. The crowds were appalling, and Marta treated him no better than a whipped dog. Why does she think it's okay to tell me off in front of the kids?

They trooped onto the ferry, and Frank felt a lingering dread, like being watched. He looked around, but there was nothing obvious. It was his fevered imagination again. He tried to throw the feeling off, shaking with the effort to keep it together. He'd been making such good progress. Damn Marta and her selfishness. You'd think if she made him come in spite of him not wanting to that she'd at least be nice to him.

Mercury peered at something on the doorframe and tried to pull away to get his father to hurry up. Frank, wary that Mercury might run off, tightened his grip, but Mercury was fascinated by a fleck of paint and picked at it. Jesus, he was turning into a panic puss like Marta. Frank let go of Mercury's hand. His son needed to do these strange things to indulge his curiosity about the world. Marta might get embarrassed, but she'd have to get over it. Mercury's behaviour might seem odd at times, but Frank figured it didn't matter if he wasn't hurting anyone.

Satisfied with the doorframe, Mercury looked around with a half-smile on his face. Frank knew that look. Before he could take his son's hand again, he was off.

Mercury shrugged off Frank, barrelled past his sister and sprinted along the deck, his head moving left and right, as he tried to find the most fun.

'Marta,' Frank yelled. 'Get him!'

Tightness grabbed across Frank's chest, and he sprang forward.

'Go sit down,' he ordered Palace. He charged ahead, saw Marta had heard him and moved to intercept, but Mercury did a neat sidestep and evaded her. The force of his movement making him trip, and sending him flying into the elbow of the mother with the pram. The sandwich she'd been holding took the knock, seemed to consider its options and then curved in a graceful arc straight over the side, spewing out lettuce, tomatoes, olives and cheese. The lettuce was the last to float down and hit the water.

'Fuck,' cursed Frank.

'Shit,' hissed Marta.

'You little bastard,' swore the young father.

Mercury grabbed the railing and bounced up and down before jumping up onto the rails and pretending to surf. Marta grabbed his coat and yanked him back down. She swung him round and launched him violently onto the bench with a crushing thud.

The young couple made a move to confront Frank and Marta but changed their mind and began bickering with each other. They stumbled quickly inside, arguing and muttering, pointing back at Mercury. Frank sat down, panting. Unsurprisingly, Mercury clapped at the fun of it all, his eyes darting about as he looked for the next adventure.

The ferry's foghorn blared out a warning, and the engines sucked the boat away from the wharf. Frank couldn't believe the day was just starting. Why, oh why, had he come?

They had to face it. Mercury was getting more manic the older he got. Soon he would be as big as Marta; lord knows how they would control him then. Maybe he would calm down when he hits puberty and chases girls – they might soothe him. Mercury would surely have a happy life once he matured. He had charm, as all energetic people do. They had to make sure he didn't kill himself first. Mercury's feet galloped on the floor like a runaway horse, but he was riveted to the spot by his mother's command. Frank felt exhausted just looking at him.

Marta's breath heaved, and tears welled up. She softly banged her head against the wall behind her.

'Three fucking invalids to look after,' she whispered, almost to herself. 'Why didn't you watch him?' Frank opened his mouth to speak, but she got there first. 'Hopeless. You said you would be good today. Make a fucking effort, Frank!'

He turned away from her, resentment curdling his guts. 'What's the point? Nothing I say is good enough.'

She stared at him with dagger eyes. 'Sometimes I hate you.' She sprang to her feet, yanking Mercury with her. 'Come on, kids, we're going inside.'

She stomped off down the deck, Mercury flailing behind her. Palace sat on the bench, looking confused. 'I don't know what I was thinking,' said Marta. 'A fun day out. What a joke.'

Frank couldn't agree more.

CHAPTER 14

Surprisingly, Palace did not go inside. She shuffled along the bench seat and reached across to hold her father's hand. She was trying to look after him. He sat quietly. He was still smarting about Marta, how antagonistic she was. *Doesn't she know I'm trying? Mercury is hardly an easy kid to take on a ferry. What a stupid idea.* They had barely left the wharf.

Palace was still squeezing his hand. Frank realised how stressed he was. She gently rocked backwards and forwards, humming to herself. He felt some calm. She was a kid, a sick kid, but she knew what she was doing. He breathed in some air. He felt grateful; he would be okay.

The engines revved up, and the boat throbbed. The sea boiled, and the world turned majestically. Frank gazed into the blurry middle distance, and the harbour seemed to slowly turn around. He had the feeling that he wasn't moving at all, but instead the world was turning around him – a peculiar perspective, slightly unnerving but curious.

He took stock. The cold wind fluttered on his cheeks,

but they weren't *his* cheeks. The wharves were right there in front of him, but they didn't belong to *his* field of vision. The smell of the salt water didn't belong in *his* nose. All these things were there, but at a distance. They were *other*. He was disembodied, unlocated. It was … pleasant, and he floated.

The ferry lurched and cut through the waters. The wharves shrank away, and the Opera House sailed by. The Harbour Bridge in the distance enlarged. Frank snapped out of his *otherness*. Everything belonged to him again. He leaned back, the odd sensation lingering but diminishing. He was surprised to feel peaceful. It was curious to feel quiet again after all these weeks of turmoil.

Palace nudged him back into the present. He'd completely forgotten about her. He looked into her face, and she frowned, as if neglect was added to his sins. Neither spoke, so they watched the water glide by. She looked inside to see where her mother was. Frank felt protective and wanted to reassure her, but her hand was cold as clay. She didn't respond – it was like holding a dead hand. He recoiled and let go of it.

'Mercury's crazy,' she said.

Frank snorted. 'Yes, he takes some looking after.'

'Who do you like best?'

Frank was startled and looked into her eyes, weighing his answer. 'Both of you.'

'Does Mum like both of us the same too?'

'Yes, Mum too.'

'I'm the eldest.'

'Yes, only just.'

'I like you and Mum the same as well.'

He was silent for a moment.

'I think Mum's going to take us away from you.'

Surely, it wasn't that bad.

The air felt cooler. They were under the shadow of the Harbour Bridge now. Frank stood up and looked down into the water again, darker now – and inviting. *Maybe it was that bad.* He shook his head and covered his face to get those thoughts out of there. The boat hit turbulence, and his hand grabbed at the rail. He felt a force tipping him over if he didn't hang on. It would be easy to give up and fall in. The depths of the harbour pulled him forward. A siren's call – come to me, come to me. Oblivion would be merciful. All the guilt gone, and the shame. Everything finished. The fights with Marta, the chaos of Mercury, the cruel cancer of Palace. A worthless life, but at least a finished one. *It would be so easy.*

Suddenly, he was seven years old. Young Frankie was helping his father haul the gear onto the fishing boat.

'C'mon, son, don't be a slacker.'

Frankie pulled harder, even though he was already trying his best.

Two of his dad's navy mates, who were going out fishing with them, waited on the wharf. They looked amused at Frankie's straining efforts with the big box of gear and smirked at Frankie's father.

'I'll sort him out.' He gave Frankie a little shove to indicate to his mates that he was on the case to toughen up his son. He pulled the box away from Frankie and took over hauling it towards the boat.

Frankie was left waiting on the wharf. The two mates walked past him towards the boat, and the one called Karl rubbed the top of Frankie's head whilst getting on the boat. Frankie didn't know if he liked that or not.

'Leave the kid alone,' said the one called Stephan.

The boat's engines exploded into life. Frankie ran and leapt onto the boat before it took off. He sat breathlessly, and they sped towards the open water. The sun boiled high overhead, and the beating engines hammered the fishing boat towards the horizon. The dry land disappeared rapidly behind.

'More beer?' said Frankie's father. The other two nodded, and he threw them cans, Karl not quite catching his, and it went over the side.

'Fuck it,' he slurred. They all laughed. Frankie tried to laugh as well.

'Think that's funny, do ya?' Karl gestured that he would throw him over the side. Frankie looked at his father, but he was too busy laughing to care.

'Never mind, kid,' said Stephan. 'Karl's an idiot.' Frankie tried to join in the fun, but the game was too hard for him, too mysterious, too rough. He descended into a silence.

A pile of caught fish was flipping around, dying and smelling at the back of the boat. Frankie thought his father looked like a pretend commodore – at the wheel, cutting through the water, swaying the boat crazily from side to side, jostling everyone around. Frankie hung on with both hands. Dad's eyes would be glazing over now. Frankie had seen his father drunk before. *Don't look at his eyes, don't look.* Instead, he stared across at the reflected sunlight on the water while the sunburn roasted his face. He frowned at his father's mates and wished he were at home.

The big commodore noticed him, heaved a huge breath and flared his nostrils. He leaned forward, flipped the key, and the engine noise stopped. Frankie fought back a shiver.

Look at the water, don't look at him. The laughter stopped. The whole hot world of sun and sea went quiet. There was only the soft hissing of the boat gliding through the still water. His father turned and raised his arms in a huge lavish gesture. The beer can in his hand spilt a big arc of brown foam through the air, spraying everyone. It hit Frankie's mouth, and he spluttered the foam out in disgust. Something was coming, but he didn't care; he hated his father. He cowered in the back of the boat with the dying fish.

'Come here, boy,' his father slurred and growled. 'Want to stay at home, do you? I'll toughen you up.'

He grabbed Frankie's ankle and dragged him like a dead fish across the deck. At the boat's edge, he pretended to hurl him over the side. Frankie dangled there, above the big sea, arms and legs waving about. The upside-down Karl was laughing and Stephan was frowning, but Frankie heard nothing. The water below wanted to drag him under. His stomach felt sick. He knew what his father wanted. He wanted him to be tough, to not cry, to not scream, to not show anything. Don't show any feelings at all.

A voice came into his head. If you really want to scream, scream. He didn't care about his father, his father's friends, or his father's pride. He wanted his father to be disgusted, to give up on him, to lose interest and let him go. His stomach burst with a galloping ache, and he retched out a monstrous howl.

Laughter started up again on the boat. The two mates pointed at the humiliated, pretend commodore. Frankie screamed and struggled. His father turned to his two mates, getting their attention.

He let go of Frankie's ankle, and he plunged into the sea. Suddenly, Frankie didn't care. His life had already ended. Let the water take him. The water rose higher, and he felt his father grab his other ankle. The wild and cruel man who used to be his father grunted and pulled Frankie back onboard. He flung him across the deck and into the pile of fish.

'Fuck!' said Karl.

'That was a bit harsh,' said Stephan.

The boat moved quietly through the water, back to land. Frankie was done with his father.

Frank reared up onto his toes, still grabbing the ferry rail, frozen like a diver waiting for the starting gun, his hands stuck there. His thoughts shimmered between two worlds. A female voice in his mind told him of the beautiful release from life. Why would he want to live after what he had done and seen? Follow her for blessed death. Another voice, male, was filled with curiosity about life. What would life be like now? Could he survive? Was it worth it?

Then his lungs breathed, and his heels lowered back onto the deck. He chose the male voice. The death wish subsided in the way the wind leaves a sail. He would take back charge from his misery. The harbour became water again, not an evil spirit trying to pull him down.

An exhausting wave of regret travelled through him. The chance at merciful oblivion was gone. He let go of the rail and shakily sat back in his seat.

Palace pulled at his arm, irritably. His mind wanted to stay in the past, in those warm and cruel memories, but Palace kept shaking. He pulled his arm away from her, but she wasn't about to be refused. He struggled to return to the present. She didn't like him back there in those memories. She wanted him here, right now. He was sucked out of the past. He looked into her big eyes.

'You're back!' Her face eased, and she let go of his arm as though tired of the effort of being the adult. She inhaled her oxygen.

Frank's mind cleared, and he embraced the relief of being in the present moment, leaning back against the wall. His own child protecting him. Not right, not how it should be.

The ferry emerged from the giant shadow of the bridge,

back into the sunlight, and the world brightened. Maybe Marta was right, and he really was hopeless. He couldn't even top himself. Couldn't do it. Yo-Knee came into his mind, wagging her fat little finger, admonishing him that if he didn't confront the past, it would haunt him because it hadn't been processed properly.

The ferry gently nodded up and down and glided towards the giant Luna Park clown's face entrance. A splash hit Frank's face, and he breathed deeply, grateful for the air, the morning air. Recent days had been bad, but today could still be a good day, a thankful day.

The clown's face reared up, eyes glittered, eyebrows manically raised. The grotesque mouth of a thousand teeth invited you to come in for some playful lunacy. The water splashed again, and Frank's attention was pulled back to the deep and its promise of oblivion.

He approached the railing again, was instantly taken by the patterns in the water, the swirling gushing eddies along the side of the boat, mesmerised by the strict formality in the seeming chaos. He leaned over the side a little more to get a closer look.

I'm always here, said Oblivion. *Here when you're ready.*

The clown's face was closer now, its manic eyes gleaming with the promise of delighted release from the humdrum. It was entirely up to Frank whether the kids had a good day out or not.

The face was low set, and the harbour seemed to flow into its mouth where the missing lower jaw should be, the water going straight down its throat. Giant Chrysler Building towers replaced its ears and the improbably rosy cheeks flushed in the horizontal sunlight.

'Dad! Dad!' shouted Mercury.

Frank turned to him with a smile, and he even offered a smile to Marta. She gave him a half-smile in return. They would be okay. Every family had issues.

'I see the clown, I see the clown,' Mercury shouted.

'Yep, we're nearly there, mate. We'll be at Luna Park soon and having lots of fun.' He pulled his son in for a hug and swung a grin back to Palace. 'We can go for rides on the big dipper. When I was a kid, the big dipper was the best. The big dipper and the ghost train.'

'Mum, when you were little, did you like the ghost train?' Palace asked. His baby girl – always trying to keep the peace.

'Yes, sweetie.'

The wharf got closer, and Frank noticed a grizzled old man waiting there, leaning on a post and smoking a pipe. He had a patch over one eye. You didn't see many people smoking pipes these days. He seemed to be looking towards them. Was that the same guy who was on the train?

The ferry bumped into the wharf, and Frank grabbed at the railing, and he felt grateful that those feelings of dread were leaving him. The ferryman tossed a rope and pulled a gangplank. Frank breathed in and heartily braced himself for a fun day. Mercury shot towards the shore, Marta close behind him, while Palace held Frank's hand.

The gigantic bridge cast a morning shadow across the clown's face, and the Ferris wheel in the distance turned slowly, catching shards of sunlight. The faint sounds of children screaming and laughing rolled down the hillside. Palace guided her father across the gangplank towards Marta, who was deliberately busying herself with Mercury. *Has she given up on me again? Surely not.* Luna Park really would snap him out of his funk. He would stop brooding. Stop fixating on the horrors. Marta wouldn't have given up on him. They love each other. Frank took in the untroubled world of the bobbing ferry, swishing water and excited children.

On the wharf, the old man with the pipe was definitely fixing Frank with his one eye. Palace held Frank's hand tighter to make sure that his last couple of steps off the gangplank were steady ones.

'Palace, we're here,' yelled Mercury. 'Come on!'

'Go join your brother,' Frank urged. It wasn't right, her babysitting him.

He watched her slowly make her way up the hill to the others near the entrance. He was happy to trail along behind.

'Frank,' said a gravelly voice.

Frank spun round to see the shambolic one-eyed old man. He wore a loose and dirty beige overcoat with a black eye patch over his right eye, and the pipe smoke swirled around his left eye, half closing it. Frank blinked. He examined the stranger, whose single eye swivelled along towards his family.

Frank stepped forward to protect them from whoever this person was. 'How do you know my name? What do you want?'

The stranger held out his hand. 'Harding's the name. Duggy Harding.'

Frank didn't move.

'I'm looking for the truth. Maybe you've got some?'

What the fuck is this? Frank's stomach turned over. He ignored the offered handshake and tensed, ready for anything.

Duggy Harding dropped his handshake with a laconic shrug and waited for Frank's reaction. He sucked on his pipe, and a slight gurgling sound came out.

'Maybe I'm mistaken.' He puffed out a plume of smoke. 'About that truth.'

Who was this guy? Up ahead, Frank noticed Mercury

break free from Marta, and she spun around to retrieve him. Frank jumped.

'Mercury! Wait!' Mercury halted underneath the gigantic gleaming clown's teeth.

He wasn't letting this guy get in the way of his family day. 'Look, I don't have time for this. I have to get my son.'

'I want what we all want, Frank. I want the truth.'

Nutter.

Marta dashed ahead to get hold of Mercury. Frank turned back to the stranger, the smoke billowing around his face, his one eye twinkling as if he'd got what he wanted. 'Listen, you better leave us alone. We're here for a nice day out, nothing else.'

The old man's lips curled into a slight smile. 'Satisfying my curiosity, that's all.' He waved his pipe in Frank's face. 'I'll let you be.'

He shuffled off and leaned against the entrance wall and watched, deliberately fiddling with his pipe, as Frank ushered the family into the funfair.

Marta half squinted into the distance to keep Mercury in view. 'Who were you talking to, Frank?' She had that crinkled brow of worry, and her chest and shoulders caved in a little as if she was cold.

'No idea.'

Frank looked around again, and Harding had disappeared. The stink of smoke still hung in Frank's nostrils, tightening his stomach. Had Border Force sent him? Was he being followed to make sure he kept quiet? No, the army wouldn't be following him. He hadn't spoken to anyone about Narus. They had nothing to suspect. But how did this Harding character know his name? It was spooky. He must have overheard Marta talking to him as they were getting off the ferry. She must have mentioned his name. Yes, that's it! He breathed out. A weirdo, taking advantage. He shook his shoulders and tried to blow off the feeling of dread.

They passed through the entrance, and the rollercoaster was right there, full of screams, making Frank cringe. *Stop it! It's kids having fun. Nothing to fear.* Frank looked up at the rollercoaster. Harmless fun. But maybe he could delay things for a while.

'Look, let's go get some food. Want some chips, Mercs?'

But Mercury jabbed his finger to the top of the rollercoaster. Frank saw that familiar determination in his face, but he couldn't face it yet. Not even for Mercury.

'Let's get some coffee first.'

Marta half shrugged, raising one shoulder the way she did and tilting her head to the side.

'Let's go, let's go!' Mercury grabbed the hands of his mother and sister and dragged them towards the big dipper.

'Mercs, stop it,' yelled Marta. 'C'mon, Frank, let's take them on the rollercoaster. That's what we're here for.'

Mercury had already forgotten the offer of chips. He wouldn't be content till he was at the top of that big dipper, looping over the top, stomach lurching, scared out of his wits and screaming on the downhill ride. It was the last thing on earth that Frank wanted. He needed some time to get used to the idea of a rollercoaster ride. Maybe in a little while.

Marta looked at Frank. 'C'mon, we'll take them for a ride.'

Mercury let go of Marta and pulled at Frank's hand instead. 'Yeah, come on, come on.'

Frank tried to calm himself down. *I am grateful, I am grateful,* chanted through his mind. It would be good, harmless fun up there, might blow away his demons, bring all the family together. Frank closed his eyes and listened to the chanting going through his mind, calming him. At the same time, he could clearly hear the screaming of the children. His mind was split in two, each side fighting for dominance, the quiet chanting trying to overcome the sounds of screams. But the screams got suddenly louder, and a lightning bolt of pain shot across his eyes, from temple to temple.

'Arrgh!' he yelled and clapped his hands to his face. 'You go up. I'll wait here.'

Marta spun towards him. 'What's the matter now?'

Mercury, not to be thwarted, grabbed his mother's hand and pulled her towards the entrance. Palace adjusted her headscarf in anticipation.

'You take them. I'm getting coffee.'

'What's the bloody harm?' She marched the kids off in a huff. 'Whatever!' All three disappeared into the rollercoaster entrance.

Frank trudged well away to the other side of the park to get away from the screams. He sat on a wooden bench and put his head back, relieved to be in the quiet. Trying to be normal was bloody exhausting. In the distance he heard the foghorn blast as the ferry left the wharf. Seabirds screeched and squawked. People talking. Normal conversations, no manic screams. Peace at last.

Way, way in the distance, he heard the rollercoaster screams again, barely audible. Gradually, they got louder and louder, insistent. *That can't be right. I'm way across the other side of the park.* He leaned back, and the morning sun streamed into his face, soothing. But the screams got louder, screeching.

Then with a jolt he realised something peculiar – he wasn't hearing screams at all. The screams were coming from inside his own head, from his own thoughts. The memories started juddering through his mind. His teeth scraped, and his temples tightened up.

No, don't go there. He jumped up and hurried to the coffee cart. *You are here for a nice day.*

'Flat white,' he said and furtively looked around, expecting to see that Duggy Harding character. Oh, to be at home. He bought a cappuccino for Marta, a mocha for Palace and a hot milk for Mercury, with sugared doughnuts all round. Sugar didn't make the slightest difference to Mercury, but caffeine made him even more frenzied.

Back at the rollercoaster, they were just coming out, flushed and animated after the ride. Even Palace's face was red with delight. She was breathing so hard that she'd blown the oxygen pipe out of her nostrils, and the tubes dangled from one ear like some wanton facial decoration. Frank's gruesome thoughts of screams floated away, and he smiled. Her headscarf was long gone, and her bald head shone like a beacon. Marta took the coffees from him, her cappuccino with the chocolate on the one side only, just as she liked it.

He hooked the pipes back over her ears and thought what useful things ears were. He held the back of her head and patted her flushed cheek and gave her the mocha, which she gulped at. Mercury grabbed his hot milk. Marta's hair was all over the place. She looked exhilarated and a little surprised at herself but was still trying to be surly. She took his arm. He felt like he'd fixed it.

'C'mon, c'mon.' Mercury pulled them all along towards some more fun somewhere. The screams from the rollercoaster faded, and Frank's mind filled only with his family.

Mercury broke free and ran towards the Big Top. He started doing his little awkward dance that always made them laugh. His playacting increased, and he deliberately banged into the wall, pretending to be shot and fall down dead. He might be exhausting, but he sure was a lark.

Marta and Frank grabbed an arm each as they always did and dragged him to his feet. He was getting heavier by the year. Palace clapped her hands and squealed. Mercury stood against the wall with head dropped to the side, trying to hide his grin and still pretending to be dead. Marta poked a finger into his ribs, and he crumpled in laughter.

'You're not dead,' squealed Palace. Mercury bolted away from the wall, and Marta and Palace ran after him.

Frank made ready to chase after them, but he caught sight of a big blue plaque on the wall where Mercury had been standing. In gold letters it said:

> *This building stands on the site of the Ghost Train, destroyed by fire on the night of Saturday 9 June 1979, with the loss of seven lives. They are remembered.*

'That must have been terrible.'

Frank looked up. It was that nutter Duggy Harding again, leaning against the wall and fiddling with his pipe. His black eye patch caught a glint of sunlight.

'That fire must have been awful. Those children frightened and screaming, people outside thinking they were having fun till the smoke choked them. Terrible, terrible. All that screaming, so many screams.' Duggy Harding looked straight at Frank.

He knew. He knew about the explosion. Frank's face went cold. But how? Border Force wouldn't have this crazy fucker following him around. Harding poked around in his pipe, lit it carefully and puffed up a cloud of smoke. Harding's single eye glinted like a diamond, forever waiting and hardening.

Marta came back clutching a struggling Mercury.

'I must be off,' said Harding, and he rushed away.

Marta touched Frank's arm. 'What's wrong?' she said. He was dimly aware of her. The screams in his head were getting louder and seemed much more real than the outside world. She came closer, but he shoved her away.

Arrgggh! A severed arm flew out of the dust cloud in his mind, again and again, like a gif. He grabbed his head. Vaguely, he noticed nearby people shuffle off. The howling screams were getting louder and louder. He clapped his hands over his ears.

'Frank, Frank! What are you doing?' Marta cried.

A piece of flying glass spun through the air, coming out of nowhere. It severed half of Palace's face.

It's not real.

Another flew into the stomach of Mercury and left a great bloody gash in his side and then, for once, Mercury was silent.

'No!' Frank panted. He tried to focus, but all he could see was blood. The screams and the blood. Then Marta was struck down by a dozen slivers of flying red arrows of glass and slumped mute next to the memorial plaque.

'Marta,' he groaned and fell to his knees. His family – all he had wanted was to protect his family.

Like an angel, Marta was lifting him up.

'Bloody hell,' she seethed through clenched teeth. 'Frank! Frank – snap out of it!'

Marta shook his shoulders, and he came back from the nightmare. She had that look of fear and anger. That vein on her neck was twitching, and he wanted to stroke it to stop. A crowd of strangers surrounded them.

He shrank away. 'Can we go?' he pleaded. He looked

at Palace. She was shaking. He looked around and saw the people watching. Cringed from their attention.

He had to get out of there.

He turned and raced for the entrance, pushing through the crowd. He looked back and saw Marta holding both the twins close to her. Duggy Harding waited in the distance.

'What do you know about that explosion, Frank? What did you see in that bunker?'

No, he mustn't talk. He'd be in too much trouble. Marta gave him that ferocious look as if to say, *don't you dare embarrass us in public again*. Frank stood frozen. The panic wanted him to run, and the father in him wanted to act normal. The panic was winning. He went into a low moan and waved his head around. The twins huddled into Marta. A blinding shriek blasted through his ears. Marta's face changed from anger to disappointment to despair. In a maddening haze, Frank howled and grasped at his ears. Marta clutched her children tighter. The nearby people shuffled back and formed into a circle, like they were watching a show. Frank looked up, mortified, and made a mad rush for the exit. He crashed through the ring of gawkers and out of the funfair.

CHAPTER 15

Broken body parts rushed at him - arms, legs, hands, a splattered piece of finger, a human scalp, each more gruesome than the last. And that severed head. Frank knew he was dreaming.

These dreams were familiar to him, knowing you were asleep but still dreaming. He could direct his dream. He ducked and batted away the missiles of human flesh, feeling no pain – in control. Was he awake yet? No, not yet. He flung away a few more pieces of the evanescent dream. Awake yet? Still not. Then, with barely a shiver, he was alive to the world and felt cold on his back.

He opened his eyes, uncomprehending of his surroundings. This wasn't home. He appeared to be crouched forward on a park bench, and his eyes homed in on the huge rectangular pool of shimmering water in front of him. It was shallow enough to see the bottom, and he could just make out the reflection of the dawn twilight sky and the grey, upside-down Brutalist architecture of the peace monument. He knew this place. It was the Pool of Reflection in Hyde Park, the Anzac Peace Memorial. How did he get here?

Down in the pool, an upside-down kookaburra flew across the granite block of a building and circled off into the dawn sky. The slight ripples through the pool turned into reverberations inside his head, throbbing like an old motor trying to start. He was now fully awake, and a vice gripped his skull.

'Owww,' he wailed. Where had he been? Had he been here all night? Where did he sleep? He must have been wandering the streets all night, sleepwalking. His worst hangover could not come close to the pain and confusion he felt. Fuzzy memories of Luna Park swirled and formed in his mind, and that scruffy old man with the one eye. He tried to recall what happened to Marta and the kids, but the appalling memories at Luna Park raced back. Oh God, Marta was going to be livid. He should call her and tell her he was all right.

The childhood voice of his friend, Jimmy Budabuda, came to him. *It's a brand-new day, Frankie. Everything's going to be okay.* Inexplicably, he felt the tension ease. Jimmy's memory always had that effect on him. He smiled. The smile of nothing left to lose. Jimmy had always taught him, always sure, always steadfast. He was right, of course; whatever had happened yesterday was gone. He expelled a long, tight breath, lifted his head and rose to his feet, straightening the cricks out of his back. He stretched up his arms and felt stronger as a lightness of spirit came over him. It was time to go home. He had the whole train ride to think of how to make it up to Marta.

He looked across the park towards the city, and way, way in the distance, despite the low light, he saw the unmistakable form of that old guy from Luna Park, the black patch on his right eye clearly visible. He'd followed him! Startled, Frank quickly looked away. He couldn't face that Harding man again, and what if he followed him home? He'd never get rid of him. No, it was better that he lose him here. He looked for a hiding place.

Without thinking, he turned and went to run up the memorial steps, but his legs were like molasses, every step as slow as treacle. He struggled upwards. His legs trudged, but his footsteps were loud and sharp, echoing in the quiet of the morning, booming around the place. Again, he had the sensation that he wasn't moving at all, but rather the entrance at the top of the memorial was coming towards him, moving to the rhythm of his painstakingly slow progress, enveloping him.

After an eternity, at the top of the steps, he entered the monument. No, the monument entered his field of consciousness – *it* entered *him*. Everything came towards his eyes, then moved past him. He caught his breath.

Inside, the polished stone walls echoed his footsteps, a spooky sense of solemnity, like an empty church. A little gas burner sat on an altar-like stone table inside a cavernous apsis. A sign said, 'The Eternal Flame of Remembrance'. The domed ceiling, emblazoned with thousands of stars, saluted the sacrificed dead. He had never been inside here before, although he had walked through the park many times and never given it a second thought. The building was part of Hyde Park. He must have driven past a thousand times.

He looked down over a circular stone balustrade at the life-size bronze sculpture, a naked soldier lying dead on a shield and sword, arms outstretched along the blade in a Christ-like pose, shocking in its polished nakedness. In another place it would be erotic, but not here. The man was limp and dead, heroically sacrificed in battle, held aloft by … what?

Frank peered closer. Three women held up the dead soldier. According to the sign, it was his mother, his wife and his sister. The soldiers gave their lives, gave away their existence! But the women had sacrificed too. He imagined his own family torn apart like thousands were back then. What if Mercury was taken away by a war? How it would break them, all three. Frank's body filled with a shuddering gratitude for the sacrifices of those soldiers, those families. His arms shook. He gripped the balustrade and bowed his head in shame. He had mindlessly obeyed a bad order when he could have resisted. The heroic soldier below had died for him. Frank felt ashamed of his own cowardice. He pulled away from the soldier and shuffled outside into the dawn gloom.

The building was surrounded by a terrace, and Frank looked at the bas-relief carvings slightly raised from the surface of the granite, telling tales of the quarrelsome nations from the war of 1914–18 – for King and Country. The nurses, the engineers, the officers and the diggers. All toiling, screaming and dying for the empire.

He looked up higher still to see a giant plinth. It seemed like it should have something on top of it, like a statue was missing. Curious.

Frank caught a whiff of pipe smoke and stiffened.

'They made a giant statue for that plinth but never put it up there – too controversial.' It was that voice again, that Duggy Harding. 'Hi, Frank.'

Frank spun around to see the expression of haughtiness on Duggy Harding's face. Who did he think he was, following him all over the city? Frank narrowed his eyes and tried to put on his own haughty mask. He would not tell this snoop anything.

'Second Lieutenant Francis Bargen,' Duggy bowed. 'Third Home Detachment, Border Force Army, Victoria Barracks, recently moved to Gunderman.' Frank frowned. How could he know that? Was Frank under surveillance?

'How is it out there, Frank? Nice to be by the river, back in your childhood home? Or is it *Captain* Bargen yet?'

'Piss off!' Frank spat, hurrying away. The man was a goddamn bloodhound. What did Harding know about anything? Frank had been following orders. There was a chain of command to be followed, and besides, he had to look after his family.

He realised he'd inadvertently run back inside the safety of the memorial. Damn it, where was his head at today? He turned around to leave again, but Harding was already inside and blocking the exit.

'Take your mind back to that bunker, Frank. How did you feel about that?'

The suddenness of the question catapulted Frank back there, the dust-filled images on the monitor and the silent screams from those victims. He shivered and looked down. It wasn't his fault. It wasn't his fault. Even Torus said so. Didn't he?

'That bad, huh?' Harding played with his pipe, scraped it out and knocked it insolently against the balustrade, the sound echoing around the stone walls.

Harding studied his pipe, his face contemplative. 'When I was a young man, I was stationed in India with the British Army. Saw many things I'd like to forget.' He stuffed his pipe with tobacco, lifted it to his mouth and fished around in the pocket of his overcoat. 'But I also saw things I'm grateful for.' He fiddled with a matchbox.

Frank had no idea how anyone could be grateful for

seeing humans torn into pieces by a bomb blast. The thought made him sick. A wave of nausea made him unsteady, and he moved closer to the nearest wall in case he collapsed.

'Up in the Himalayas, one cold morning, I had a sweeping vision of oneness.' The match flared up and brightened Harding's ancient face, beatific in the memory, eyes shining. 'You get that in the Himalayas; maybe it's the thin air up there.' He sucked the match flame into his pipe and blew out a big cone of smoke. 'If you've never experienced it, it sounds a bit queer, but – everything was connected.' His moist eyes looked towards Frank.

Was he talking about that feeling I had a few minutes ago? That everything was contained inside me? That I wasn't in the world, but rather the world was in me?

'You know what I'm talking about, Frank. I know you do.' Harding leaned forward and looked directly into Frank's eyes. 'In the following years, this feeling never went away, even though it dimmed from time to time. I thought about what made this feeling come back, and it was the ability to relax and feel clear in the heart. I was the centre of my world. I *am* the centre of my world.'

The centre of my world.

Yes, Duggy Harding was describing exactly what Frank had just experienced. As if in confirmation, the dawn sun came in through the window, and the gloom filled up with swirling dust motes.

Everything is contained inside my mind.

'I became headless,' said Harding. 'I realised we can't see our own head – no one can. We can see other people's heads, of course, but not our own, not from our own point of view. Sounds peculiar, I know, but it made me want to find the truth of things. To find out why we all assume we have a head, just because everyone else has a head.'

Frank peered at Harding. The words sounded a bit crazy, but the old face looked like it knew what it was talking about – not crazy. Yes, he'd just felt like that – he was central and connected. Maybe it was the same thing. Maybe he was headless too.

Harding moved forward towards Frank's face, and he smelt his smoky breath. 'You'll feel better if you get it off your chest.'

Frank felt how glorious that would be, to tell the truth, to unburden his conscience. Let go of the awfulness of keeping quiet. But he would be in real trouble with the army. Was he ready for that? He looked into Harding's face again, dimly illuminated by the dawn sky. Better keep quiet. Frank's head bowed, and he stepped away from the wall.

'I – I have to go. My family is waiting for me.'

'There's an honourable history of disobedience to authority, you know.' Harding wouldn't shut up and poked his pipe into Frank's face. 'When the order is evil.'

Frank lifted his head. This old guy's badgering was beginning to irritate him.

'The Nuremberg trials, Frank. The Nazis said they were following orders, but that was no defence.'

Is he saying I'm as bad as a Nazi?

'Also, Mee Lai in the American War in Vietnam. Again, obeying orders inside the blind madness of war.'

'I'm not a Nazi,' Frank muttered, shooting him a dark stare. Harding's head was silhouetted against the stained-glass window.

'I know. You're a good man, Frank, following a bad order. That's why you understand that some orders are bad and you have the right as a soldier to disobey them.'

Frank was silent. What did this man want from him?

Harding took a breath, puffed out his chest and pointed with his pipe again. 'Even earlier, there was the Glencoe massacre in the Scottish Highlands.'

A history lecture now. Frank had heard enough. He turned to go.

Harding put a soft hand on Frank's shoulder. 'Do you hear me, Frank? Three hundred years ago, the English court determined that disobedience would have been dutiful.'

Frank's eyes welled up, and he looked down at the sacrificed soldier, wobbling in the dim light. He turned away from Harding. My God, he thought, rubbing a hand across his wet face, he didn't even know this guy. Why was he standing here listening to him?

It was something about this place. Frank stared again at the sacrificed soldier and felt an easing in his chest. The memorial was not condemning him. It was taking him in, comforting him like a magic hex. The soldier was forgiving him. For the first time in weeks, some dreadful plague was leaving his body, replaced by that uncanny, even pleasant feeling of being at the centre of everything, of being made of nothing. His uncontaminated awareness expanded and swaddled the objects around him. The dawn light streamed into the building, and he felt pulled out to the portico. The red sky scintillated in the Lake of Reflection. Effulgence poured into his dazzled eyes. Duggy followed him out and waved his arm back towards the building.

'You feel it, Frank. This place has magical powers.'

Yes. Maybe it can protect me, somehow.

'A chain of command can't always help you,' said Duggy. 'Bad orders are bad orders.'

Frank thought about what Harding was saying. Was he

right? He thought he was doing right by his family, but maybe Marta would be proud of his courage. She would understand. Maybe he would even get another medal for blowing the whistle. He imagined a proper ceremony with pomp and pageantry for his new medal, with everyone present, not like his grubby little promotion.

Then he thought of Torus's smug face. No, that fantasy was nonsense. He would never be safe while Torus was alive. His confusion was running riot in his mind. Harding lived in a world of history and ideas. Frank lived in reality. He would serve his country and take care of his family by keeping quiet. He breathed out. Yes, that's what he would do. Definitely keep quiet. He strode down the steps and waved an arm back at Harding.

'Keep away from me.'

'That order didn't come out of nowhere, Frank,' Harding shouted after him. 'There is a chain of command, and the orders come from up high.'

Frank shook his head. He had to get home.

~

Frank sat at his kitchen table, gazing out the window to the river. He clutched a whisky in one unsteady hand and the other cradled his chin, elbow on the table, trying to feel the calming river. Many times, as a child, he'd sat here watching the waters flow.

The whisky tasted hot and nauseous. Out the window, the gardener spread manure, and the stench stuck in his throat. He took another slug.

He had a plan. First, he had to tell Marta. Make her understand. Get her advice. Explain why he might get kicked out of Border Force. Then he had to confront Torus. He couldn't get Harding's words out of his mind. Why did Torus do it? Maybe he was following orders after all, and his bravado was all show. Or is he evil? He had to talk to him.

'Where have you been? And drinking whisky?'

He jumped and looked up, eyes barely focusing.

Marta stood in her dressing gown, looking sour. Where was the young girl he had married ten years ago? There was no sign of her now. No smile, no joy or affection, just a hurt arrogance that sent shivers through him. He wanted her to put a hand on his shoulder. He wanted to tell her everything. She crossed her arms, in no mood for any kind of reconciliation.

'Where've you been? I had to bring the children home.' Her feet were spread, locked to the ground.

'At the war memorial.' He sounded pathetic to himself.

'What the fuck?' Marta sniffed. 'You were supposed to be with us, not abandoning us like a piece of rubbish.' She turned away, looked out at the gardener, and pulled her dressing gown tighter. 'Anyway, what do I care where you've been?' She opened the back door, and the whiff of manure stung Frank's nostrils.

He noticed the little rip on the sleeve of her dressing gown that had torn way before the twins were born. They'd been drinking and laughing so much that they'd fallen into her mother's rosebushes. Frank felt the dull thud of despair and slammed his glass down. She flinched.

'You're not who you were,' he wailed, 'ten years ago.'

She spun around and rolled her eyes as though he were a child. 'Neither are you, Frank.'

He scowled and poured another drink. 'I'm going mad with grief,' he slurred.

She spun around, and her lips curled. 'Yes, yes, we all

know how hard it is for you.'

'Not who you were.' He shook his head.

'You and your damn misery. Call yourself a soldier?' She pulled out the cutlery drawer. 'You're an armchair officer. You never had to fight anyone. You're pathetic. What's going on with you? What have you done? What will happen to the children and me if you screw up and get kicked out of Border Force?' She rattled the drawer full of cutlery, shook it wildly with both hands. It jangled like the clashing of wild hostilities and pierced his ears. 'We'll be a laughingstock,' came her voice through the cacophony. 'I'll be humiliated beyond tolerance.' She collapsed into a chair, head in hands.

She didn't understand. She acted like it was all his fault. It wasn't! The drunkenness drained out of him, and he was suddenly stone cold sober. He sat upright. The heat spread through his body and up to his cheeks. He pushed himself up from the table, and the chair legs scraped a mournful grumble. Maybe if he told her, she would have sympathy for him, hold him like she used to. The smell of the manure started a wretched churning in his insides. He slumped back down into the chair. His hand trembled, and the whisky burned his throat.

'What if I tell you what happened?' he mumbled. 'It might help.' He knew he shouldn't, but she was a child of the military. She wouldn't tell anyone. It would be so good to share it. Maybe he could carry on, then, forget it had ever happened. It could be their secret.

Her face screwed up like she was done with him and could endure nothing more. 'Tell it to the river.' His body quivered, and she tramped back into the bedroom.

'Okay, okay!' he shouted after her. Seemingly by themselves, his hands grabbed the table and upended it, scattering plates, cups, cutlery and whisky all over the floor. The unholy noise seemed to calm him. Out on the river, a canoeist paddled by, and a kangaroo drank on the far bank. His head sank.

Oh my God, I'm crazy.

He looked at the unholy mess on the floor with glazed eyes. He must tidy it up, make amends and take the reins back of his life. He hauled the table onto its legs and threw the whisky bottle in the bin. He was halfway through the tidy-up when Marta silently came back in. He braced himself for more fight, but she was standing there, leaning softly against the doorframe. Maybe it was over. These violent storms were part of their life. Gone as quick as they started. Maybe he could tell her now. They looked at each other across the sorry kitchen.

'The kids are both still asleep. They didn't hear anything,' she said.

That was a relief, at least. Marta sat on the kitchen chair and glanced out towards the river. Frank finished tidying up and sat at the table.

'What happened at work? You know you've been acting crazy.'

'Look, I'm sorry.'

She nodded, wanting more of an answer. Frank's mind threatened to retreat back from the horrors, but a part of him stayed detached and cold, away from the dread. He took a breath.

'We were watching the refugees on Narus Island, and Torus ordered an explosion. He made me press the final trigger.'

She didn't move. Kept her eyes on the river. 'What happened?'

'I killed dozens of people. I saw arms and legs flying about.

All those innocent people.' He crumpled into the chair and grabbed the table for support.

She turned back to look at him. He looked up and was relieved to see confusion rather than disgust on her face. She frowned. She put a hand on his shoulder. 'But it was an order.'

He shook his head. 'I should have refused.'

'Is that why you got promoted? To keep you quiet?'

He nodded silently.

'Well, what can you do about it?'

He looked up at her. 'I need to confront him. Make him see what he did.'

'Won't you lose your promotion?'

'Of course. And I'll lose more than that. I'll probably be tried for murder.'

Marta's hands shot to her mouth with a sharp intake of breath.

'But I might get my sanity back. At Luna Park, I kept hearing the screams of those victims getting torn apart. I felt a howling horror at what I'd done.'

She stood up and put an arm round his shoulder, and the wind outside rustled the trees.

'After Luna Park, everything is blank. I woke up in the morning, and I was at the Anzac Memorial in Hyde Park. I don't know how I got there, and I felt very strange. I've been getting these peculiar feelings that I don't exist in the world, but instead the world exists in me. I'm so large that everything around me is actually inside me. It's disturbing, but strangely blissful.' He looked at Marta. There was no way she would understand.

'Blissful?' She frowned and sat back down on the chair, looking outside for some kind of guidance.

'Those statues seemed to have some kind of magical

quality. There were sculptures of dead soldiers. I went inside the building, and right in the middle was a golden statue of a dead soldier lying on a cross made from a sword. That soldier spoke to me, told me what a coward I was. All those soldiers had sacrificed their lives, and all I did was kill innocent people.' He looked into her face. She had a faraway look.

'I know about those statues,' she said. 'They were made in the 1920s at the National Art School, down the road from Hyde Park. I was a student there for a while. My dad was really into military history. It was a really big deal at the art school. Even one of the buildings at the art school was named after the sculptor, Rayner Hoff.'

Frank listened, rapt. Rayner Hoff. He must find out more about him. How had he made this magical building that could have such an effect on people?

'We met the guy who originally modelled for the central statue. He was very old by then. He told us that every afternoon he would lie on Rayner's table, naked, with a broomstick under his outstretched arms for Rayner to sculpt in clay. But some of the statues were too controversial to put on the finished memorial. One of the statues was a naked female Christ. It was hidden away and forgotten. No one knows what happened to it.'

'What do you mean?'

'The Catholic church down the road flexed their political muscle, and there was an almighty row. There was a lot of talk about what the church actually objected to. Was it the naked female? No, lots of those in churches. Was it the crucifix? No, also lots of those in churches. It was the central *male* saviour being replaced by a woman. The church won in the end. Those old men couldn't cope. Still can't. The same thing would probably happen today.'

Frank thought about how the memorial had had such a profound effect on him and that maybe if he got Torus to go there, it would have the same effect on Torus – loosen him up and get him to admit the truth. It was half a plan, at least.

CHAPTER 16

Torus poured himself a whisky with a slightly quivering hand, not offering one to Frank this time. He slugged it down, and his mouth opened and stiffened out wide. A tight little scraping noise came out of his throat. Frank couldn't tell if he enjoyed the whisky or not.

'We'll go for a little walk, Frank,' instructed Torus, and led the way down to the parade ground. Trailing behind Torus was a gruesome experience for Frank, like you were part of the walking dead. Frank recalled his nickname round the base was Zombie. Nobody would say that to his face, of course. You would be in all sorts of trouble. Torus had no feelings, kept them well in check, but his whisky drinking and that tremor might mean something. He was impossible to reason with, but maybe some emotion was leeching to the surface against his iron will.

Frank would have his work cut out, trying to get Torus to admit responsibility for the explosion. Did he have any humanity in him at all? Was he given an order from higher up? Frank shrugged. He had only the inkling of a plan – somehow to get Torus to talk to him about the explosion and admit they were both given bad orders so they would be off the hook.

Torus sauntered out to the edge of the parade ground and looked across at the recruits practicing drill. He lit up a cigar. Frank remembered when he first came here, serving under Torus, but they had never been mates. Frank shivered at the thought. Torus didn't seem close to anyone. Frank did feel some pity; Torus had never married and didn't have a family. Maybe a visit to the memorial might move him a little.

'That little incident back in the bunker, it was an accident. We're all clear on that, right? Your promotion took care of that, okay?'

Frank cowered. Even through all his confusion, Frank knew it had definitely not been an accident. It had been a direct order. Torus looked straight into Frank's face. Frank felt a revulsion as he looked at Torus's eyes. They looked ninety percent dead, so black you couldn't see the iris from the pupil. A shudder ran down his body. The two men peered at each other. Frank detected a small something in Torus's eyes, something he'd never seen before. Was it fear? Surely not. Torus had all the power, held all the cards. Had he gone rogue and acted on his own, and now Border Force was in damage control? Was Torus getting hassled by his superiors? But Bradsleap was onside, surely. He had promoted Frank to keep him quiet. Was Bradsleap in on it? He sighed. Maybe there would be a forensic investigation and Frank would lose his promotion.

Torus looked back out towards the parade ground. 'It's looking like we won't be able to keep this little incident under wraps, Frank. It's going to get out, and it will definitely be an accident.' The marching soldiers stamped out their metallic rhythm. 'I want you to forget what happened,' he said. 'Completely get rid of it out of your mind. It's the best thing. You can go back to how it was before. You've been promoted. I can tell you feel guilty – I did too the first time.'

First time? So he could feel guilt!

'After a while, those guilt demons inside you will calm down, and you'll relax back into normal life again.'

Frank stiffened. The squad of soldiers advanced towards them, and the marching got louder.

'Squaaad! Halt!' the barking Sar-Major shouted across the parade ground. The squad stamped in unison. 'Stand-at! Ease!' One giant stomping of feet and then a silence echoed round the square. The quiet was solid, comforting. The beautiful tidiness. Torus stood taller.

Frank remembered the revelation he had felt in the memorial, the promise of freedom if he came clean, and wondered if Torus had ever been there. Would it be possible to get him to admit that the orders came from higher up? Or at least that he was sorry. How could Frank get him to go to the memorial?

'There could be consequences,' Torus said. 'A danger to us all.' So, did that mean Torus *was* in trouble from his superiors? Torus gave Frank a warning look. 'A danger to us all – and to our families.'

Frank flinched. *Was that a threat?*

Torus fixed his eyes on the distance again. 'All the families in Australia would be in danger if we are prevented from carrying out our work. All the families in the world.' Torus sounded like a deranged lone actor.

'Of course,' Frank muttered. They nodded, as if an agreement had been reached.

'Atten-SHUN! By the left! Quick! March!' The squad took off in unison.

Torus put a fatherly hand on Frank's shoulder, and Frank felt a cold shudder like it was a claw clutching him.

'Of course, the families,' muttered Frank. Torus was definitely threatening Frank's family. 'Some one-eyed guy called Harding has been following me. He knows something. I think he might be a reporter, but I haven't told him anything.' Frank tried to shrug off Torus's hand, but it dug in tighter.

'We are doing our duty. You know that. There will be the worst consequences if we don't do what we have to do. All the good people of the world rely on us. Where would we all be? Where would your family be, Frank, if we didn't do our duty?'

Frank's face flushed. He cut across, took a chance. 'I went inside the memorial at Hyde Park. It spoke to me.'

'Oh, yes?' Torus nodded distractedly as he watched the squad way across the other side of the parade ground.

'It told me about the noble sacrifices that have been made in the name of protection.' Torus's hand squeezed tighter into Frank's shoulder. Frank took a breath.

'Were you acting under orders down in the bunker?' Torus glowered at Frank like a master who had been insulted by his slave.

'Maybe we could talk about it,' Frank went on.

Torus groaned. 'Not your concern, Frank.' He looked down at Frank from a great height, disappointed. 'Memorial talking to you? What a nutty idea. I've never been inside one of those memorial places.' He dug his claw hand deeper into Frank's shoulder, and Frank recoiled from the pain. Torus watched, then shoved Frank's shoulder away, releasing the claw. Frank rubbed his shoulder and felt a flash of hatred.

'It's your fault. I'll tell that reporter what happened.' Frank was astonished by the words that had just come out of his mouth.

'Reporters are sewer rats!' Torus spat out.

'Squaaad! Halt!' The drill sergeant's command echoed across the square. 'Squaaad! Dismissed!'

Torus squinted at Frank, then looked out over the parade ground and puffed on the cigar.

'Sewer rats! Take care, Frank, take very good care. Let's get things clear. I'll be following you wherever you go.' He slowly turned his back and walked away. Frank would be monitored everywhere he went. He breathed heavily, but with a flash, he realised something.

Okay, follow me, follow me to the memorial. But how could he even think that would do any good? Torus was a completely lost case. He had no empathy at all.

On the other hand, there was definitely something spooky about the memorial that might affect Torus. Frank knew it.

CHAPTER 17

1999

Micky Torus arrived at the party early. It was being held at his mate Rick's house over near Centennial Park. Rick's parents were Paddington artistic types and lived in the last house standing on Cook Road. All the other houses had been sold off to build apartments. There was a drum kit in the front room as you walked in, and as always, Micky sat down on the stool and started banging.

'Enough!' shouted Rick from the next room, as always. 'You'll wake the dead.' Micky thought he was pretty good on the drums, but Rick rushed in and screwed up his nose. Their other mates, Globba and Bainsey, were already there with him. Micky's cheeks flushed, and he dropped the drumsticks.

'G'day,' they all said solemnly in unison and nodded to each other. Micky thought Rick was lucky he'd even bothered to come to his stupid party. *He's a Paddington snob. I'm only here to get laid.*

He was feeling okay in his Mambo flame shirt and baggy jeans. Yeah, his dick felt free in there. Looking good and feeling good, despite Rick's comments about his drumming. But he'd gotta get laid tonight – just had to. It was shameful that he'd missed out last time and in front of his mates too!

Rick claimed he'd been fucking since he was fourteen, and Globba was always going on about how the chicks at South Sydney Girls' were the hottest anywhere, even better than Randwick Girls'. The shortest skirts, right up to their crack, and bigger tits. Even Bainsey, who was more like a girl himself, laughed when Micky always messed up in the *getting fucked* department. He was eighteen, for fuck's sake, and not getting any younger. Tonight was the night.

He looked round the room, and a gang of chicks in the corner caught his eye. They were all sucking straws, in that blue eye shadow, and with chokers round their necks. He tingled at the sight of the chokers. An episode of *Sex in the City* played with no sound on the TV, and another gaggle of girls in spaghetti straps with that Reese Witherspoon look cavorted around to some boy band. They all wore bucket hats and looked stupid.

He spied Leslie by herself in the corner, sucking on a red drink through a straw and chewing gum at the same time, ogling at the dancing girls. Everyone said she was a lezzo. They were all lezzos at Sydney Girls' – too smart for their own good – but Micky didn't care. That would probably be easier. She'd do, even if she wasn't from South Sydney. Girls are girls, and if she was a lezzo, she probably didn't know how to do it anyway. Perfect. He snatched down his rum and coke and sauntered over there.

'Woo, hoo!' his mates yelled. 'Micky's going for it.'

Leslie sucked on her straw and looked straight at him. He went in for the kill.

'G'day,' he said.

Her chewing got bigger. 'G'day.'

It was going well. 'Wanna go outside?'

Leslie seemed keener than he expected and lazily pushed herself off the wall. She shrugged.

The back veranda was pretty dark. He was laying it on thick and thinking it was going well when Lezzie gave him this exasperated, bored look and grabbed the bottom of her shirt. She whipped it up to her neck. Micky was boggled and stunned at the sight of her magnificent chest – no bra. Her tits were shaped like a dark fulsome statue. Not like you see in magazines or on your computer, but better in real life, way better. He figured she liked his reaction, because she pulled her shirt up higher so he could get a better look. She swayed a bit from side to side, and they wobbled. They actually wobbled! That must be what they do if they're not in a bra.

He took a big breath and slowly approached the swaying breasts with both hands. His mouth was dry. She looked like the best gift anyone could ever get. Two tits, two hands, perfect. She was pretending to be a bit bored, but he knew she was playing. He touched her softly, and his fingers tingled. She pushed her head back and let him feel.

'Let's go somewhere,' she whispered.

This is really going to happen! Lezzie dragged him by the hand through the house. Micky gave his dick a quick comforting squeeze and followed.

They found Rick's little sister's bedroom, empty for the weekend, and Leslie hustled them both inside and slammed the door. She grabbed his cheeks, pulled his face towards her, and banged their lips together. Their teeth collided.

'Ugh! Rough cheeks,' she said, rubbed her lips and pulled away. She looked at him, wiped her mouth, then shrugged. 'Whatever,' she said and pushed him back onto the bed. He bounced there and waited, watched her take off her shirt.

A kid's picture on the wall caught his eye. The Handsome Prince was kissing Snow White back into life. There was something about the picture, Snow White's pale skin and inert body were like his mother when he had laid with her for hours after she'd died. He felt suddenly melancholy.

Lezzie fumbled at his belt buckle.

What's she doing? My mother would never do that. He wanted her to lie still and be passive. He shivered in fear. She dragged his pants off him and grabbed his dick. It was as soft as a kid's fluffy toy.

'Huh!' she said. 'Not much going on there.'

A burst of shame and anger shot through his head. She'd got no right to say that. It must be her fault. He grabbed at her furiously and rolled her onto her back. He'd show her. He'd get on top. He felt under her skirt, but she struggled. He grabbed at her flesh, not sure what to touch first. There was a hole down there somewhere, and he fumbled around between her legs. His dick hardened up good and strong now. He'd definitely get his carrot in there this time. It was suddenly the best stiffy he'd ever had. Better than when you do it yourself and think about your mother. He found Lezzie's hole, and it felt a bit wet and disgusting. But anyway, he shoved his finger in there. She yelped and pushed at him. Why wouldn't she stay still? She tried to push him off.

But he was so close now, there was no stopping him. At last, he got his dick inside. What a relief, he was doing it! Now what? What do you do now? It never occurred to him to move in and out. He lay there, even though his enormous weight made Lezzie fight and flounder. His mother came to him with her silky white skin, her smooth gentle movements. Why wasn't this girl like that? She was trying to get away. Hold her! Hold her still!

'Whatsa matta? Thought you wanted it?'

'Not any more, dickhead.' A sharp hurtfulness shot through him like a glass shard, and he grabbed her round the neck. She froze in shock. That's better. He breathed more easily.

She shoved at his chest. 'Get off me!' she gasped through her strangled throat.

This was so difficult. Not fun at all. He pulled back slightly, softened his hand. Maybe she would cooperate then. Instead, she screamed and pulled his hands off her. She tossed him away, slipped out from under and ran from the room half clothed. He heaved and panted. Stupid, he thought. Girls are stupid.

CHAPTER 18

Frank sat in his back shed, sheltered by the enormous gum trees. Kookaburras laughed high above. What had Marta said about the memorial? Something about missing statues. Frank searched his iPad. There, plain as day, were the original drawings of the memorial showing where the statues should have been at the east and west sides of the building. The statues were giant, naked, female Christs crucified on the sword and shield of Mars, the god of war. The plinths were waiting there on the memorial, but the statues had never been erected.

Frank scrolled down to the next search item, a journalist's article about how the nearby St Mary's Church had prevented their installation. Frank clicked on the article.

It didn't help that Rayner Hoff's depictions of the human body were always sensual. He was a vitalist, said the article.

I suppose I don't really get art, Frank thought. What's a vitalist? I suppose it's because the statues are so lifelike.

Hoff's intention had been to show the sacrifice that women had made in the war, the article said. No lists of dead and dedicated women were ever memorialised. The wife, mother and sister holding up the dead soldier in the middle of the memorial symbolised their sacrifice. The article had a quote from Hoff at the time:

'Thousands of women, although not directly engaged in war activities, lost all that was dearest to them. There was no acknowledgment of them in casualty lists, lists of wounded, maimed and killed. In this spirit, I have shown them carrying their load, the sacrifice of their menfolk.'

Frank pushed away his iPad. Even way back a hundred years ago, there were people who thought that war was not glorious, not courageous, but low and pathetic.

Rayner Hoff had been in the trenches in the Great War and seen the sickening slaughter. He'd seen the accusing, skeletal fingers of the rotting corpses. But in the memorials, no one had thought to remember the women. In Rayner Hoff's memorial, the wife, mother and sister holding up the dead soldier made him think of Marta. She kept their family together. She was enduring enormous strain because of his actions and craziness. He bowed his head. He started reading his tablet again.

The female Christ statue was declared revolting and offensive. The fake moral outrage by the church had turned the sculptures in the public mind into tawdry sexualised imagery. The archbishop, just for good measure, threw in the observation that the memorial was obviously only intended for protestants. It must have been a crazy time of prejudice, Frank thought. It always seemed to him that one church was much the same as another.

The article continued. The journalist theorised that the real reason for the ban was that a female Christ would have meant the theft of the central Christian patriarchal symbol.

Frank assumed they meant Jesus. Hoff insisted that the female body could be as symbolic of sacrifice as the male. But the church up the road insisted the statues be prohibited. At the time, Nazis were also censoring degenerate art on the other side of the world. Hoff was devastated, never recovered from the controversy, and it contributed to his early death.

Frank had never been religious, but his encounter in the memorial was the closest thing he had ever had to a spiritual experience. These people from the past, creating memorials, and others banning the same memorials, were all acting out of their own religious feelings. How could they be so different and hostile towards each other? Frank had only felt an enormous sense of awe and peace in the memorial.

Would the same banning happen today? Probably, Frank reflected. The restoration of the memorial back in 2018 had ignored the neglected statues, and their plinths were still vacant. The moral guardians were still prowling. Frank was beginning to feel that his adventure in the memorial was almost religious.

~

The clock ticked. A faraway bird squawked. The blue, blue sky filled the window. Frank looked around Yo-Knee's office, and it was all somehow different. They had just finished their fifty minutes.

The whole world was different. For a start, he saw his arms in front of him, but his hands resting on his knees seemed so far away. His legs were the same; his feet were miles away and tiny. He tingled with excitement at this peculiar vision. He looked down at his chest and then … he realised something. Something he had never noticed before. A vast thing! There was nothing above his chest! It was amazing now that it was so obvious. He could not see his own head! A bit of a blurry nose, but that's all. No head at all. He looked at Yo-Knee, preparing some notes. She had a head. Those people outside the window had heads, one each. He was the sole recipient of this blankness at his centre. He was the only one without a head. His mind fell back into a silence. He felt surprised, but vaguely untroubled.

What does this mean? What is Yo-Knee doing to me? Was this part of the amending? If it was, it was good. But he didn't really care what it meant. It didn't matter what it meant. He didn't even care what he felt. It only mattered what he *saw*.

'I want to stay here.'

Yo-Knee looked at her watch, and her big forehead creased. 'Okay,' she said. 'Just for a while. You've been through a lot. Your mind is reacting to it. It's not dealing with reality yet.'

'No, I mean this headspace. I want to stay in this headspace.' He felt empty in the middle. He was blank but filled with the world. The room, Yo-Knee and the people outside the window actually seemed to be inside of him. Why had he never noticed this before? He looked at her as if he was asking her to explain it to him. Yo-Knee peeked over the rim of her glasses and chewed on her pencil, as though slightly puzzled. *She doesn't know about this stuff! She's got power that she doesn't even know about.* My brain must be affected by the trauma of seeing all those poor people.

He walked to the window and held his thumb out at arm's length, covering the building across the road with it. He had lost his sense of space. He had no perspective, no depth. Everything was the same distance from him, on the same plane. His thumb and the building seemed to be the same distance from him and the same size. He pointed to his feet – yes, there they were, where he was pointing. Then he pointed to his knees and chest – still there, same as his feet. Each time his finger was pointing correctly at the object. But then he pointed at his head and saw only the end of his finger, not his head, only a blank space, a vast space ready to be filled with his universe. It was magical. He looked at Yo-Knee and could tell she wouldn't get it. Nobody would get it. He was alone with it. Was he mad? He didn't care. It was more real than anything he had ever known. This would change everything he had ever thought about the world. He felt grateful to the whole world. Yo-Knee and the world had given him this vision. He must thank them somehow.

Yo-Knee was scribbling notes. Frank slowly turned his head around the room, fascinated by his new world. But he seemed to be still, and the room was moving instead. He dreamily looked at the corner of Yo-Knee's eye, with its years of listening to other people's problems and worries. Her face was profoundly inside him, inside his consciousness.

She knew that he'd seen inside her. She looked up, her face relaxed, and she had a little faint smile. Frank saw that some of her own anxiety had fallen away. *I love you.* The words catapulted round his head. He loved her. She was inside him.

'Thank you,' he said. She smiled slightly and fussed around with her pencil.

'If people would only do what they damn well need to do,' she muttered and stood up. Then she realised she'd spoken out loud, smiled, then shrugged. It hit him. He must *do* something. He must confront Torus and try to find out if the orders came from higher up. The world had been good to him; he must be good to the world.

He observed the dusky skin of Yo-Knee's cheeks. He had never really looked so closely at the skin of a black person before. It was shiny. She was blushing!

'Anyway, good to see you. I have another appointment.' He was startled by this abrupt dismissal. She was losing a bit of her professional manner. He felt pushed away. But she was blushing! She knew he'd noticed, and she became more abrupt. She felt something for him too. He smiled as she bundled him out the door.

'Okay,' he said, 'my wife's coming to pick me up.' But he had a mission, and his mind felt stable at last. Weird, but stable.

~

Marta's knuckles sharpened into a vivid whiteness with her grip on the steering wheel. Mercury bounced around in the back of the car, seemingly everywhere. She wouldn't be surprised if he had taken his seatbelt off. She couldn't bear to look. Palace sat quietly beside him as usual. It was unbelievable how she managed to tolerate him, but the child was a saint.

Marta pulled up outside the address in Palmer Street, East Sydney – the dingy red-light district. Why did Border Force have their broken soldiers come here? Anyway, it would be nice if Frank came out smiling from his session. She hardly dared think it. Mercury's feet stamped into the back of her seat for the umpteenth time, and her neck jolted back.

'Stop it!' she screamed. Today had been relentless. If Frank was in one of his moods, she thought she might throw Mercury to him and leave. Take Palace and keep driving. The thought was delicious. Imagine it.

'Where's Dad?' Mercury yelled as he saw her gathering her handbag and opening the car door. He grabbed for the door handle, but she quickly exited and flicked the modified central locking system for the car.

'Wait here in the car and don't move.' Nobody could get out now, but just in case of trouble, there was the big red button that would open the doors. Marta pointed to the button, and he knew he mustn't touch it. It had taken months of professional training to get him to understand that the big red button was not a toy and was for emergencies only. He slumped back into the car seat.

Marta looked back at Palace through the car window and suddenly felt weary. Her daughter gave a small smile, but it couldn't hide the fact that she was pale and the brown circles under her eyes had darkened, and her hair was thin and watery. Was she getting worse?

Marta dismissed the idea from her mind and hurried down the little lane to the back of the building. At least Frank should be fixed up now, after his visit to the amender. She really needed him to be better. They worked wonders these days, those amenders. They had to help him, they had to.

She walked into a small entrance lobby, and a man sat at the desk looking bored, dressed in orange clothes with beads, like an Indian holy man. The place smelt of incense. He didn't say anything, just idly pointed along a corridor. A woman hurried towards Marta, her face crinkled up in some kind of anguish, holding a handkerchief to her face. She gave Marta a sharp, desperate look as she bustled past and out the door. *Well, that one's not so fixed up.* But Frank would be better, she was sure. The man in orange didn't react.

Marta crept along the corridor to a door with a sign that said *Doctor Yo-Knee Thompson – Amender.* A small pair of wooden steps was outside the closed door.

I wonder what that's for?

The door opened, and Frank strolled out. He looked

… lighter. At least he wasn't doing anything crazy. Was he actually smiling? Frank looked startled when he saw her.

He's forgotten I was coming to pick him up.

The smile dropped from his face like a falling curtain. He quickly looked away, and then just as quickly recovered his composure. He became sullen again. Marta was puzzled.

He was followed out of the office by a child – no, not a child, a dwarf! A woman dwarf, a black woman dwarf.

'Hello, Mrs Bargen. I'm Darcta Tarmsun.' The dwarf held out her hand. Before she knew what had happened, Marta found herself shaking the dwarf's hand. A distaste built up in her mouth. It didn't make any sense. A dwarf?

What in the world is Frank up to now? It's unbearable. I'm sure he's doing it on purpose to annoy me. And look at the way she's dressed and made up. She looks like a circus tart.

The dwarf climbed to the top step and hugged Frank. Her Frank! He wasn't much, but at least he was hers. They broke out of the hug, and the dwarf looked at Marta with a mischievous smile, which Marta was sure was malevolent. Why was she laughing at her? This wasn't professional, surely. What was going on here? Marta would make a complaint. If that woman thought she could come between their family while Frank was sick, well, she had another thing coming.

Marta grabbed Frank by the arm and marched him out the door, back to the car. Any recent affection for him was gone. She spun him around to face her.

'What are you doing with that creature?'

'What creature? She's a professional amender.'

'When I told you to get some amending done, I didn't think you'd …' It was too much. On top of everything, now this. 'She touched you!'

Frank recoiled from her, then slouched towards the car.

Palace leant against the window, slumped sideways. Marta hurried over and flicked open the door.

'Baby, baby … you okay?' She went to pull Palace upright, but she opened her dreamy eyes and sat back into the seat. She seemed okay.

'Yes, Mum.' Her poor, brave daughter. It was heartbreaking.

Mercury grabbed the opportunity to leap out of the car.

'Frank,' Marta screeched as he was about to get into the passenger seat. 'Don't ignore him. Do something!'

Frank seemed to snap out of a dream and he yelled, 'Get back in the car!' Mercury scuttled back into his seat, followed by Frank and Marta.

What had she ever done to deserve this life? She side-eyed Frank, who had put his seatbelt on and was sitting there, clearly distracted, like he had dropped back into another universe – separated from his hyperactive son and his dying daughter. Was she the only normal one here? She gritted her teeth and spoke under her breath.

'Palace is getting worse.'

Frank said nothing. Did he even hear her? She wanted to repeat herself, to punch him, to force him to look and really see their child. It was like Palace was someone else's problem. Marta's. Everything was hers and hers alone. It was unbearable.

~

The car screeched into the bumpy gravel driveway at Gunderman. Frank had been biting his lip all the way home. He wanted to tell Marta about Yo-Knee, how he found her so wonderful to talk to. How she made him feel so protected and ethereal. Marta would be happy for him, surely. He would need a few quiet moments in the house with her. Once she understood, he would be able to tell her everything, and they could work on his plan together. He would confront Torus to find out if he was coerced into the atrocity by higher-ups.

Their grumpy neighbour, Drovis, draped his arms lazily over his side fence and watched them return home. Frank groaned. Drovis was a quick and nervy little man who had lived alone next door since Frank was a child. He got his entertainment from watching the comings and goings of this small insular cluster of houses on the Hawkesbury. Frank's parents had been forever quarrelling with him about next-door neighbour trivia.

Marta skidded to a halt and flipped open the back doors. Mercury was out in a heartbeat and raced for the big swing dangling from the enormous gum tree in the front yard. Frank looked to see if Marta was calming down, then carefully got out of the car.

'I want a word with you, Frankie,' shouted Drovis. 'I know you've got a gun back there. It's dangerous. You shouldn't be shooting a gun.'

Frank halted. Not now!

Marta disappeared towards the front door. Frank watched and thought it wasn't looking promising to talk to her. What on earth is wrong with her now? He turned back to Drovis. 'It's not a gun. It's machinery from work. It's classified.'

'Classified?' Drovis gave out a nasty, brittle laugh. 'How do I know it's classified? It sounds like a gun,' Drovis muttered and retreated back towards his house. 'I'll find you out, Frankie. You always were a secretive little kid, hanging around with that aboriginal. You won't get away with it.'

Frank imagined a little bullet from his Scarlatti X3

penetrating the back of Drovis's skull. That felt good, but only for a moment.

No!

You're not allowed to feel like that! Drovis was a lonely old man. Frank dropped into a sullen thought. Why not? Why couldn't he feel like that? The man was a prick. A righteous, blazing anger raged through him.

'Everyone, get in the house!' he shouted and turned rapidly to face Drovis. 'Come back here!'

'He's got a gun in his back shed,' Drovis yelled to the sky and anyone who would listen.

Marta shooed the twins into the house.

'He needs sorting out,' shouted Drovis. 'He's not a good neighbour. He's dangerous. He's never been a good neighbour.' Drovis threw his arms in the air and retreated into his house. 'I'm calling the police,' were his last mutterings.

Frank's breath slunk out of his body, and he was tired, so tired, but at least Drovis would be quiet for a day or two now that he'd had his rant. He wiped his forehead and trudged into the house after Marta.

Mercury was finished with the swing and was now running round the house in circles. It was his favourite go-to adventure when he was too agitated to sit still. He ran to the TV, then to the window, then the couch, then to the TV again and round and round. Palace sat, waiting for him to calm down. Marta slammed her bag onto the table and slumped into a chair, her face in her hands. Frank was confused. Should he go to Marta? Should he shut Mercury up?

He looked at Mercury, and the swirling and running around dug deep into Frank's head. He pointed with a ramrod finger to the seat next to Palace. Mercury immediately froze like a statue. It was another game. He sat down, fidgeting next to Palace. Marta was sobbing, her shoulders heaving. Frank put a tender hand on her back. She stiffened, then stood up and wiped her eyes and nose.

'What was happening with that amender?' Marta demanded.

She was still on about that! Frank was tempted to sit down next to her, but remained standing. 'She was comforting me.'

'Comforting! Why did she touch you like that?'

'She's my amender.'

'It looked like more than that.'

'Nothing more than that.' Frank went silent. Was it more than that? What did he really feel about Yo-Knee? He felt beautiful about her. She was the most wonderful creature he had ever met.

Marta waited. 'Well?'

Mercury bounced on the couch and started to hum to himself.

'Quiet!' shouted Frank. Mercury slapped his hand across his mouth, rolled his eyes in mock horror, and waggled his feet. Frank turned back to Marta. 'She's very nice. She's a very nice person.'

Marta heaved in a big breath. 'Very nice, was she?'

Frank cringed at her loaded sarcasm. 'She was helpful. She understands me.'

Marta's eyes and mouth widened out like a Luna Park clown. 'Understands you? I've been fucking understanding you for years. I'm sick of understanding you. You can have her. It's disgusting. A dwarf! Thrown away for a dwarf!'

What did she mean? Frank recalled the tenderness of being in Yo-Knee's office, her listening to his every word, her seeming to understand all his pain. He smiled at the memory.

'You don't understand. You've got it all wrong.' But right

now, he would rather be with Yo-Knee than Marta.

Marta's face creased up. 'You bastard! What did you two get up to in there? She's the right height for you, is she?' An image of Yo-Knee came to him. She was standing in front of him, undoing his fly and rummaging around in there.

'That's horrible!' Frank yelled, too loudly. He shot to his feet, then suddenly realised the twins were watching and lowered his voice. Even Mercury was stock still. 'That's disgusting, a terrible thing to say,' he hissed.

'No, you're the one who's terrible,' Marta spat. 'And what's with that sleazy neighbourhood? If you think I'm going to let you humiliate me this way, you're crazy.' She shoved him in the chest, and then without another word, strode over to the couch, grabbed the twins, one in each hand, and marched them out of the room.

CHAPTER 19

The year 2003

Micky Torus checked out the mirror. Mirror, mirror on the wall, who's the ruler of them all? He straightened his white silk tie over his black t-shirt and adjusted his Lance Armstrong rubber bracelet. On his other wrist was his big-faced digital Timex. Too cool. His red trucker hat said *girls gone wild,* and his mauve skinny jeans pulled at his crotch. Two-tone black winkle-picker shoes finished him off. Not bad at all. *There's a treat for you tonight.* He checked his pockets for the Rohypnol. Yes. This time, this time, everything would be all right. He was twenty-three.

He'd had a couple more bad attempts at sex since he was nineteen, but always, always, his mother appeared in his mind. Her soft white skin glowed in his mind. It was like his mother was reaching out from the grave, jealous, refusing to let her miracle child go. But this time, he would find the perfect girl and root her to death. She would be compliant, so still, like that very last time with his dead mother. She wouldn't laugh, she wouldn't be sympathetic. They were the worst, the sympathetic ones. Why didn't they shut up? That rubber doll at the last party was almost perfect. He had taken it and ravished her. She was compliant, so natural. He had almost turned a rubber doll into a girl. Tonight, he would turn a girl into a rubber doll. He squeezed his dick. Was it toughening up? It was! He pulled it roughly out of his fly and gave it a couple of slaps. That's good, that's better. His dick was going to love it, love it. He shoved it back into his pants and headed for the party.

It was cranking. The lights were sharp balloons scraping across the ceiling. You could hardly hear yourself think, but Micky had enough chat to get the girl unaware enough to slip the drug into her drink. She was half willing anyway. Why would she be talking to him otherwise? Once again, without ceremony, into the bedroom they staggered. The drug was quick; she flopped straight back onto the bed and snored. Micky faltered. His mother had never snored. But he got to work, lifted up her flimsy dress, and rolled her over. No underwear! *I knew she was willing. She deserves this. What kind of girl goes to a party with no underwear?*

He pushed apart her knees and struggled out of his pants. His dick wasn't very hard, and he had to jerk it off a bit, but he somehow got it in there. He was warming up. The girl groaned in her sleep. His dick went flat again. *Shut up, shut up.* He put his hands around her neck and shook her. That felt good. His shoulders broadened out. He was powerful, like a god, the God of the Universe. Goooood! He shook her more, more. Good, good. He could feel his dick throbbing and gristly. It was really going to happen. He was inside her again, shoving, shoving. It was happening; it was happening. He came in a quick spasm of reassuring pleasure and let go of the girl's throat. He felt great, elevated and noble, like the god he was. He threw his arms up in the air and rolled off her. *She's not snoring now. That's woken her up.* But she looked weirdly tangled up. He gave her a tap.

'Hey, wanna go back to the party?'

She didn't move. He shoved her, but nothing. Her chest looked still. He leant in close. She didn't seem to be breathing.

What the fuck! What's she done? She's gone and killed herself. She was very quiet now. Her skin was glistening. She looks way better than the rubber doll, way better.

He straightened her out and climbed on top of her again. There was no need to choke her into silence anymore. He lay with her for many hours that night. By the end, he knew he loved her. Really loved her. He was so grateful they had met.

CHAPTER 20

Frank wandered out to his back shed and slumped into the creaky old chair. A pungent pine smell filled the place. His feet were up to his ankles in wood shavings from the desk he had been making before his life had gone to shit. Seemed like ages ago. He relaxed into the tangy wood smell, and his mind filled with disbelief at his predicament. His life had been so perfectly normal, going to work and coming home, quiet and content. Then, suddenly, bang! His mind raced through the recent crazy events. Did Torus really mean to do him harm? Why did he have to give that order anyway? He wished, oh, he wished he'd been out of the room. That shiny red button, and now all those people were dead. How many? And Frank had killed them. So easily. He slumped further into the chair.

He was a killer now. He had never seen a dead body until all those bits and pieces of arms and legs. His cheeks burned. His guts were ripped apart. The terrible shame of being exposed. The guilt that he had actually done such a dreadful thing. The awful fear that Torus would come for him. His heart pumped. The chair creaked.

There was a rustling in the wood shavings at his feet. Frank looked down, and the kids' black cat, Thomas Traherne, strolled into the shed. The cat took one quick look at Frank, then sprang onto the bench. He licked his paws nonchalantly. Frank stroked the cat. Maybe he should keep quiet. No one would know. Torus had promoted him. It might be all right. His trauma would fade.

'What do you think, Tommy?'

The cat yowled. It had always been a vocal one. Frank was filled with his eternal indecision.

Thomas Traherne let out a piercing cry. Frank jumped. What was wrong with him? It was like the cry of the dead. Like all those people were screaming through the cat. We must be avenged, they cried. Frank was exhausted from his own brain going round and round.

He reached into the small drawer underneath the bench and pulled out the disassembled pieces of his tiny gun. Shooting practice was Frank's secret vice. Could he kill Torus and get away with it? It was absurd. What was he thinking? But what if he killed him in self-defence? What if Frank admitted he was a witness to the atrocity but had nothing to do with it? Torus would come hunting for Frank's family to keep him quiet, and then Frank could shoot him with the legitimate excuse of protecting his family. It would work perfectly. He would be an even bigger hero.

He began to assemble the gun. Another gorgeous neat plan. Like the beautiful mechanical workings of the little gun. Yes, it was the simplest course to follow. His mind felt clear. It would be easy. Kill Torus, and everything would be all right again. He wiped his forehead and took a long, easy breath. The old chair beneath him creaked. After all, he really was a killer now. Thomas Traherne jumped into his lap and purred. Frank felt some pride. Was he a real soldier now that he'd killed?

Frank finished assembling the little Scarlatti X3. He screwed the tiny barrel to the body and locked the three-slug chamber into place.

The Scarlatti was a miniature palm gun. It would almost fit in your wallet, almost hang off a keychain, but at close range, with good aim, it could be lethal. One, two, three tiny *point 22* lead slugs slipped into the chambers, ready for the Scarlatti to propel them from the muzzle at the speed of sound. Frank had practiced a lot, just for fun. He could shoot the straw out of a bottle at five metres. But you had to watch yourself with the Scarlatti. It was designed to be as light as possible; the safety catch was small and flimsy and had the disconcerting habit of releasing spontaneously. The trigger guard was optional, and he habitually left it off because it felt more daring. He weighed the gun in the palm of his hand, no bigger than a small cake of soap. A clean kill. Thomas Traherne jumped off his lap into the wood shavings and shuffled around. Frank jumped.

The cat had a lizard. It poked at it, and the lizard darted about. The cat slammed down a paw, holding fast to the wriggling creature, then let it go. The lizard scrambled about, only to get slammed with the paw again. Frank watched, mesmerised. This was the truth of life, the way it was. Fragile and cruel. You had to survive, and sometimes that meant doing what had to be done.

With his claws, Thomas Traherne gently lifted the lizard to his open maw, softly closed his mouth and carefully held it there, the tail wriggling from the side of the cat's mouth. Frank shivered, then swallowed.

A quick gulp from the cat, and the lizard was gone. Frank shivered again; a life could be finished that quickly. Thomas Traherne licked the side of his mouth, then casually scratched the side of his ear. *The cat doesn't care; he couldn't care, he's not made to.* Frank sighed. To not care would be the greatest thing.

Frank stared into the wood shavings and noticed his gun hand was shaking. Could he be like Thomas Traherne? The cat had killed a lizard with a complete lack of remorse. Torus could die just as quickly. Was the cat still thinking of that lizard? No.

Thomas Traherne jumped up onto his lap again, and Frank cradled the satisfied cat's head in his hand and stroked his neck. To kill and be happy. What joy! Thinking about it felt so freeing. But could he really do it? He tried to imagine shooting a bullet into a man's head. Would it go straight through neatly? Would brains and blood splatter everywhere? He might even get some mess on his arms and face. He was still shaking. He couldn't kill anyone in this state. Maybe he needed some killing practice.

The cat. Frank hadn't wanted the cat to come with them to Gunderman anyway. But it was the kids' cat, and Marta had insisted. Thomas Traherne was already doing untold damage to the wildlife around here – lizards, birds, bats. Frank held Thom Cat's head in one hand and the gun in the other. He slowly put the barrel to the cat's head. One tiny squeeze, and a life would be over. That simple.

'What are you doing?' screamed Marta's voice from behind him. Frank spun around. Thomas Traherne sprang from his lap.

'Nothing!' Frank slumped back into his chair.

'What are you doing with the cat?'

'Nothing, I'm doing nothing.' He tried to hide

the Scarlatti.

'What are you doing with that gun?'

'Just practicing.'

Marta retreated back a step. 'On the cat?'

'No, I was just thinking.'

Marta picked up the cat. It purred and rubbed itself against her chest. Marta was shaking as she drew the cat into her.

'Listen, Frank, you've got to get your shit together.' She checked on the cat, but it seemed okay. 'You're getting weirder and weirder.'

He shuffled his feet in the wood shavings. What would Marta's father do? What would his own father do? Neither of them would have let it happen in the first place. He felt like a skewered rabbit on a turning spit.

Marta towered over him, hugging the cat. 'Frankly, *Frank*, if you don't get your head fixed up, I don't know what I'll do.'

I know what you'll do. You'll leave. Take the kids and go. Frank stared at the ground. He had to say something.

'There was a terrible accident at work. People died.'

'I know, you told me.' She looked concerned for a second, then closed down again. 'But you're okay now. You've been promoted.' Marta was halfway out the door with the cat.

'I've got a plan to get everything sorted out,' he mumbled.

The mocking expression on Marta's face cut through him like a knife. 'A plan? You have another plan? Well, get on and do your plan or … I don't know what.' She sighed. 'My parents warned me not to marry you. There I was thinking you'd make a good military husband like my father, but no, you're a bumbling fool.'

Frank braced himself for more insults and humiliation. He couldn't help but think of when they first met at the summer camp for servicemen's children. They were both seventeen, too young, too young. They would lie for hours on the couch, legs intertwined, not daring to go any further.

Then it happened. They were forced into marriage. It was okay, they both said to each other, and they'd grown to like each other for a few years, especially caring for the twins.

'I can barely face those wives at the Officers' Club. Their smirks and innuendos.' Her voice got shriekier. 'Do you ever think what it's like for me? Do you ever think about anything more than your own fucked-up head? Pull yourself together, or I'm pulling the plug on this so-called marriage.'

She started for the door, then halfway through, paused and turned around. 'So, what's your big plan, Napoleon?'

'I'm going to commit a murder.' She stopped dead, mouth half open, ready for her next tirade. Frank saw that, for a second, she thought he was serious, then a crooked smile formed across her face.

'You are a fucking joke!'

Frank hardly registered in his own mind what he had said; it just came out. He was getting less able to control himself. It was as though he was being taken over. He slowly realised that he had said he was going to kill someone. He jumped out of the chair, then realised that she hadn't believed him. What a relief!

The world suddenly went into slow motion. He felt his finger tighten by itself on the trigger of the Scarlatti. He felt the little recoil into his palm, and then a large piece of splinter dislodged from the wooden beam just above Marta's head and ricocheted across the shed. He saw the splinter turn end-over-end towards him and fly past his head.

Oh Christ, what have I done?

Marta's mouth opened, and a noiseless scream came out.

The world came back to normal, and Marta dashed from the shed.

I really need serious help.

He heard the rustle of bushes from next door and knew Drovis was listening. The image of a bullet going through Drovis's head came back to him, satisfying. He picked up the gun and turned up the radio to blast out the sounds. It didn't matter what was on, but it appeared to be ABC RN. That would do.

Crack, crack.

The two remaining bullets straight into the straw in that bottle. He reloaded. Crack, crack, crack again. He sat down, exhausted. The radio crackled.

The Hyde Park Memorial was opened in 1934 to much anticipation and controversy. There was a huge turnout of enthusiastic Sydneysiders, but there were detractors as well. The Celtic Australians had been against the 1914–18 war, but the Anglos were all for King, Country and Empire. Conscription for the war was defeated at two referenda. After the Australian and New Zealand invasion of Turkey, Edith Granville, already well known for her humanitarian work during the Armenian genocide, began to organise for the collection of money for a peace memorial in Sydney. Edith's son had died on that first day at Gallipoli. She organised women around New South Wales to raise funds. The momentum built as the realisations came to the population of what the war had cost in lives and suffering. Fifteen years after Armistice Day, as the memorial was nearing completion, the religious divide opened up. The monument was never completely finished because certain controversial statues have never been erected. The statues were blasphemous — a naked female Christ. St Mary's Cathedral across the road would not tolerate it.

That memorial again! What was going on?

Frank imagined the horrors of World War One. What he had done to the refugees would have been reproduced hundreds of times a day throughout that war. It was unimaginable. His mind reeled from the thought of it and pulled back. The horrors became a numbness, and again he had that feeling that he was at the centre of everything; that the whole world expanded out from himself. Some peace came to him. The Memorial seemed to be calling him back. Somehow, it understood him. It knew both the violence of humanity and also the benevolence. It was humanity at its best and worst. This contradiction was also building inside Frank, day by day. Frank needed to find a way to resolve this conflict inside himself. It was tearing him apart.

CHAPTER 21

Frank stood on the top steps of the memorial and felt that now familiar feeling of relief. He looked up and let the grace wash over him. So nourishing to be protected by the benediction of this building.

He descended the steps down to the Pool of Remembrance, glanced across the park, and yes, he saw Torus's black van parked in College Street. He sat down on a park bench. So Torus was following him to make sure he kept his mouth shut. But Frank felt sure that Torus would be beneficially affected by the memorial the same way as Frank had been. If only he could get him inside. How could anyone not feel the poetry here and be changed accordingly? Torus would then have to admit his guilt, and Frank would be off the hook. He could go back to normal life, and things would be just as they were before that awful day. A breeze came up from the city, and Frank shivered. But would it be right for Torus to take all the blame? After all, Frank had pressed the final button. Frank shook his head. No. He didn't care. It was all Torus's doing. Out of the corner of his eye, he saw some movement over in the bushes. Torus! His plan was working. How was he going to get Torus into the building?

An old man, must have been a hundred, hobbled out of the memorial, his coat covered in medals. He held the hand of a young girl around ten years old and tottered toward the steps leading down. He struggled, one step at a time, held up by his stick and his granddaughter.

'Gramps, why did that man in there have no clothes on?' The morning air was still, and her voice carried across the park. 'You could see his willie and everything.'

Frank smiled. Children! The bushes where Torus was hidden rustled a little. Obviously, Torus had heard the girl as well. The old man leaned over towards her and spoke in a quiet voice, probably telling her not to be silly. They slowly moved away from the memorial back towards the city, heads together, talking.

Frank was vividly aware that Torus was watching the pair, when suddenly Torus strode out of the bushes and stood at the bottom steps of the memorial, looking up, hands on hips, a latter-day Mussolini, like the monument was something to conquer. Torus completely ignored Frank, but instead looked over at the retreating figures of the old soldier and the child. Then looked again up at the building, went up the first step and halted. He glanced around, then carefully walked up, occasionally glimpsing back at the child and grandfather. Had he forgotten that Frank was here?

Why had he suddenly decided to go up the steps? It must have been what the girl said. Torus stood at the top and looked around as if he was about to go into a forbidden and secret place. He suddenly darted inside.

Frank's memory of the statue inside was vivid, a sacrificed

naked soldier on a shield and sword. Frank crept up the steps, thrilled that Torus was inside. He had no idea what he would say when he confronted him. Torus was leaning over the internal balcony, looking down at the statue, and rubbing himself against the balustrade.

Bloody hell, he's wanking!

Frank gasped. His hand shot to his face to cover his mouth. A great smell of dead and rotting flesh seemed to penetrate into his throat. His knees weakened. He turned to run, and Torus heard and rapidly twisted towards Frank. Frank caught a look at the face of Torus. A face he had never seen before. Oh, what a blessing to have never seen that mask of terror!

Go! Go! Get out of there!

Frank pelted out of the building and scampered away, stumbling down the steps. Breathless, he took stock behind some bushes. He could not believe it. Was Torus really masturbating? Yes, definitely. Torus was even more demented than he thought.

CHAPTER 22

The Year 2003

After several hours of rapport with his new lover, the first light of a new dawn crept around the edges of the curtains. Mike's eyes shot open in a blazing panic. His breath coming in pants. But then the cold, calculating part of his mind took over. He knew exactly what to do.

His recent work in the army had involved removing old statues out of some bank vaults in Martin Place and taking them for future storage to the tunnels underneath Hyde Park, left over from the abandoned eastern suburbs railway. He had spent the last few months in the tunnels and knew them well. This would be an excellent place to hide the body.

He looked at the girl lying crumpled in sheets on the bed. He softened. Ahh, to have more time with her, but no, he must hurry. He picked her up, drove her to the tunnels and hid her. His panicked mind was a helpless and mute passenger while the disciplined Corporal Michael Torus did the work. He was in a battle zone, and his life depended on it.

At last, he relaxed and looked at the girl's body on the ground, crumpled and sad. She was broken and blackened. Dead, really dead. His iron discipline wavered, and his chest filled with a great sob. A rising panic coursed through his body, and his arms shook. He knelt before her and could not move.

I will fix this. I will make it better. He tenderly lifted the girl's body and placed it against a wall of the tunnel. He arranged her hair to look like it was when they first met back at the party. He placed a small rock in front of her as an altar. But no matter what he did, he couldn't erase the gut-wrenching fear and remorse at what he had done. Even blaming the girl for tempting him didn't help. He trooped away from this melancholy place.

He couldn't work, he couldn't think straight, he couldn't sleep, and a few weeks later he crawled back into the tunnel – for what reason, he didn't know. The nameless, rotting corpse shrieked at him. But he didn't see a corpse. He saw her alive and resting peacefully. He placed a small cloth and a candle in front of her. Now he felt better. The altar was complete. He didn't see death here; now he saw life.

Over the years she made him come alive whenever he came here. The memory of their one night together would come back to him, and he would kneel in front of her and masturbate, fully and completely.

CHAPTER 23

Torus hurtled down the memorial steps. Frank's plan was now in tatters. The memorial definitely did not have the same effect on Torus as it did on Frank. Torus was depraved. His years of debasement had taken him to a place from which there could be no return.

At the bottom of the steps, he adjusted his clothes and looked furtively around. Frank was shaking with anxiety because of what he had just seen. Torus turned to the right and disappeared! It was as if he had vanished into thin air. Frank blinked, shocked out of his nervousness. Where had Torus gone? After several careful minutes, Frank approached the memorial like a prying cat. No doubt about it, there was no sign of Torus. He saw a small door at the base of the steps, ajar. He must have gone in there.

Frank thought about what he'd seen, and it occurred to him that he had some leverage now. Surely, Torus wouldn't want his perverted practices getting known about. Surely, Torus would take all the blame now to keep his secret.

Frank breathed easier and felt some brave recklessness as he entered the small door. It was black as night inside, and he waited till his eyes adjusted. In the distance he heard Torus's hasty footsteps. It was dusty and dank in there. Where was Torus going? Frank wanted to follow, but what if Torus caught him down here? The look of terror on Torus's face earlier told Frank that he would go to desperate lengths to keep his secret. That was good for Frank, right? Or was it reason enough for Torus to kill him? Frank got the creeps thinking about it. But he felt he had been given a prize jewel.

He had heard about these tunnels. Left over from when they were building a railway under the park. It was never finished, and the tunnels were abandoned. Frank was overcome by his rash curiosity. He walked further into the tunnel. There was a dim light in the distance. He felt his way along the wall. His heart pounded.

He heard Torus ahead of him, way ahead. He waited. The gloom cleared more. He felt the wall, and it was smooth now, not rough like before. He saw shiny, smooth rock to his side, and as his eyes adjusted further, he saw it was a huge statue. It was a naked woman, three metres high, crucified on a sword and shield, head bowed in death, the helmet of Mars ironically crowning her, the ruins of war at her feet, broken men, broken machinery, cogwheels and diggers' hats sluiced together in the mud, all dead. He was mesmerised by the beauty of the statue, and that feeling of grace overcame him again. These were sacrificed soldiers! This must be the statue that Marta had told him about. It was never erected, hidden away because it looked like a naked female Christ.

This is too weird. Get out of here.

He heard a shuffling sound, unmistakably a rat. It squeaked, then another. He could see them moving about in the gloom. More of them, more squeaking, a cacophony. Bits of human body parts flew across Frank's mind. He clutched at his stomach and grabbed the statue for support. The rats scuttled away. He heaved in the dusty air.

He could still hear Torus's footsteps in the distance, and then the sound suddenly stopped. Frank listened. Nothing. The place plunged into darkness. How did Torus even know his way around down here? Frank's breathing got faster. He needed to get out of here. The walls were leaning in, the screams ready to start up again. His heart started a staccato beat, and he spun around. *Have to find the entrance.* He took jumbled steps and crashed into a wall. Turned around, felt confused. He had no idea which way was out, and his legs began shaking. Slowly, his eyes adjusted again, and he saw a faint glow. Was it towards Torus, or back to the outside? He didn't know, but it was the only light available, so he moved towards it.

The light became brighter and flickered like a candle. He rounded a corner and saw Torus kneeling down at a shrine, naked. A candle burned on an altar, casting Torus's giant shadow back onto the wall behind him. Frank stared at the scene, taking it in, trying to work out what he was looking at. Torus had not seen him – he was relieved – but what was this place?

And that was when he realised what he was looking at. On the shrine was a plastic skeleton dressed in shreds of rotting cloth. He saw dangles of flesh attached to the ribs. Frank opened his mouth, and a silent howl came out of the depths of him. It wasn't plastic! It was real. His breath came in short, sharp jabs. It was definitely a human skeleton. Frank squinted, his eyes trying to capture every detail. Torus knelt across from the skeleton, softly stroking his erection with the back of his hand.

Frank slammed his hand across his mouth to stifle his gasp, but too late. Torus halted the rhythmic movements of his hand over his erection. His face changed to alarm and blank disbelief. He looked at Frank. His face was horrified. There was also a tone in his face that he had been invaded and he was *hurt.*

Hurt? Torus was hurt?

He looked confused about what had happened and what to do. His face crinkled up and his eyes widened and his nostrils flared, and Frank recognised the start of the fiery rage that was the Torus he knew. The two men stared at each other.

Torus suddenly jumped up, arms outstretched in his familiar choking gesture, and raced towards Frank, half a dozen steps away. His erection was still there. The candle was upturned, went out, and blackness came. Frank stumbled back, but hit the wall. Which way was out? Frank froze like a rabbit. He felt squashing hands around his throat, shaking him. Torus's erection against his stomach. Frank realised with disgust that Torus was coming on him.

Frank grabbed Torus's dick and dug his fingernails into it with such ferocity that his wrist stung from the strain. Torus kept shaking his neck tighter. With his other hand, Frank grabbed Torus's balls and wrenched them violently to the left, to the right, to the left again. Torus gave an almighty howl and let go. Frank heard him crash to the ground. *Get out of here!* Torus was so monstrous that there was no way that he would ever do the right thing.

How Frank fought his way back through the darkness of the tunnel, he'd never know. He suddenly burst into the daylight of Hyde Park.

CHAPTER 24

Frank bustled into the Oregon Ranch reception area. Crowley sat at his usual desk, raised his eyebrows, and fingered the beads round his neck. Frank ignored him. Yo-Knee's office was the last on the right. He flew past the picture of the poppy field and perched on the chair opposite the small stepladder outside her office. *Was she in there? What if she's got a client? No, she probably hasn't.* He should knock on the door. All this stuff was done by appointment. What could she do anyway? He didn't even know why he was here.

Yes, he did. Someone had to stop Torus somehow. But who? His mind went back to Hyde Park, the black tunnels, the wet stench in the air. That skeleton – who was it?

Crowley followed him carefully. 'Can I help you?'

'Need to see Yo-Knee.'

'I believe Dr Thompson is with a client at the moment. Do you have an appointment?'

'Need to see her.'

'You must make an appointment.'

Frank's fright at being turned away soared through his body. He ran to Yo-Knee's door and placed both hands on it. His forehead gently touched the door. He heard the muffled sounds from inside and put his ear to the door.

'I'm sorry, if you don't have an appointment, you can't disturb her. She's with a client.'

Frank felt his terror turn to anger. He looked squarely at Crowley, and Crowley's authority visibly shrank. He turned away, probably going to get a security guard. But Frank didn't care. He banged a fist on the door. The muffled talking stopped. Yo-Knee was his amender. She had to help. He knocked again.

'You must leave. I'm going to call security.'

Frank knocked louder. Crowley hurried away down the corridor.

'Yo-Knee! Yo-Knee!' He grabbed at the door handle, but it was locked. 'Yo-Knee-eee!'

The door ripped open.

'Frank! What are you doing here?'

'Need to see you.'

'I've got a client.'

'But Torus is a—'

'You need to make an appointment.'

'Appointment!' He grabbed his head. 'Appointment! What's with the appointment?' Through the open door in the background of the office, a woman was sitting in the white chair where Frank usually sat. She was doing up the top button of her blouse.

'I need to talk to you.'

'Wait a few minutes. You can't act like this.' She pointed to the chair in the corridor. 'Sit over there and calm down. I'll be with you in a few minutes.' She turned to Crowley down the corridor and nodded to him that everything was all right.

Frank slumped back to the opposite wall, admonished. Yo-Knee waited a few seconds to make sure that he was going to stay put, then with a quick downward tug on her skirt, she disappeared back into her room. Frank fidgeted, his mind swirling with random images of death, destruction and mayhem. It was a titanic effort to keep himself seated on the chair.

This must be what Mercury feels like!

The door opened again, and Yo-Knee ushered her woman client out with a hug from the stepladder. The woman seemed to be in a bit of a dream state and touched Yo-Knee's face gently. She beamed a hazy smile at Frank as she passed. Frank wondered what was going on here. Yo-Knee climbed down and draped a lazy elbow across the top of the stepladder.

'Okay, Frank, what's up?' Those eyebrows raised. He jumped up. She ushered him towards her room. His wild thoughts drained away. How did she have such control over him? How was she able to calm him down so completely? He followed her docilely inside, feeling like a complete fool.

'You have to tell me to go to the police,' he mumbled. She arched her eyebrows.

'Settle down, Frank. You can't barge in here like this. Our relationship is a professional one. I'm not someone in the army you can boss around.'

The panic was gone. She was his saviour. He wanted to be in her arms. She looked at him steadily. He felt a tear in his eye and looked away.

What would Torus do now? Now that Frank knows his repulsive secret? He could have his promotion stripped. No, that would be nothing. Torus would go much further than that. He could intimidate Frank. Intimidate? He could threaten him. He could threaten his family. A cold frost crept through Frank's body. Torus would kill if he had to. And now Torus did have to kill because of what Frank had seen. Torus will violently threaten and then kill, Frank had no doubt.

'Can I hug you?' The voice of Yo-Knee came through from the beyond. He nodded like a child, and for a moment, the thought of being hugged swept through his heart. 'Physical contact is therapeutic. Sit down there while I massage you.'

But he was torn. *Is this right? Can she be doing this?*

Yo-Knee came towards him and placed her hands in a prayer position, bowed her head, then put her arms around him. Her face came up to the middle of his chest. He felt his heartbeat slowing as she fingered his spine. Goosebumps tingled up and down his back. He surrendered into the feeling, and the tingling spread across the rest of his body. He felt the beginnings of an erection pressing against her body. He swooned. What was he doing, for God's sake?

A terrible thought suddenly clouded him. Marta and the kids! Torus was ruthless. Where had he gone after the memorial? What if he was at Frank's house? He had to get back home immediately. Would he be able to kill Torus if he had to? He had no choice.

He felt complete shame and pushed Yo-Knee away. He raced from the room.

'Frank! Come back. I can help you.' Yo-Knee's voice trailed away as Frank charged for the exit. He felt a new emotion that he'd never felt before. He was a warrior protecting his family from oblivion.

CHAPTER 25

It was evening twilight when Frank barrelled off the rattly planks from the ferry at Wisemans and tore down the winding, frustrating road towards Gunderman. The eucalyptus forest hurtled past and spun off the road several times. Normally, the drive took half an hour, but he did it in fifteen minutes. He finally screeched into the driveway. No sign of any other cars. That was good, but he looked down the track to the river, where a car could hide. He cautiously trod down there, but still nothing. He breathed relief and collapsed on the ground near the shoreline and watched the dark river flow. Some anxiety left him. He trudged back up to the house, all the time squinting for hidden cars in the darkening bush. At last, he was satisfied no one was there, and a weariness enveloped him, and he dragged himself into the house.

Marta was trying to get Mercury to sleep.

'I don't like sleep, I don't like sleeping,' Mercury yelled. 'I don't go anywhere. I'm not there when I sleep.'

Marta gave Frank an exasperated look. 'You do it,' she said, wiped her forehead, and abruptly left the room.

'Shush, mate,' soothed Frank. 'It's okay, it's okay. Lie down like your sister.' Palace breathed softly in the other bed, still looking pale.

Mercury jumped up and down on the bed, and Frank sat down and pulled out a book to read. Mercury pointed at the pictures, then struggled to concentrate on going to sleep like a good boy. He shut his eyes, then had one eye open, then closed, then both open again. Normally, Frank would have laughed at these antics, but he was tired, too tired.

Palace suddenly made a guttural sound, and Frank whipped around and saw that she wasn't breathing properly, her breath snatching. Mercury jumped up from the lack of attention he was getting, leaping about on the bed. 'Not sleep, not sleep.'

Marta ran back into the room, went straight to Palace's oxygen pipe and reconnected it, and Palace began to breathe normally again. 'I thought you were going to keep an eye on the bloody thing?'

'I was distracted by Mercury. He won't go to sleep.'

'Of course, he won't go to sleep. He never wants to go to fucking sleep!'

Frank tried to put his arm around Marta, but she elbowed him away.

Mercury leaped out of the bed and ran in circles round the bedroom. Marta sat on the bed with her face in her hands. Again, Frank tried to touch her, but she recoiled.

Mercury suddenly stopped and stood at attention with his head down, dramatizing his obedience – another game. Palace breathed softly. Mercury quietly crept into bed. Marta relaxed a little, let Frank put his arm around her.

Even though Torus wasn't here, Frank still had a gut-wrenching anxiety in his stomach. When would Torus strike? He definitely would sometime, after what Frank had seen.

'I'm scared,' she said. 'You're acting so strange.'

He rubbed her back softly, and Mercury turned his head to the side and fell asleep like magic, snoring. They looked at each other in surprise. Marta softly stroked the side of Mercury's cheek with the back of her fingers. The light from the window flitted across her face, and a tear welled out of her eye. Frank took her hand and led her out of the kids' room and back to the lounge.

'How was work?' she asked.

'I went to see my amender.'

Marta's face darkened. 'Okay, how was that?'

'Good, it was good.'

'And?'

He looked at her and wondered how much to tell her. 'Major Torus has got some weird shit going on.'

'Like what?'

'He creeps around inside those tunnels under Hyde Park.'

'I told you about those tunnels. They hid statues down there when I was at art school. What do you mean – creeping about?'

Frank flashed back to his fight with Torus in the tunnel. He could hardly believe what had happened. His mind had difficulty thinking about it. He breathed.

'I met him down there.'

'What were you doing there?'

'I followed him.'

'You followed him into the tunnel? Why?'

'No, he followed me.'

She lost patience. 'He followed you, or you followed him?

This is really confusing, Frank.'

He moved awkwardly. 'After the explosion, I freaked out and ended up at that memorial, and it made me feel better. All those people dying in that war. All that tragedy. I thought if I could get Torus to go there, it would have the same effect on him, make him more human or something. I knew he would be following me to make sure I wasn't going to blab, so I went to the memorial, and sure enough, he followed me. But he went upstairs and started ...' He dropped his head.

'What?'

Oh, why not, thought Frank, and shivered. 'He wanked off looking at the statue of that dead body.'

Marta recoiled. 'He what?'

'Then he rushed down through a little door at the base of the memorial that led into a tunnel. I followed him.'

'You followed him into the tunnel? Why?'

'I don't know. He had some weird kind of altar down there and was wanking in front of it. The altar had a skeleton on it.'

'Frank, what is going on here?' She pulled away from him.

'He saw me and attacked me. I managed to run out, but he's going to shut me up for good now. He's murderous. I went straight to the amender after that.'

He thought of Yo-Knee and her hugging him. He'd been turned on and was shocked. Even now, his groin tingled at the memory.

'What did the amender do?'

He looked at Marta. 'Nothing. Nothing at all. Nothing happened.' She looked at him quizzically. What was Marta thinking?

'What are you going to do?' she asked.

'I'm sure he wants to kill me. I've seen his secret. But I've got a plan.' As soon as he said it, he realised he had no plan at all, but Marta seemed to relax a little.

She took his hand. 'Maybe it's not as bad as all that. You've been a bit crazy lately. Your imagination is acting up.'

He really wanted to believe her. She was right – everything had been crazy. It was hard to know what was real and what was due to his disjointed mind. Looking at Marta now, he could see she needed him. Maybe it was the kids, maybe she was scared too, but whatever it was, his wife needed him at her side.

He nodded. 'Maybe you're right.'

'Let's go sit outside.'

He followed her meekly. The sky had darkened, and they drank a beer, the last bit of twilight silhouetting the trees over the far bank of the river. Frank flicked through the music on his phone and found some Nina Simone. He touched Marta's knee, and her leg moved slowly. They drank a whisky, and Marta took the phone and played the Pointer Sisters. They kissed. Anita Pointer smouldered out that she wanted a man with a slow hand, an easy touch. He pulled away from the kiss and, with soft astonishment, looked at her and smiled. They both whispered together, 'We're crazy.' They quickly shut down the house and padded off to the bedroom.

They did their favourite things. Frank liked it when she pulled him towards her, holding his dick, walkin' the dog. He lay down, and she sucked. He expanded. His shoulders became strong. His back arched in brawny force. He was a knight. He could do anything. Taking on Torus, in whatever manner, would be easy. Torus was a crazy person who needed to be brought down for his murderous attack on the refugees, and who knows what was going on down in those tunnels? The longer Marta caressed him, the more Herculean he felt.

His mind drifted, and he thought of Yo-Knee. That small body, so perfect. Her cheeky manner. Just the right height. That moody caramel skin and poppy-coloured lips. His hands on her tiny breasts. One hand could cup her entire arse. Suddenly, he shuddered. Was he having fantasies about a child? Marta stopped and moved to indicate that he should be concentrating on her, not some fantasy. She took his hand and carefully arranged his fingers across her labia, middle finger draped across her clitoris, ready for a slow hand.

Yo-Knee still danced around in his mind, but now she was being cruel. His whole body went cold. *What's the matter, big boy? No good?* His erection shrank and slid out of Marta's mouth. He gazed at the ceiling. There was a badly painted patch in the corner. Marta gave up and rolled over and immediately fell asleep. That was not good. She would be pissed off in the morning.

He sighed and rolled over to the far edge of the bed, tried to push those disturbing thoughts of Yo-Knee out of his head. And Torus too. They were all safe for now. He would figure things out in the morning. For now, he could rest.

~

He dreamt about Torus and an army of massive erections all coming for him. Seeking revenge, coming for his family. They pulled up in a van and ambushed him. Was he awake when he heard a car in the distance, or did he dream it?

At 3.03 am, Frank woke in a cold sweat. Torus was the first thing on his mind. He had to do something. The time for waiting was over. If he had to kill Torus, even in self-defence, could he? He believed he could. What would Yo-Knee think if he told her that? He imagined her in that yellow dress, and he started to tingle up again. He stroked his dick. No, no! He felt a burning shame. Yo-Knee was a mistake; he had to stop seeing her, even if she did help. His bloody crazy mind would have to deal with itself! She was a distraction, and his life was in enough shit already. And the kids were just as much trouble as ever - Palace seemed to be getting worse. Mercury was slowly sending Marta insane. Why couldn't anything be simple?

He heard a kookaburra in the distance. Its laugh-like squawk echoed around the trees outside. Car tyres on gravel receded in the distance. Was he asleep? No, definitely awake. The car sound faded. He leaped out of bed. Nothing seemed unusual. He checked the front and back door – both were locked. He went into the kids' room, and a stark moonlight lit it up in sharp angles.

There they were, both of them, quiet. He went over to kiss them. First Mercury, then Palace. He brought his lips towards her face, and the shadow of a moving curtain wafted across her. He whirled towards the window, and a breeze pushed open the curtain. The window was open! There, under the white moonlight, was a large pair of scissors opened with the oxygen tank's pipe going through the blades, ready to cut. His face went cold. Torus had been here! His heart pumped. Palace breathed smoothly.

A bilious rage built up inside him. Going to the authorities would be futile. Gone from his mind were any social restraints about his duty to his society and the law. His mind flooded with a much more primitive impulse – raw vengeance and survival. He would kill Torus himself. A perverse logic worked its way through his thoughts.

One: Torus had gone rogue about the explosives. Two: Frank was a witness to Torus's atrocity. Three: Torus had come to kill Frank, and Four: Frank had killed Torus in self-defence. The violence of stabbing Torus a thousand times with scissors slashed through his mind. His mind was glinted steel, and he felt peace. The first peace since this whole nightmare had begun. He knew what to do.

CHAPTER 26

There was no sign of Torus when Frank arrived at Victoria Barracks. He felt relieved. Who wants to confront a psychopath? How was he going to deal with this? Should he go see Bradsleap? No, Bradsleap was useless – he would do whatever Torus wanted him to do. He peered over into Torus's office and imagined him lying dead on the floor. That would be good. He wouldn't have to kill him. All problems would dissolve away. It was satisfying. Frank wasn't a killer anyway.

'He's not here.' It was the voice of Kain Webber. Frank spun around, as if his thoughts had been heard. Kain stood there, hands dug into the pockets of his grubby white lab coat, pulling at the material. Frank thought Webber's eccentricities were mostly endearing, but since their argument, Webber seemed like a nutcase, playing up the mad scientist thing a bit. He did look the part though: thick glasses, shock of black frizzy hair, insecure on his feet. Frank hesitated.

'Hasn't been back since …' Webber shot a quick glance at Frank's new captain's epaulettes. They nodded a cold greeting.

Frank was relieved. Something seemed normal again.

'So, what's happening?' Frank asked.

Webber shuffled on his big feet and softened a little. He had never needed much of an excuse to start an enthused monologue about his work.

'Brilliant, brilliant.'

Frank was glad that Webber didn't seem to harbour any lingering bad feelings. He had never noticed it before, but Webber's nose twitched as he talked. Frank's mind seemed so sharp with its new primitive clarity. So many new things to notice.

'We've been breeding these spiders, see, funnel webs and redbacks. We've called it the funnelback, and it's a marvellous little monster. It spends most of its life asleep, but the moment it smells *the ointment*, it jumps into life, thinks it's in danger, and attacks the nearest thing it can bite. And it's deadly – it can kill a horse in a minute. But only once though. The poison sac is so big that it burns out the fangs. The spider's brain is overloaded, and it splatters from the inside, bursts, and the little monster dies, causing no further danger. Neat. It's got one bite.'

Frank watched Webber's mouth move, and his nose definitely twitched.

'I know about the spider.'

Webber ignored him. 'And the ointment – it's miraculous. You can transfer it from person to person by shaking hands. Completely harmless to humans.'

'Huh,' grunted Frank. 'Okay.' He prowled away along the corridor, furtively looking for signs of Torus. Webber went back into his lab, but immediately Frank heard Webber's laboratory door slam open again, and he rushed out in a wild panic.

'Get away, get away!' he screamed. 'The spider's out. I've got the ointment on my hands. Get away!' Frank whirled towards the lab and saw the little monster crawling on the floor. It ran this way and that for a few seconds, then suddenly went dormant, presumably because it was now out of range of the ointment and couldn't smell it anymore.

Frank thought of Torus and smiled. He might not have to kill Torus himself. He could somehow get the spider to do it. He moved towards it. It was not moving. Webber had said it would be dormant until it smelled the ointment.

Frank stared at the little curled-up thing, trying to figure out how to get hold of it, when he heard the unusual high heels of a woman's footsteps.

'Hi Frank.' It was Yo-Knee, dressed up to the nines.

You look like a whore! thought Frank. 'What are you doing here?' he demanded.

She didn't miss a beat. 'I work here, like you.'

He got it. She was here to amend some broken soldier. He was annoyed with her. She should be back at Oregon Ranch, where he had left her. That's where she should be if he needed her. Why was she allowed out?

What am I doing?

When he was in Yo-Knee's office, he'd felt like a god, listening to her, her laughter and gentleness. Her voice made his heart quicken. The look of her stopped his words in his throat. His skin tingled with a thin, quick flame. He stared at her, and his ears hummed. He felt himself sweating and started to shiver. He slipped close to something like death.

Stop, stop!

'Ah, you little bugger,' breathed Webber, scraping the little arachnid into a cardboard box with a trowel. He disappeared back into his lab.

Frank's heartbeat slowed a little.

'You should come see me again,' said Yo-Knee. 'You're improving. You seem stronger.' Frank wavered for a moment, but then realised that he could never see her again. She was too distracting. He had to solve this himself. She would be appalled by the idea of murder. She seemed to read his mind and gave a little coquettish look and moved along the corridor.

Frank reached the door to his office, but he couldn't go in there. His mind was swirling with images of Yo-Knee and Torus.

He had an overwhelming urge to get back to his family, turned on his heels, and headed for the elevator. And underneath his thoughts a little motif was running through his mind, barely conscious – how in the world could he get hold of that spider?

CHAPTER 27

Torus prowled along the corridor, down into the kennels where Volf was kept. The dog saw Torus and cowered in the corner of its cage. Torus strapped the collar around the dog's throat. Volf rumbled a low growl, teeth bared and fangs protruding, but impotent to retaliate. Torus's mouth salivated in triumph, and he licked his lips.

He pulled at the dog's lead, but the damn thing wouldn't stop whimpering and yowling as they travelled up in the elevator. As the door started to open, Torus had a sudden vision that the dog had broken free from its genetic shackles and attacked him. The dog would go for his throat and rip it out in a bloody instant. Torus shivered momentarily and yanked on the dog's neck to pull it into line. The dog spluttered a short explosive, spitting sound, then lifted its paw in a pathetic plea.

That's better. Keep quiet.

The door opened, and who should be there but Frank Bargen! Torus's eyes quickly flickered away, so he yanked on the dog's lead, and the dog produced another yowl. It looked up at Bargen with its miserable paw held out. Bargen should normally have cringed back from Torus, but he held his ground.

'Where are you going, Bargen?'

Bargen suddenly said, 'Home.'

Torus's eyes glittered. 'How is your sick kid, Frank?'

Frank started quivering.

'You better get back there, in case anything else happens,' Torus sneered. 'Losing a kid on top of everything else would be terrible.'

Frank bundled into the elevator, and the doors closed.

Torus's power was coming back to him. He stormed along the corridor, and that idiot Carnley was outside his office like a dog waiting for its master. Carnley saluted, but Torus brushed past, grabbed the whisky, and guzzled. What had Bargen seen down in the tunnels? What had he really seen? It was dark in the tunnel, and Bargen could have been confused. Another slug of whisky. But no, Bargen had seen *everything*. Bargen shouldn't have followed him into the tunnel. That was Torus's secret tunnel; it belonged to *him*. What right did he have? *None!* Bargen needed to be kept quiet. Quiet about the explosion *and* quiet about the tunnel.

Torus mulled these thoughts over all day, and at 5 pm, he decided.

'Carnley! Get in here!' Torus barked. The adjutant ran in. 'Sir!'

'Get the van. We're going to see Bargen.'

Carnley grimaced with that look – that he wanted to say something, but didn't dare.

Torus grabbed Carnley's jaw and squeezed his cheeks. 'That's right, Carnley, keep your trap shut! Looks like we need to go on another little trip to that godforsaken place out in the sticks.'

Carnley's eyes glittered. 'Yessir!'

CHAPTER 28

Carnley skidded the black van to a stop on the gravel outside the Bargens' house in Gunderman. Carnley made to open the door, but Torus held him back.

'Wait.'

They watched. Torus's mind was still blazing with the memory of Bargen's violation of his sanctuary. Why was Bargen even in his tunnel? He didn't trust that worm at all. His wrists started to ache like fire, and his hands began making those gripping movements, like he had to choke something or the pain would become intolerable.

Carnley fidgeted. 'Bloody hell, why would you live way out here?' he said.

Torus ignored him.

Bargen's car was parked in the driveway. Over at the back of the house was a little shed.

'We'll have a little talk with the wife. That'll keep him quiet, eh, Corporal?'

Carnley's eyes watered as they often did when Torus

had a job for him. Torus liked that look in Carnley. It made him reliable.

Carnley knocked on the front door. They stood at ease, looking military. No response. Torus felt irritated and nodded to Carnley, who banged louder and insolently raised a boot ready to kick the door in. It suddenly opened, and Bargen's wife Marta stood there, eyes fixed on Carnley's raised boot. She wore an apron, and her face was sweating. The smell of frying steak wafted out the door. Torus recognised her; she'd come to the barracks one time with her kid. The one that couldn't keep still. Torus lowered Carnley's knee back to the ground.

'Frank here?' Torus barked. Snarling usually gets to people, puts them on the back foot.

'He–he's not here.' She must have been warned. The young kid came up beside her.

'Been keeping out of trouble, son?' Torus reached over and gave him a pat on the cheek, then a little slap. The kid cowered back into his mother. *Good.*

The steak from the kitchen was burning now. 'I don't know where Frank is,' she said and spun around and rushed inside, followed by the brat.

Bloody coward sends his missus out to get rid of us.

Torus pushed through the front door into the house and looked around. It was an old fibro shack. What a dump! They wandered through to the kitchen, where she was fiddling with the gas stove, trying to turn it off. Carnley grabbed her by the arm, spun her around, and forced her back against the sink. Torus pulled him off her. *He's not having all the fun.*

'We need to have a little talk with Frank,' Torus snarled. He reached out to grab her neck. 'We need to clear a few things up. Go get him.'

Torus flexed his fingers and paused for a moment as he felt that pleasantness of being in total control and about to choke the life out of something. He grinned at Carnley, who snorted. Torus lifted up his hand and widened his fingers, ready to choke. It was bad enough, Bargen defying him about the explosion, but invading his special place was the living bloody end. Torus felt his shoulders puffing up.

The bitch stood there defiantly.

Okay, so you wanna play. He stepped closer. 'Go get him, or I'll squeeze your pretty little throat till your eyes pop out of your head.'

The thought of Bargen violating his special place made his skin hot and itchy. It was embarrassing. Shame and anger filled him up. He stepped closer to the cow. This was going to be fun.

The back door burst open, and Carnley rushed towards it. Torus spun his head, and it was Bargen holding a pistol aimed straight at him.

'Get away from her!'

Torus looked at the gun. It was shaking. What a drippy coward that man was! Torus turned carefully and gave him his full chest to aim at. There was no way he would fire on his superior officer. He was a desk jockey, and a scared one at that.

'Or what, mouse?'

Torus's hands were on fire, almost shaking now, ready to punish! He marched forward and saw the fear in Bargen's eyes. Torus licked his lips. Bargen wouldn't shoot – he couldn't shoot. One more step forward, and Torus was close enough to poke him in the chest. Torus prodded him, but Bargen held his ground. Torus shoved him in the chest, and Bargen stumbled backwards.

The gun exploded. Marta screamed, and Torus felt a little slice across his cheek, then immediately a searing, scalding pain. He howled and slammed a hand to his ear, felt warm blood and a dangly bit of flesh between his fingers. The kitchen fell silent except for the steak sizzling in the fry pan.

He snapped his hand from his ear, and his fingers dribbled blood. The warm trickle oozed down his cheek. *How could he?* He felt insulted. *How could he shoot me when I knew he wouldn't?*

Torus's wailing anger was like a frenzied bull. His fingers and hands were an inferno of pain. He lurched at Bargen and grabbed his throat. Immediately, his fingers felt free, and his wrists lost their painful tension and relaxed. The grip around Bargen's neck was like a lover's embrace. All was well. The ecstasy rose in his body. He crushed with both hands and felt a profound gratitude to Bargen.

Bargen's neck throbbed with blood, and Torus squeezed and shook harder. Bargen's gun fell out of his grip and clattered to the tiles. His arms flailed about, trying to get Torus's grip off his neck. No chance; he was weakening. Torus was almost lifting him off the floor and felt thrilled at Bargen's convulsions. Blood shook from Torus's savaged ear, streaming on the floor, and Bargen couldn't get his footing.

I'll kill him, I'll kill him, I'll kill him.

Something moved to Torus's right. From the corner of his eye, he saw that woman grab at the burning steak. She snatched at the frying pan and swung it round. The steak flew across the room and hit Carnley in the face. Torus took his eyes off Bargen long enough to see Marta's two-handed grip on the frying pan come crashing into his injured ear.

A colossal yowl came out of him, and he crashed to his knees. Frank grabbed his fingers round Torus's grip and shook his neck free. Marta banged the frypan right on to the top of Torus's head. He tried to hang on to Frank's neck, but his wrists weakened. He collapsed completely and groaned on the floor.

He grunted and struggled to his feet, slipped on his own blood, and sank into a chair. He looked down and saw a black cat licking up his blood. He felt a defeated rage and hate. He hated defeat like nothing else. He put his hand to his forehead and panted for breath.

The bullet had traced across Torus's cheek and split his earlobe in two. Frank watched blood pulse out. Half the earlobe dangled from his face, jostling like a little pearl earring, shiny with sweat and blood. Frank watched it swing from the tiny thread of skin, hypnotised by its little dance. Torus lurched up from the floor and took another step towards him, hands outstretched, ready to choke again. A gurgling sound came from his throat. Frank and Marta backed away against the sink. Every deliberate step that Torus took, the miniscule thread of skin holding his earlobe stretched longer and the little glob of earlobe danced livelier. Torus shambled closer, and his fists clenched, opening and closing.

'Mike?' yelled Carnley.

Torus rapidly twisted his head to Carnley, and the little thread of skin, now as thin as cotton, slashed across his face and mouth. Torus spluttered, and the thread snapped. The earlobe broke loose and splatted to the floor. Marta and Frank looked wide-eyed at each other, neither believing what they were seeing. Bargen's black cat sniffed around in the blood. His paw delicately pushed and pulled at the earlobe, and he picked it up with his claw. Suddenly, the earlobe was gobbled up.

'Mike! Let's go,' yelled Carnley. Torus sighed. Frank knew

Torus was beaten, but also knew that he would be back, worse than ever. Torus slowly went to the sink, washed his mouth, then whispered to Marta, 'Your husband is a dead man.' He strode to the front door, pushing Carnley out of the way.

Their van screeched down the road.

CHAPTER 29

Marta slumped breathless on the kitchen chair, shaking. 'What was that all about? Who were they, Frank?'

Frank gazed at the blood-splattered floor. 'That was Major Michael Torus, my commanding officer from work.'

'What the fuck did he want? I was cooking, and he burst in.' She put her hands to her face. 'In my own home. What did he want, Frank?'

'To intimidate me, keep me quiet.'

Frank saw the twins standing in the kitchen doorway. Mercury was quiet as a mouse and was as pale as Palace. He was holding a toy gun and shaking.

Marta clutched at her stomach and suddenly threw up on the kitchen floor. She ran to the sink and wiped her mouth with a disgusted growl. Frank approached, but she turned rapidly towards him, and the lowest guttural sound came from her throat.

'Get out!' she blazed at him.

Frank was shocked by her vehemence. He looked over

at the children, but she screamed at him again. 'Get out, get out, get out!'

He slumped towards the door, held the doorframe, then turned and looked at the blood and vomit. Marta clutched her stomach.

He walked away from the house and saw Torus's van disappearing round the corner, under the moonlight.

That's not the end of it.

He waited a few minutes before going back inside. Marta was crying on the lounge chair, a child on each side of her.

Oh my God, what have I done? Trying to keep my family out of all this, and look what I've done.

He crumpled onto the sofa. Hands across his ears, head down, muttering into the floor. I will fix this, he thought. Fix. Fix. Fix.

'I will fix this, Marta.' Maybe if he said the words out loud, she would believe him. And he would believe himself.

He jumped up and grabbed a mop and swirled the mess around the kitchen floor. The trio of Marta, Mercury and Palace watched dumbfounded as he manically whirled around the kitchen, bumping into things. The mop wasn't helping, so he reached under the sink for paper towels.

Fix, fix.

He slipped in the mess and landed on his butt in the disgusting mixture of blood and vomit. Mercury yowled in laughter. It wasn't funny. Didn't they know they were all in danger? Frank jumped up and rubbed around with the paper towels, but when he got to his feet, he banged his head under the kitchen table, making him lose his footing again. Mercury loved it. Bent in half, beside himself with laughter. Frank wanted to scream at the little shit and saw even Palace was grinning. Marta had a slight smirk on her tense face too. Instead of feeling nettled, there was a sense of relief rising in his chest. The kids were already looking less scared, and Marta's emotional ice pack was melting. Maybe he should be grateful that he could provide them with some amusement! Frank threw the steak at the garbage bin, and Thomas Traherne ran for it. Frank was impressed by his own accuracy and saw that Marta was too. She relaxed a little, but still clutched each child in her arms.

'I've got a plan,' he said. 'There's a spider.'

Marta's brow furrowed. She turned to Palace, who was holding her oxygen tank and shivering slightly.

'Look, I know it sounds crazy,' Frank went on.

'*Anything* sounds crazy at the moment.'

Frank shrugged. He had to get Marta and the kids to a safe place.

The kids watched, then looked at their mother, picking up her doubts. Mercury held his toy gun. Palace gripped her oxygen tank tighter. A big shiver went through her body. Marta tried to hug her, but she recoiled at the sight of her mother's battered mouth. Frank rubbed the soiled paper towel across Marta's face. She spluttered out the crap on the towel with a huge UGGH! and pushed him away. He fell back and slipped on the floor again.

'Owww!' His final resting place was sitting deflated on the floor.

'This is too much, Frank.' She looked at her kids and tried to hug Palace, but she pulled away. Marta grabbed at her, but Palace struggled. Marta at last let go of her daughter. Marta covered her face in her hands and groaned. 'Poor, poor kids.'

Frank struggled up from the floor and looked at the scene before him. Marta with her head in her hands, Palace terrified, and Mercury about to go into a manic fit any minute now.

He gestured to Marta's mouth. 'Please let me make this better.'

Frank cleaned Marta's bloody mouth with a new tissue. Palace sobbed and at last allowed her mother to hug her. Mercury held out his hand with his toy gun and fired it at where Torus had been. He held out his other hand.

'Here, Dad, use this.' It was the slug that Frank had fired at Torus. Frank took the bullet from him and realised what a relief he would feel if the bullet went straight into Torus's brain. Everything could go back to normal.

'Kids! Go watch TV. Your mum and I have to talk.'

Marta lifted her head up and looked at the kids. She nodded at them. 'Go watch TV – and Mercury, no arguing.'

The kids shuffled off without a word.

As soon as they were out of earshot, Frank grabbed Marta's hands. 'You have to go to your parents – take the kids.'

'What do you mean?'

'Torus will be back.'

'Why?' She threw off his hands and stepped away from him. The distance felt like a cold slap. 'Why is he here in the first place, Frank?'

Frank sat on the sofa. He knew she deserved answers, but he also didn't want to risk her with too much knowledge. 'He wants to keep me quiet.'

'But can't the authorities take care of him?' She wiped her hand across her mouth, smearing the blood. 'Go higher up.'

She didn't get it.

He looked down at his hands. They were shaking. 'You don't understand. He *is* the authority! There *is* no higher up.'

'What do you mean? How can he be in charge? He's a nutcase.'

'Since the new government came in, there's no telling

what will happen.'

As soon as the words were out of his mouth, he knew it was the truth. There was no one who could save them. It had to be him. As if in agreement, the cat started retching and threw up the little blob of Torus's earlobe. He had to be the one to deliver the final death knell.

Frank stood up to his full height, and the image of the sacrificed soldier from the memorial came to him. He felt an enormous violent strength, and he imagined Webber's spider biting, biting into the flesh of Torus. Marta looked up, and he saw that she almost believed in him.

CHAPTER 30

Torus breathed heavily from exhaustion and anger as Carnley sped along the road back to Sydney. A steady drip of blood dropped onto his arm from his severed ear. Carnley screeched the van to a stop.

'Fuck me, boss, you're damaged. There's blood everywhere.'

Torus clamped his hand over his ear. 'Never mind. Keep going.'

But Carnley reached across in front of Torus to the glovebox and fumbled around for a bandage or something. Who did this imbecile think he was, his mother? Torus pushed his arm away. Carnley pulled a worried face.

'But boss, let's put a bandage on that ear.'

'Drive!' Torus's anger overcame his exhaustion. He grabbed Carnley's wrist and pushed it back towards the steering wheel.

'I want to help you. You're bleeding.'

Torus's exhaustion flooded back into him.

'You're hurt. Let me put this bandage on your ear, boss.

It'll stop the bleeding.' He pulled the van over and looked appealingly at Torus.

Through the fog of his weariness, Torus suddenly felt an unfamiliar tenderness. He fought an urge to pat Carnley on the head and tickle his neck like a dog. He didn't like these unusual feelings, but was too tired to resist. He suspiciously pushed forward his ear for Carnley to repair.

Carnley enthusiastically went to work and applied the bandage. Torus felt more and more uncomfortable, something close to nausea. What was Carnley up to? Torus dared not think. His throbbing ear made him feel wounded to his core. The only time he had felt this maimed was when his mother died. His mind screamed back to that dreadful day. She had wonderful tenderness for him. Then she had abruptly left him, tearing his world apart. His anger boiled up again, flinging away his fatigue. There was no going back.

'Get back to their house!' He pushed Carnley away.

'But we're halfway back to Sydney.'

'Get back there, I said. We're going to scare the shit out of his kids. That'll shut him up.'

Carnley finished his bandaging, then screeched a rubber donut on the narrow highway and raced back towards Gunderman.

An hour later, they pulled up nearby, but the house was in darkness, lit by the silvery moonlight, the corrugated iron roof gleaming. Torus had a mind to barge right in again, but remembered that Bargen still had that gun. Obviously, the house would be locked up.

'What's the plan, boss? Why are we even here?'

Torus gave him a withering look, and Carnley shrank.

'We're going to scare the living daylights out of this fucking family.' Bargen had proved to be a tougher nut to crack than Torus thought, figuring that he would be squashed like a peanut under the first pressure, but he was proving to be as tough as a walnut, needing hammer blows to crack open his resistance to Torus's frenzied will.

They sneaked around to the back of the house, and that black cat ran in front of them and yowled. Torus involuntarily clutched at his mangled ear, the pain still smarting. He wanted to kill that bloody cat. It disappeared into a broken louvre window in the toilet window next to the veranda. He'd deal with the cat later. The louvred window slats would come apart easily. He manoeuvred each slice of glass out of its slot until there was enough room to climb in.

'Wait here,' he ordered Carnley.

'No way, boss. I have to look after you. You look after me all the time. Your ear's hurt.'

Torus gave Carnley a quizzical look, then his soft, dead mother flashed through his mind. He couldn't figure why, but he relented, and they both climbed in the window.

'Anyway, what are we doing here?'

Torus turned back to look at Carnley. 'You know that sick kid? The one with the oxygen tank? Well, she'll be sleeping peacefully now, but we're going to pull out her oxygen and turn this whole damn house into a bloody freakout session.'

Carnley giggled at the prospect. Torus grabbed Carnley's cheeks between his fingers and shook his face.

'Bargen will be a quivering wreck after this. He won't cause any more trouble.' He slapped Carnley's face like you would if you were trying to revive an unconscious man. 'Got that?'

Carnley deflated into silence.

Inside, the house was black as pitch, and they had no idea where that sick kid's room was. Torus waited till his eyes adjusted to the dark, strangely calm. Gradually, the shape of the corridor appeared, and he stepped forward. His shoe heels clacked on the floor. Torus turned back to Carnley with his finger on his lips, indicating to keep quiet. He took his shoes off and gestured for Carnley to do the same.

They slunk along the corridor, and it turned left at the end. A bright shaft of moonlight slanted across the hall and into the kids' room. The light illuminated the oxygen pipe hooked up to the girl's face. Torus looked at the other bed, and the manic kid was wide awake, eyes glistening in the moonlight. He held his toy gun straight at Torus.

'I'm going to shoot you,' he said. Torus pulled out his real gun and pointed it at Mercury.

'Keep quiet, kid,' he growled. Torus moved towards Palace.

'Get away from her.' Mercury jumped out of bed and lunged for Torus's arm. This kid had more backbone than his useless father. Torus was impressed. A worthy opponent. He slammed his gun across the child's face and pushed him back onto the bed. Torus took a moment to look at the sprawled child, then felt a glorious victory. He grabbed Palace's oxygen pipe and pulled it out of the machine.

Mercury screamed.

Torus and Carnley scurried from the house. They drove back to Sydney shoeless.

CHAPTER 31

Frank's dream was a shriek from Hades. His eyes opened bright with the trauma of the exploding refugee camp. But no! It was no dream. It was real life Mercury, like Frank had never heard before. Marta was already awake. They scrambled to the kids' bedroom, and Mercury had turned on the light, his legs pumping up and down on the spot.

'Calm down, mate. What happened? Did you have a bad dream?' Mercury pointed frantically at Palace's oxygen pipe. His other hand held his cheek.

Palace breathed irregularly. Marta screamed at the unhooked pipe. Frank scrambled to fix the pipe back into its socket. Palace's chest took a big breath, and she began to breathe normally. Marta's legs collapsed a little, and she hugged on to Mercury.

'That bad man was here. He hit me with his gun. My face hurts. It was a real gun.'

Frank pulled Mercury's hand away from his cheek, and it was inflamed and scratched. Frank felt an electric fire exploding into his cheeks. He fled along the corridor and stumbled over the discarded shoes. He slammed open the fly screen door. Mercury grabbed his toy gun and ran after him.

'Let's kill him, Dad,' he said, holding his sore cheek.

Frank heard the sound of a high-speed van receding down the road. He quivered, stood upright, then squinted into the darkened roadway. There was a hill ahead, and he caught a glimpse of the receding rear lights of Torus's van. He couldn't believe he had dared to come back. And the same night!

This was war.

~

Frank couldn't sleep for the rest of the night until the morning light crept through the window. It took him right back to his early life, and he felt a serene gratitude for his childhood home. The gratitude let him fall asleep.

The rough pushing of Mercury woke him.

'We got them, Dad. We scared them off.'

The night's memories came flooding back, and he started to shake. 'Where's your mum?'

Mercury pointed towards the back door, and Frank went out there. Marta was sitting with her knees up to her chin, rocking backwards and forwards. Frank made to touch her, but she brushed him away, catatonically looking into the distance. Frank sat next to her on the veranda chair. Frank had never seen her so afraid. All his reluctance to confront Torus was gone. But he had some thinking to do. The river flowed. The house seemed eerily serene, the ringing cicadas in the eucalyptus trees the only sound.

He sat upright and felt the return of the unusual and pleasant feeling of what he could see, his arms seeming to sprout out of the sides of his awareness, his legs floating downwards. No, wait – they weren't floating downwards; they were floating *upwards*.

He was astonished – he was upside down. His feet were at the *top* of him, not the bottom. He jumped up and ran inside to get his phone. Marta barely registered. He took a photo of his legs and feet to confirm this surprising fact. Yes, definitely. His tiny feet were at the *top* of the photo. Below that were his knees, then thighs. And below that, his chest and then nothing. Nothing at all.

Marta was curious now. He showed her the photo on his phone, but it was incomprehensible to her, and she shook her head at this latest madness from him. She shrugged and went back inside.

Frank sat for a while and looked at the photo. Why was that upside-down point of view so pleasant? He must be wrong. Everyone knows that your head is above your feet. And with that thought, the pleasantness gradually faded and, in his chest, fear tightened. That fear felt more like home to him, but which was the real Frank?

He got up and paced out the fifty-five steps to the river's edge – he had counted them many times. The flowing river brought back his childhood. This land had been in his family for generations, ever since the English colonists finally dominated the Dharruk people and took over their river, Dyarubbin, after decades of bloody conflict. He remembered Jimmy Budabuda's stories, from before, long time. Stories about spearings and guns, all around, and diseases. Dry times were the worst. Dyarubbin couldn't feed everyone in drought.

After a time, the Hawkesbury aborigines had learned to make exquisite Georgian furniture for the colonists. Jimmy Budabuda was a furniture maker, learnt from his father, and he'd taught Frank about dovetail joints, mitres and glues made from saps and widgeries. Jimmy never used a nail or screw in his furniture. Jimmy told stories as young Frankie had watched him work.

Spears made of the hardest woods were fashioned and shaped using sharpened shale. The Dharruk were the axe people, and the downstream Eora were the sea people.

'Once them spears with the barbs go in, he won't come out. You die.' He sighed. 'But bullets better, make bigger hole, bounce around inside body. Bullets win fight. Bullets and smallpox.' Frank could hear the voice of Jimmy Budabuda and his elders always echoing around this part of the river.

Frank's eyes stared at Dyarubbin. The injustice shoved his emotions into a trance-like rage. He watched his own mind from a mighty distance, calculating. He crawled back to his bed.

CHAPTER 32

Frank woke with a start, and the light streamed in through the northern window. The cicadas were ringing – it must be mid-morning. He knew the inevitable, even without putting his arm across the bed to feel for Marta. She was gone. He threw the blankets off, jumped up, and ran for the kids' room – empty. They hadn't even taken clothes. Mercury's toy gun lay abandoned on the floor. *Gone back to her parents in Woollahra.*

Torus had destroyed his family. They wouldn't be back till Torus was dead. He had threatened Frank's sanity, tried to destroy him, but Frank would fight. Marta had done what she had to do, and now he will do the same. Torus must die. Frank shocked himself at the violence of his own thoughts. It's not like him to be this way. Look what Torus had done to him. He shivered. His rage filled him, but he knew what he had to do.

Out on the veranda, he flicked on the old radio and hummed along to some ancient jazz. He imagined a thousand ways to kill Torus. Beheading, poisoning, up against the wall as an execution, eaten alive by ants. Frank knew exactly what Marta's father would say. That Frank was basically useless, not a real soldier, a coward. But he would show him. And her. He would show everyone.

He thought of Jimmy Budabuda's story about Pemulwuy, the Bidjigal Aboriginal who fought the colonists with guerilla tactics after they were dispossessed of Toongabby and Parramadda. Pemulwuy escaped so often that everyone thought he was immune to British bullets. He was a clever man, bringing up spirits out of the land to fight the British robbers.

~

As Frank drove to Victoria Barracks, each fantasy about Torus became more gruesome than the last. By some means or other, Frank vowed that Torus would be dead by the end of the day. Disembowelling was the last thought he had when the elevator doors opened on his floor at Victoria Barracks.

Torus was on the other side of the corridor and spun round at the sound of the elevator. The two men stared at each other. Torus was haughty, unmoved, smug. There he was, the man he'd been fantasising about killing for the last two hours. Despite this, Frank had no coherent idea at all about what he would do. He controlled the urge for an immediate attack. He had to be strategic. Torus stood transfixed, his hands opening and closing with titanic control. He obviously wanted to murder Frank.

'Hey, Frank.' It was Kain Webber. 'How's it going?'

Frank snapped his head round towards Webber, who recoiled from the glare. He squinted into Frank's face, puzzled, then looked over at Torus. Down to Torus's flexing fingers, then back at Frank. Without further hesitation, he stepped directly between the two men and placed his hands on Frank's chest. 'No.'

Why was Webber trying to keep him away from Torus? He couldn't be in on it too! Frank couldn't bear another enemy to face.

'How're the kids?' Torus sneered over Webber's shoulder.

Frank's mind flashed back to this morning and his empty bed and abandoned house. The exhausting fear and rage swept through him, sapping his energy. He flinched and grabbed Webber's arms with his enfeebled grip, but Webber stood firm.

'Ha!' yelled Torus, and he turned briskly away down the corridor.

'What was that about, Frank? What's going on?'

Frank breathed heavily. 'Gonna fuckin' kill him,' he muttered.

'Oh yes, aren't we all?' joked Webber, patting Frank on the back. 'Let's go have a cuppa.' He tried to push Frank along, but he shook him off.

'Why did you do that?' Frank cried at Webber. 'I was going to kill him.'

'Oh yeah? What are you going to do? Stab him with a paper clip?' Webber chortled to himself. 'Look, I could see you two were going to get into it, but it's not worth it, mate.'

He was in on it. Maybe they all were!

Frank felt like smashing a sharp elbow into Webber's face. Webber picked up the hostility and shook his head at Frank. 'Okay, whatever.' He turned away like he was never coming back.

All the violence seeped out of Frank at the sight of his friend scurrying away. Had he overreacted? He couldn't tell.

He couldn't see anything anymore. He needed Torus gone so he could breathe.

Frank shuffled to his office. On the way, he passed the canteen, peeked in and saw Webber sitting there staring out the window, probably dreaming about some new crazy animal he was going to create. He continued on. He had plans to make. But when he walked past Webber's lab, he saw the door was wedged open. Somehow, Webber still had no sense of danger, even after the spider had escaped. One day, it would cause big trouble.

He remembered the sickening way Torus treated Volf, Webber's giant dog that he'd created in the lab. Suddenly, the three elements of Volf, Torus and the spider collided together in Frank's mind, and he knew exactly how he was going to kill Torus.

He shot back to Kain Webber's lab. There was no one around. It didn't take him long to find the spider's glass cage. It was a tiny five-centimetre cube – the top was a hinged lid. The spider was dormant, as Kain said it would be. One sniff of the ointment, and the little bugger would bite. The ointment was safely on the other side of the lab, clearly labelled *Funnelback Ointment*. Frank scooped it up.

He had to get it into Torus's office unseen. He thought about Torus hanging out in the hall. Had he been waiting for Frank to taunt him, or was he on his way to the canteen? With any luck, it was the latter. Back at the canteen, Frank sneaked a look inside. He was in luck. Torus was in there, which meant Volf was in Torus's office by himself for a few minutes. If he hurried, he could do this.

The thought of it all finally being over drove Frank to the office. The door to Carnley's anteroom was open a little. Bad luck! Carnley was in there, sitting at his desk. Bold as brass,

Frank went straight up without thinking.

'Major Torus wants you down in the basement.' Carnley looked up in surprise at the sight of Bargen. A few hours ago, Carnley had been terrorising Frank's household. Carnley's hands fidgeted.

'Why are you suddenly the errand boy?'

Frank ignored him. Carnley would be nervous about not giving Torus immediate and complete obedience.

'You don't want to get him offside.'

Carnley sneered at Frank and shoved his chair back, put on his hat and left the room without a word.

~

Frank went straight through into Torus's office. Volf recognised Frank and right away licked his hand. Frank wondered if his crazy plan was really going to work.

We go way back, don't we, Volfie?

Frank wondered where the best place was to put the ointment. It needed to be somewhere that Torus would touch as soon as he got back from lunch. The dog's neck! Torus would strangle anything he could get his hands on, either seriously or in cruel jest. He rubbed ointment into the giant dog's neck.

Frank heard the distinctive marching steps of Torus outside in the corridor. Could Frank get back out into the corridor without being seen? No. Was there another way out from Torus's office, a back way? Frank had never seen one. After a few moments of panic, he pointed to the floor.

'Stay!' he ordered Volf. He crept back into Carnley's anteroom and squeezed himself behind the door, hoping the dog wouldn't follow him. Torus barged in past Frank's hiding place and straight into his office. Frank could hear him handling the dog. Torus now had the ointment on his hands!

Torus's habits were like clockwork. After tormenting Volf for a few minutes, the dog would be returned to his kennel for the afternoon. Torus would then be alone in his office. But now he would have the ointment on his hands.

Now for part two of the plan.

Frank scrambled quietly out into the corridor, hurried down to the lab and meticulously cleaned his hands with sanitiser, hoping it was thorough. If he had any ointment left on his hands, that would be the end of him if the spider got out. He grabbed it, still in its box, and scurried off to the internal mailroom. He took a small cardboard posting box, tipped the dormant spider into it, addressed the parcel to Torus and placed it in the mailbag. If the internal mail delivery worked as usual, it would be delivered in the next half hour.

CHAPTER 33

Frank scurried back to his office. He didn't want to be anywhere near Torus when it happened, or the mail room, or Webber's lab. He sat at his desk, staring at the endless banks of numbers in the open spreadsheet that he'd last been working on. It seemed like years ago. A different person, a person that he knew only vaguely. The numbers meant nothing to him – no meaning, just a blur. In the back of his mind, his thoughts turned to the imaginings that he'd had before, about killing Torus in the most vicious ways. He added a few extra versions. Tied to an anthill in the desert sun was another good one.

Then he panicked. He'd actually done it. He was too agitated to sit there. He must watch the end of Torus for himself. He imagined Torus's instant death and Frank's panic eased, replaced by overwhelming relief. Torus would be dead! Frank had to be there to see it.

He got to Torus's office just as the private arrived to drop off the mail. Frank's mind was filled with a calm elation, and he leant back against the corridor wall. The private stopped at Torus's office, knocked on the door and entered. Frank peered through the open door. Volf was still there. Not supposed to happen! Frank was mortified.

The private left the small cardboard mailing box containing the spider. Through the doorway, Frank saw Torus open the little box. He saw the spider and threw himself backwards. The box fell to the floor, and the spider scuttled out of it, darted this way and that. Volf jumped forward and sniffed at the spider. Torus clambered to his feet. Frank looked on in horror. The spider was going to bite Volf! Frank tried to yell out a warning, but not a sound came out of him. He'd unknowingly slammed his hand into his mouth.

The funnelback scrambled about and latched itself straight onto Volf's neck! The dog jumped back and wailed a midnight howl. The poor creature snatched at the air with its jaws and shook its head. The dog's feet grappled for the floor, made two steps, then collapsed, panting. Volf half lifted his head, eyes rolling and pleading. He slumped to the deck, and Volf was no more. Frank's hand was still across his mouth, and he chomped into his thumb to stop from yelling out. *The dog's dead, Volf is dead.* Frank had killed it. Frank at last took a breath. It's Torus's fault! He felt a pummelling nausea.

Torus jumped about, stamping on the floor till the spider was squashed. He bent down to the prone Volf, who lay still as Thanatos on the floor. Torus gave the dead dog a soft kick, and the corpse responded gently. Frank snatched at his stomach. He felt disembowelled. Torus ran from the room.

'Webber, you fucker! Where are you?' he yelled. He almost ran straight into Frank in the corridor. 'What the fuck, Bargen! What are you doing here?'

Frank felt like a rabbit in the spotlight. 'Just walking past.

What's happening?'

Torus squinted into Frank's face, convinced that something was up. 'Come with me,' he ordered.

'Why? What's going on?' Frank was sure that Torus could see right through him, but he had to keep up the pretence.

'Don't fuck around, Frank. What are you and Webber up to?' Torus gave Frank a rough shove in the shoulder. 'That spider killed the dog. Come with me.' Torus bundled Frank into the elevator, down to Webber's lab.

Webber was innocently amusing himself with a new toy when they burst in.

'I know that spider was meant for me, you little turd.'

'What spider? What are you talking about?' Webber looked at Frank, and Frank shrugged, like you do when Torus is on a rampage. Webber's blameless manner made Torus doubt his conviction that Frank and Webber were responsible.

'The dog's dead. You killed my property.'

'Dead? How?'

Torus was now convinced that Webber had nothing to do with it. 'That bloody spider killed him. Somebody mailed it to me, but it got the dog instead.' Webber looked at Frank, but Frank shrugged again.

'Where's the spider now?' asked Webber.

'Squashed flat.'

'You destroyed my funnelback as well? You're a destructive monster. I'll report this.'

'You killed my fucking dog!'

'He's not your dog! He's my scientific experiment.'

Torus grabbed Webber by the throat. 'It's my dog if I say it's my dog!'

Gasping for air, Webber gripped Torus's arms and managed to wrench his hands away from his throat.

'Anyway, it's no one's dog now,' yelled Webber, 'if Volf is dead!'

Torus walloped Webber a mighty blow across the face with the back of his hand, and Webber collapsed to his knees. Frank couldn't believe it! Torus had gone mad. Some crazy impulse made Frank rush forward, but Torus had his fist out ready to punch. Frank halted and watched Webber struggle to his feet. Torus glared at Frank, and a flicker of suspicion flashed across his face. Frank was impassive and stood to his full height. He felt a strange sense of power, knowing that he was the only one who knew the truth.

'If you had anything to do with this, Bargen, I'll strangle you.'

Webber wiped his face and looked at Frank. Frank felt a gulf of guilt, but said nothing. Webber and Torus looked at each other, then Torus turned his stare back to Frank. Frank returned it.

'Don't look at me. Nothing to do with me,' said Frank. Torus grunted, turned away and strode off.

'What happened?' Frank asked Webber. Frank felt mountains of remorse, pretending he knew nothing, wanting to tell Webber what happened, but he kept silent.

'So the spider got out and killed Volf? I don't know how it happened. Did you see anything?'

Frank shrugged. The admonishing voice of Jimmy Budabuda reverberated through his mind.

'Only a few people know where that ointment is kept,' said Webber, rubbing his face.

'Maybe the spider doesn't need the ointment anymore?'

'Course it does!'

Frank could tell that Webber knew he was responsible. Frank's mind filled louder and louder with the full-blown singing and clapsticks of Jimmy Budabuda.

'It's not wise to get too attached to your experiments,' Webber said. He shook his head. 'But I loved that dog, loved that beautiful Frankenstein I'd created. Never mind, I'll make another. Next time, I'll keep it away from Torus.' He sat down, exhausted. 'What's going on with you and Torus anyway?' he sighed. 'Besides the normal shit.'

Jimmy's voice subsided a little in Frank's mind, but he couldn't reveal himself yet. He wanted Webber to stay right out of it.

'Just the usual.'

'Okay, okay. Have it your own way.' Webber rubbed his face where Torus had clobbered him. 'But something's going on with you, Frank. You're so … so cold.'

Frank was taken aback. That stung. 'Never you mind. Stick to your animals, and let me mind my own business.'

'Y'know, Frank, I thought you were in some kind of trouble, but now I think you're just plain ugly.'

Frank jolted upright. He felt all his energy fall out of his guts. How could Webs say that? He felt terrible about what he'd said and held his arm forward, but Webber turned away.

Frank was the only one who had really loved the dog. To Torus, it was property. To Webber, it was an experiment, but to Frank, Volf was a pet. Just a friendly dog, like any other dog. He felt cold and alone, and his rage came roaring back. He wanted to immediately go upstairs and put Torus in his grave.

He quickly left the barracks. What else could he do? What price was he willing to pay for Torus's death?

CHAPTER 34

Frank needed to think. He drove back to the labyrinth in Centennial Park where they'd recently had the picnic. It seemed like an eon ago. He recalled Mercury carefully working his way through the labyrinth, not allowed to cheat and leave the winding path, working out his own way to defeat his temptation to cheat. He was a good kid. They both were. They would be okay. Frank became dimly aware that he was preparing for their life after his death. Was he willing to die to keep his family safe? He roused himself with a shock. He had to get his life back so he could be normal again. A strange thought hit him. Instead of the nightmare visions of mutilated bodies, now he was consumed by anger at Torus. He must go see Marta to make sure she knows that he understands why she left. She has to know that he cares about their safety. Tell her he's dealing with the problem. Even after the fiasco with Volf and the spider. Every failure seemed to send him grovelling back to Marta. He drove the short distance to Marta's parents' house.

He pulled up outside a three-storey terrace nestled under Woollahra trees. Its louvred French windows huddled behind a large eucalyptus tree canopy, with a driveway down the side, one of the few terrace houses on Ocean Street with its own driveway. Next door was a narrower, two-storey terrace, overshadowed by the giant eucalyptus.

Marta's car was parked outside the narrow house. Her parents had come down in the world since their bankruptcy. He strode up the gateless pathway, up to the shabby stained-glass front door, and rang the dull brass doorbell. There was shuffling and hurried whispering from inside. At last, it opened and Marta stood there, looking like she owned the place and had never lived anywhere else. Frank's heart sank. Was she really back here permanently? The past ten years flashed in front of his mind, and then seemed deleted as if they had never happened. Marta was back in Woollahra like when he first met her. He would have to prise her out of here all over again. He tried a joking angle like they used to do in the old days.

'Need some help getting out of the middle class?'

She smirked a little in spite of herself.

'I can take you for a spin,' he went on.

She grinned, then suddenly seemed to remember that she was angry and dropped the jokes.

'We've got to stay here until Torus is in jail. He's a dangerous man. He scared us all to death back there.'

'I know, I know. But I've got a plan. Another one. The last plan blew up, but this time...'

'What did you do?' She slumped, and alarm crept into her voice.

'Webber has this killer spider, but it killed the dog instead.'

'What ham-fisted exploit did you get up to?' She

almost laughed.

'Frank?' Marta's father appeared from around the corner. He was tall and imperious. Older, but still master of the universe despite being thrust into poverty. He had never given up the idea that Frank was a thief who had stolen his daughter.

'Hello, Charlie,' said Frank.

'Charles, if you please.' He lifted himself up even taller. 'Marta stays here where she belongs.'

Frank looked up at the man he'd already fought once to get Marta out of her suffocating debutant lifestyle. 'You stay out of this. This is my wife and my family.'

'Hah! You should have thought of that before you brought all this misery home.' He stepped forward in front of Marta. 'I was in the military for forty years and did not endanger my family once!'

Frank sneered. 'She was trapped here like a decoration. You made her so dependent on you that every time you came home, she peed her pants.'

Marta's father looked stunned. Marta stared at Frank in disbelief.

'She never told you that? What else didn't she tell you?' Immediately after he'd said it, he felt like a scoundrel.

Marta crumpled, and Frank pushed past Charles and into the house. 'Where are my children?'

Marta's mother Grace was standing next to the twins, mortified.

'Get out. Get out of my house,' she growled.

Frank looked at them all and nodded. He'd gone too far. Bitterness pierced him.

'Okay, okay,' he muttered. 'If that's how it is.' On his way out, he slammed the door in one final gesture of defiance.

CHAPTER 35

He pulled up in Palmer Street, East Sydney, and sat in the car with the engine running. Maybe he should reschedule. He wasn't ready for the police. He knew that's what Yo-Knee would say to him – go to the police. Underneath, that's what he wanted her to say. But then he would have to admit to being a murderer. His whole life would come crashing down. Marta would never come back. He would be drummed out of Border Force.

He shivered as he watched his finger push off the engine button and his hand open the car door. His body seemed to be taking over again – a mind of its own. He really did not want to go in there. He seemed to be floating out of his body. He observed himself as he slowly paced up the back lane and into the dingy reception area.

The orange-clad Crowley sat at the reception desk and eyed Frank warily. Frank sat down, and Crowley relaxed and nodded. Frank had that feeling again of being the still centre of things and everything else was moving around him. He looked up, but it didn't feel like he was looking up – it felt like the whole world was moving down. The whole world! He moved his head to the left, and instead, the world moved to the right – Crowley whizzing across his vision. When he looked right, the world moved to the left. He felt calm here in the centre. He was a camera. His unmovable self. It had been like this always, but he had never noticed it before.

Crowley stood up and looked quizzically at Frank moving his head around. He fingered his beads. He seemed to decide that it would be okay to leave Frank on his own in the waiting area and lightly shuffled away along the corridor. The volume on the TV was turned down, and the incense wafted through the room. It tickled Frank's nose and brought him back into his body. It annoyed him. He shivered. *Why do they always do that in waiting rooms – silent TV and incense?* If it was to calm people down, it wasn't working.

I have killed Volf.

It wouldn't be long before Torus put the pieces together that Frank had tried to kill him. Torus would come for him directly. There would be no more veiled threats.

Frank leaned back and thought about Torus. *He is weird. Why does he have that skeleton down in the tunnel? I'm sure he was masturbating down there.* Frank swooned and grabbed the side of the chair to steady himself. What was he even going to tell Yo-Knee? He couldn't tell her that he tried to commit another murder. Client/amender privilege didn't go that far. What was he even doing here? The best thing to do was get away, but his body felt like lead, and it wouldn't move. The sweet-smelling incense seemed to get more acrid.

'Hi, Frank.' He spun around. It was Duggy Harding, looking nonchalant, smoking his pipe. 'How's things? Not good by the looks of it. Anything I can do to help?'

What is he doing here?

Frank squinted into Harding's face. It was pretty blank as usual – you couldn't read Harding.

'Are you following me? You can't do that.'

'Just trying to find out the truth about that explosion. So, it was you and Torus in the control room at the time? You said earlier that it was Torus in there. Where were you?'

Oh God, thought Frank, *just what I need*. They were way past this. So far past the explosion, past the event that started it all. Frank could barely remember it all now. Was that really what had unravelled his life? It felt like he and Torus had always been in this struggle.

Whatever the truth, he didn't want to talk about it with Duggy Harding. He looked down at his hands in his lap. 'You can't be here. I'm waiting to see my amender.'

'So she's a real shrink, huh? How long have you been seeing a shrink, Frank? Something happen?'

Frank looked up to see Harding had moved over to the far wall and was peering at the graduation photo of Dr Yo-Knee Thompson with his hands clasped behind his back.

'I think you should leave.'

Harding looked at his watch, then up at the TV. 'Have a look.' He walked over to turn up the volume on the TV, which began to play the intro to the news.

Frank couldn't believe how brazen he was and hoped Crowley would come back and tell Duggy Harding to leave. He couldn't be hanging around here doing what he pleased. This was supposed to be a safe place.

Then the voice on the television permeated his consciousness.

Tunnel workers under Hyde Park had a

*gristly surprise this morning when they discovered
a human skeleton. Forensic investigators are trying
to determine how old the skeleton is. The tunnel
was originally built a century ago, so the skeleton
could be very old.*

Frank's cheeks went cold, and he looked at Harding. Is that why he was back? But that didn't have anything to do with the explosion.

'I happen to know' — Harding tapped the side of his nose with his pipe — 'that the skeleton is modern. And that it was placed carefully against the wall to look like an altar. There are some very sick human beings around.'

Frank recalled what he'd seen down in the tunnel. Was it true? Was that skeleton real? Torus was masturbating in front of a real skeleton? Who was it? What was going on? And Torus had caught Frank inside the tunnel. Torus had two reasons to kill him now. Frank looked at Duggy Harding.

'You were in Hyde Park that day, Frank. I don't think you've got anything to do with this, of course, but you might have seen something.'

'I was at the war memorial,' Frank blurted out.

Harding tweaked his head. 'Yes … and?' Harding waited.

Frank had the feeling of slipping on wet ice. He'd better shut up.

'Okay, Frank, if that's all you've got to say. But if you ever want to talk, get in touch.'

What does Harding know?

Harding walked up and squinted again at Yo-Knee's certificate on the wall next to her picture. 'This diploma says she's a tantriki, Frank, devoted to goddess worship and divine female energy. She looks cute.' Harding nodded and walked towards the door. 'Have a nice time with the shrink.'

~

Frank's mind was spinning. So it was a real skeleton. What in the world was Torus capable of? There was nothing to do except get away somewhere. He would have to leave his family, but they would be better off without him. He jumped up out of the chair, ready to run. But the door to Yo-Knee's office opened. Maybe she could tell him what to do. But what if that put her in danger? Oh God, he didn't know what to do!

Yo-Knee had a puzzled look for the smallest second. She wore a bright yellow dress with dark brown trim. She was immaculate as usual and smiled her bright southern smile through her never-changing red lipstick. There were some crinkles around her eyes that Frank hadn't noticed before. Looking at her was calming.

'Hi, Frank,' she said. 'How y'all doin'?'

He managed to nod, though he wasn't sure what he was nodding for. Should he leave?

She assessed his mood and, with a smile, beckoned him into her office. He felt hypnotised, slowly got up and trailed her into the consulting room. He sat on the squeaky, sticky couch, and she hoisted up her little frame onto a chair. Her legs dangled towards the ground and swung like a child's. Frank's throat was dry. The incense was in here too.

'How've you been, Frank?'

This was what made Yo-Knee so intoxicating; she had the ability to somehow crowbar your deepest secrets out of you. One part of Frank's mind was telling him to run, to get Marta and the kids and disappear. The other part was telling him to leave Marta and the kids and disappear himself. Kill Torus, don't kill Torus. There were so many voices in his head, he didn't know who to listen to. He gripped the sides of the couch as if he needed to anchor himself down to stop from running from the room.

She looked down at his white knuckles, then back at his face. 'What's on your mind?'

Frank sighed. He was beginning to figure out how Yo-Knee could put you at ease. She would move towards you, watch carefully, move back when she had to, get through your defences. She was dancing with you. Dancing with your mind, following you, flowing around. Frank felt a ripple of gratitude in his chest. It was beginning, the seduction of his mind again. His hands loosened their grip on the couch.

As if taking that as her cue, Yo-Knee launched right in. 'Come on, Frank, are you going to the authorities about the explosion or not? There are obviously rogue elements in Border Force.'

Frank surprised himself by not seeming to mind her bluntness. He was in her presence, so everything was okay. He had already known that this was going to be her first question, and it was odd that Duggy Harding had been here talking about it at the same time. Was this a sign Frank shouldn't kill Torus, that he should follow the channels of the law?

'Do you think I should?'

She rolled her eyes. 'You know better than that, darlin'. What do *you* think you should do?'

He nodded. As soon as he'd asked the question, he knew what she would say. They understood each other so well. Was she like this with everyone? Surely not. He began to imagine what it would be like to be with someone like Yo-Knee. Would she be the same outside of this office? Not that it was worth thinking about, because he'd probably end up in jail.

And then there was Marta. But how could he live without her? Maybe Marta wouldn't mind?

Then he remembered Marta had gone anyway – taken the kids. He would be in prison and without his family. Would Yo-Knee care? Would she wait for him?

I'm sure she would; look at that dress.

'Yes, I'll go to the police.'

The words were out of his mouth before he could stop them. What an amender! She was marvellous – and that dress. And her accent. And that red lipstick. And her stature. She was a dwarf, but he hardly noticed it. Going to the police would be okay. After all, he was following orders. It would be okay, it would all be okay.

An image of Torus choking Volf suddenly came into his mind, then of Torus masturbating in front of the skeleton. His mind recoiled into a tight ball. Don't think about that. Think about Yo-Knee.

Frank was still seated. Yo-Knee pushed herself off the chair and stood in front of him, their heads at the same level. She reached her arm out. 'Can I touch you?' her bright, painted lips asked.

He tilted his head forwards and nodded.

She lightly touched his shoulder. 'When you're ready, honey. Talk when you're ready.' She pulled back and sat back on her chair. Frank licked the dryness off his lips. Where to start?

'He killed the dog. No, I killed the dog. If he'd died instead, Volf would still be alive.'

'Take it easy, hon. What happened?'

Frank's mind flashed back to Torus attacking him in the tunnel. He recalled Torus's erection against his stomach. He could feel it now as he looked at Yo-Knee. Frank jumped up from the couch. He towered over her. How to make her understand?

'He was always choking the dog, like this.' His outstretched hands approached Yo-Knee. He saw a flicker of fear in her eyes, but it was quickly replaced by his imagination of Torus's erection pumping against him.

Torus. He had to be stopped.

He grabbed Yo-Knee around the throat, and she squeaked a little, and then there was a gurgle. The sound threw him immediately back into the consulting room. *What was he doing?*

He sprang back from her, saw her crumpled clothes, and slumped back on the couch, sobbing. He was a savage. No better than Torus. A fiend. Is that why Torus had chosen him to stay in the control room, because he saw that Frank would be capable of monstrosities?

Yo-Knee stretched her neck and rubbed it. Frank saw the hurt and fear in her eyes. He had damaged her. He held his hand out in a half-attempted apology, but it was useless. She was going to call the cops. She had every right.

Instead, she looked him in the eyes and, with the barest shake to her self-control, said, 'We made some progress today, darlin'. We have to tame that energy of yours. I've got an idea. A ritual of atonement.'

Frank had no idea what she meant, but it didn't sound like she was calling the cops, and for that, he was grateful. His head was fuzzy. His thoughts went back to his previous comfortable life in the leafy suburb of Woollahra. What had happened? He had blown up and killed innocent people, seen his superior officer in some strange satanic ritual, been threatened by him, killed Volf, the dog he loved, and almost strangled his amender. But worst of all, he had frightened the living daylights out of his family by his bouts of public madness. They didn't deserve this. He needed things to go back to normal. He would do anything to figure out a way how to leave it all behind. Even go with this ritual of atonement.

CHAPTER 36

Yo-Knee kept close to Frank as she led him down the steps to the abandoned crypt of Saint Mary's. After the debacle of George Pell, the catholic church had split, and a furious fight for the church's assets was underway. Saint Mary's was boarded up, empty.

Frank felt frigid. *What are we doing here?*

Yo-Knee spoke in a whisper as they descended the steps into the gloomy bowels of the church. 'Crowley and I broke in a few months ago, and we do our rituals here. It's the perfect place.'

Frank followed like a lamb.

'First, we're going to take some psychedelic mushrooms.'

Frank barely registered what she'd said.

'It's a very important part of the *Ritual of Atonement.*' She positioned a cup containing ink black fluid on a small candle-lit table with a dazzling green cloth flecked with brilliant scarlet trim. 'Green is the colour of atonement, of reconciliation, and red symbolises the living organism. We are going to connect your daily life back to the cosmic oneness – the thing that you really are at the most basic level, which is everything there is, the whole universe. After that, you will feel more confirmed about the decisions you have to make and the actions you have to take, because you will see that you have no free will, only the feeling of free will. And we must follow our feelings. They are older than our thinking.'

Frank gazed at the table, then at Yo-Knee, then at the sombre walls of the crypt. He felt a bit disturbed. What was going to happen? Did she say something about mushrooms? He'd heard of druggy mushrooms. Weren't they illegal? He sighed. He'd broken enough laws as it was; one more wouldn't hurt. Yo-Knee handed him a bundle of golden cloth.

'Wear this gown. You can change over there.' In a daze, Frank obeyed. He moved to a curtained-off part of the room and got undressed. He put the gown over his head. It was the softest material he had ever felt. So soft that he shivered.

He went back out to the green table. Yo-Knee was also wearing a gown, the same golden colour. She was sitting on a small stool with a vacant stool next to her, and she motioned him to sit down. He hesitated. He looked at her mouth; she was different somehow. She had removed her lipstick, and her hair was freed from its tight top knot.

'It's okay, Frank. This is way beyond being amended.'

What could be better than being amended, having his mind freed from its torments? But he believed her, and so he sat.

They drank the black liquid from the same cup. It tasted foul. Like drinking dirt. Yo-Knee's face registered the tiniest distaste, but Frank was ready to throw up. She stroked his arm.

'The bad taste won't last long.'

But Frank was ready to gag. Yo-Knee came over to him,

and her hand hovered over his stomach. She looked at him as if asking silent permission to touch him. He nodded. She rubbed his stomach in a circular motion.

'This is known as *The Twisting of the Space*. It will calm your digestive region so you can absorb the potion.'

Frank's stomach felt soothed and comforted by the motion of her hand. He relaxed a little and closed his eyes. She reversed the direction of the circle of her palm on his stomach. The soft cloth felt like warm cotton wool against his abdomen. His insides gurgled with delight, rumbling like soft, distant thunder. His toes curled in velvet rapture. The strange drug was definitely affecting him. He wanted to open his eyes, but his mind was pulling him inwards, keeping his eyelids shut.

Yo-Knee's hands traced up to his chest and employed the same circular motions. He felt electric tingles where her hands traced across his torso.

'This is *The Enthusiasm of the Breast*. It will enhance the will to love all creatures.'

Frank felt a beautiful feeling of oceanic majesty coming out of her hands.

Yo-Knee's fingers trailed up to his throat and gently drummed a rhythmic pattern on the front of his neck. It seemed to be a language, talking clearly but incomprehensibly, communicating with someone or something far away. Frank was becoming more invigorated.

'This is called *The Dancing of The Lord of Creation*. You will be able to talk with every creature.'

Her hands were soft across his shoulders, then down his arms to his fingertips, which seemed to be pulsating with blue electricity. She held his waist for a few moments.

'Frank?' Her voice was coming from another dimension.

'Are you still here?'

He lifted his head and opened his eyes. He saw her in iridescent outline; the air around her seemed alive. Her eyes were huge crystals, glittering with knowledge. She moved her hands to hold his cheeks and kissed him full on the lips. They remained locked together for an eternity, fused in rapture. His body arched back, and he felt his erection against her. She pulled away from his lips and lay him down on the cold crypt ground, the roughness scraping and tingling at him.

'The next part is *The Taming of the Lingam*. The emotional connection with yourself will be inflated beyond what you have ever experienced.' She pulled up his gown and cupped his balls, shooting a thousand pleasures up through his body, his nipples stinging into stiffness. She squeezed his dick. His tight shoulders, without his will, decided to rest flat on the floor. When he closed his eyes, the world was a thousand shades of lightning.

He heard her footsteps move towards his head. She put her fingers on his eyelids and opened them. She had removed her gown, and her legs were straddled between his face. He smelt her cunt.

'Now we have the final piece of the ritual, dearest Frank – *The Revelation of the Yoni.*' She held her fingers to herself and opened her labia to reveal her glistening clitoris. Frank immediately felt the beginnings of ejaculation. 'No!' she yelled and reached over to put a finger on the tip of his penis. He subsided, and tears welled in his eyes. They felt like molten steel on his cheeks.

He screamed.

His whole head disappeared in the scream. He covered his ears so he couldn't hear his own screaming. He screamed and writhed among the dirt, and still the screaming wouldn't stop. Then he left his body.

He was at the centre of a raging tornado. Chaos was all around him, but he was cool and fixed and calm. In slow motion, he saw his own body writhing on the ground, but he wasn't occupying it. Yo-Knee's legs straddled his face, and her finger pressed against the tip of his penis. He wasn't inside his body. He saw himself screaming, but he couldn't hear a sound.

Why couldn't he hear anything, and why was everything in slow motion? The whole scene was barely moving, and he was planted there inside it all but not belonging to it. He wasn't part of it. The goings on had nothing to do with him. It wasn't him.

Who was he, then? If he wasn't this, who was he? Torus grabbed at Frank, shouting, '*I'll get you. I'll get you,*' but Frank didn't care. He couldn't care. He couldn't care less.

A rumbling sensation of liquid light formed around his anus. With a slight amusement, he watched it grow and vibrate in the most astonishing colours. Still he was screaming. The volcanic lava in his arse exploded up into his lingam, and the whole universe became purple and black. The liquid light pushed and pushed and pulsed and flowed, filling everywhere with a tremendous burst of pressure. It ruptured through into his stomach, and a big, yellow vomit of black, bitter liquid lurched out of his still-screaming mouth.

The fire filled up his stomach and spread like living lightning across his abdomen. It rested there a while, waiting. Still he was not part of it all. Where was he? What was he? The pressure built, and the liquid fire filled up all crevices. The whole of the bottom half of this body, which was not his, was filled and pulsating with liquid fire, daffodil yellow, tangerine, blood red, magenta, azure, sapphire, shamrock and pear. Blue, black, yellow, indigo fire forcing its way upward through his spine. His chest suddenly exploded in flames as the lungs caved under the pressure. His heart became a spinning wheel, radiating sparks and tendrils of fire to the edges of the universe. His scream stopped, choked by the fire's passage into his throat. His breath was short, sharp gasps. His neck turned golden and black, swirling and throbbing with colour, unimaginable colour. His head was floating on a sea of fire.

It was alive, this fire, whatever it was, living, pulsing inside his body. The fire forced its way into his head. His whole face blew away with sparks, his head filled with light, liquid light, throbbing and … alive. It had taken his body, owned it and … transformed it.

His whole body was filled with it, bursting with it. The pressure built up in his head. His stomach filled with a nauseous horror as this … this thing was trying to force its way out of the top of his head. The crown of his head broke open, and the light showered forth. His head split apart, and the fire pulsed away, shimmering into infinity. It flew away to the farthest reaches, and in an instant had circled the universe and come back and connected to his arse again. His body was part of the fluorescent pulsing cosmos.

He felt … he felt … amused.

Then it was gone. He entered his body, and he lay still on the ground under Yo-Knee's legs, his throat hoarse.

Oh my god, I've been sick.

Yo-Knee stepped away from him. He dragged himself to his feet. What the fuck was going on? He sat dazed against the wall of the crypt. Yo-Knee quickly put her gown back on.

'Welcome back, Frank. You're home.'

CHAPTER 37

Frank loaded the three chambers of his little Scarlatti X3 with its point-two-two slugs and aimed it at the bottle with the straw sticking out placed at the far end of his shed. The first bullet snapped off the straw. His aim was good today. Everything was good today.

It had been several days since the *Ritual of Atonement* with Yo-Knee. The sun was setting through the light evening rain. In the silence of the surrounding bushland, he heard the stealthy approach of a vehicle. He came back into the house and spied the black van parked outside, and his temples cut like a knife. He flashed back to his father torturing him on that fishing trip. He heard his father's voice, laughing, *kill someone, kill something, anything.*

A scarlet mist descended across his eyes. He was still holding the pistol, stopped for a moment and stuffed it inside his sock, then grabbed Mercury's baseball bat near the front door and ran outside.

He hurled a wild swing at the windscreen of the van, but

the bat bounced off the reinforced glass. Carnley raced out of the van, but Frank caught him a lucky blow to the side of the head. He went down, grabbing his face. Torus jumped out, and Frank swung a mighty blow to him as well, also smashing his ear. Frank went for the van again, shattered a headlight, and at the same time cursed himself for being such an idiot. His arms were pinned behind him, and a mighty punch to the stomach winded him. He crumpled to the ground and felt a kick to the head. The world spun around, and he was bundled into the back of the van, crumpled on the floor.

He had been planning his next move on Torus, but Torus had come to him instead, and Frank had blindly provoked him. At least his family seemed to be out of trouble now.

The van screeched off with a gravel roar, and Frank rolled around inside. His stomach lurched, and he gasped for air. His head throbbed, and he put his hand to his temple. It was sticky. He lay down his head on the crumpled, lumpy rug on the floor of the van.

Where are they taking me? What is Torus up to? Torus had nothing to lose now by keeping secrets. He must know that the game was up. Was he going to kill Frank and put him in the tunnel with his other trophies? The van lurched around a corner, and Frank rolled across the floor, bumping against a soft, furry lump. His hand clutched a handful of fur. Fur? He recoiled and jumped back against the van wall. He saw the unmistakable open jaws of Volf, dead on the floor.

Frank panted and strained to get away from the corpse. He saw Torus's smirk looking back at him through the window from the front seat. Volf seemed to be alive as the van rolled around the corners. Frank imagined Volf's avenging teeth clamping onto his face and shaking the life out of him. The van lurched, and the corpse slid across the floor. Frank clambered to the other side. He breathed heavily, and his eyes got more used to the dark.

There was a small cubic transparent glass container near the front containing the unmistakable form of a curled-up, dormant funnelback. Frank did a gasp of breath as he watched Torus open a small door at the top of the glass container and poured a vial of liquid into the spider's glass cage. Torus snapped the trapdoor shut as the funnelback sprang into life, racing around its glass cage. Torus watched to make sure that Frank was looking. He had his hand on a little catch that would open the glass door and release the funnelback into the back of the van. Torus waited. He had a strange, manic look on his face. Hurt and revenge around his eyes and loathing saliva flecked his mouth. He brought his hand closer to the catch to watch Frank's reaction.

The funnelback clambered around its glass cage, this way, that way, ready to bite. It had been bred for a fight to the death, bred to kill. Frank remembered the look of terror on Webber's face when he came running out of the laboratory. No one knew what the spider was capable of more than Webber. The spider seemed to see Frank and know that he was its target. Torus had his hand on the catch. He was nicely protected in the front of the van, where he would have a ringside seat of Frank's death, revenge for humiliating him and killing Volf. Frank scrambled around and dragged Volf's carcass across the van floor and jammed it up against the glass cage. Torus laughed at this pathetic attempt of protection. Frank saw the pleasure in Torus's eyes.

Frank drifted in and out of consciousness for what seemed like hours. The van pulled up, and all was quiet. He heard the rattle of the back door being opened. They were at Hyde Park. It was dark and raining.

'That was just for fun,' growled Torus. 'Now the real entertainment starts.'

'Why are you doing this? I wasn't going to say anything.' Torus seemed genuinely puzzled, but only for a moment. Frank's desperate attempt at lying didn't fool Torus for long, and Torus's eyes narrowed into a cold squint.

'You disturbed me!' he shouted. 'Disturbed my offering! Now, you're sacrificed!'

They dragged Frank out of the van onto the street and across into the grass. He felt agonising kicks to his stomach and face. He was almost unconscious when the giant dog landed on top of him. He couldn't move, and he drifted into sweet oblivion for a moment till he felt a violent pain in his rib. Surely, it was cracked. He heard metallic sounds and clicks around him. Torus approached with a huge hunting knife and shook it in front of Frank's face. Frank was too tired to even feel fear. Torus grabbed Frank's hand and placed the knife in it. Frank gripped the knife instinctively. Then he heard the sound of the van screeching off at speed.

He was taking in short, sharp breaths, not enough air to keep him alive for long. The dead weight of the enormous dog pressed on his broken rib. The words of Kain Webber came back to him. *We'll build a dog as big as a pony. It'll be able to kill by just leaning on things.* His breath started to come a little easier. He still couldn't move from under the dog, but at least his arms were free. He thought of the mocking face of Torus in the van. He struggled and pushed at the dog. He kept the hated face of Torus in front of his mind to give him strength, and he heaved away at the dog. At last, it began to move. It slumped to the side, and the dog's giant head slid off him and slumped to the ground. Immediately, Frank's neck jerked sideways, and the serrated knife fell from his grasp.

There was a metal strap around his neck with a short chain to another metal strap around the dog's head. He was out from under the dog, but they were chained together by the neck.

He lay on his back with his arms along the ground. He picked up the knife and tried to cut through the metal, but it was hopeless. Frank realised what Torus was playing at. What to do? Wait for help to come in the morning and free him? He could be dead by then. He picked up the knife and held it against the body of Volf. He cut some fur. The knife was sharp. He closed his eyes and chanted in a groan, '*Oh-Oh-Oh*', as he held the dog's snout and cut into the neck. Revulsion paused him, but he kept chanting his frightening '*Oh-Oh-Oh*' with greater ferocity. The blood made him stop, the dog's head half severed. He must wait till the morning, and someone would come. The dog's body weighed heavier on his ribs, and he could hardly breathe. He would be dead soon. He grabbed at the knife and sawed away again. He reached the bone. His arm ached. Then through the bone and easier on the other side. He sawed and sawed, all the while chanting his pathetic '*Oh-Oh-Oh*' until the job was done and the head was severed. A wave of nausea went through him as the head detached from the carcass and the metal clasp fell to the ground.

CHAPTER 38

He lurched halfway to his feet. The dawn rain sprinkled into the pool of Volf's blood. He was exhausted and collapsed onto the ground again, heaving in front of the gently tinkling waters of the Archibald Fountain. He looked up at the statues and saw the giant sword held by Theseus, ready to slay the most muscular male body he had ever seen, bull-headed and bigger than life.

Ancient Theseus clutched the horn of the Minotaur, his sword ready to kill the bull-headed monster. The fountain's waters glistened off the sensuous bronze in the dim light. Frank remembered the myth of how Theseus descended into the labyrinth to slay the Minotaur. It lived off the blood of youth. Frank must kill Torus. He felt a wave of weakness go through him, and he collapsed to the ground into his world of pain.

He looked up at the outstretched arm of Apollo bestowing light on the world. Frank struggled up to his full height, the shackle round his neck like a hellish instrument of torture.

He drank in the noble statue. He felt the strength of Theseus filling him with courage. He would pick up that sword. He looked at the harmonious Diana and Pan playing the joyful pipes of youth. He raised his body up to copy the hero's pose, ready to bring down the sword and slay the Minotaur. He would slay Torus. He felt down into his sock. The Scarlatti was still there. Two bullets left. And now he also had a knife.

Frank shambled his way to the other end of the park, to where he had first seen Torus disappear underneath the memorial. The entrance to the underground tunnels had police crime-scene tape stretched across it. There was a broken padlock, and the door was ajar. Frank listened. He heard nothing. He edged into the tunnel. He grasped the knife. The bloodied serrations glistened from its recent obscene work. He waited till his eyes adjusted to the gloom and crept further into the tunnel. Each crunching step was an eternity.

Frank turned a corner, and the huge statue that he'd seen before loomed above him. He took a closer look this time. It was a naked woman, arms stretched across a sword in a Christ-like pose. At her feet was the devastation of war: dead soldiers, broken equipment. It was in the same 1930s brutalist style as the rest of the statues on the memorial outside.

He waited, his breath sounding like thunder. There was a dim glow further down the tunnel. He crept forward, knife shaking. He turned a corner, and he saw the shrine. The skeleton had gone. The police must have taken it, but the rest of the shrine was still there. A candle was burning. Torus must be nearby.

Cold hands gripped his heart, and his chest seized up in a spasm. How in the world could he imagine killing Torus? It was insane. He turned and bolted for the exit.

He reached the entrance and scrambled out into the dawn

light. It seemed totally normal out here. Had he imagined that Torus was chasing him out of his own fear? He relaxed, panting, and looked at the steps to the war memorial. The early sun shone off the polished walls. The tranquil Pool of Remembrance shivered as a morning zephyr coursed across the park. Frank's hairs on his arms stood on end.

A giant roar came out of the tunnel, and the lumbering form of Torus materialised, blinking into the sunlight, arms outstretched, lurching forwards with bulging eyes, nostrils flaring and imagining he already had Frank in his clutches. Frank jumped out of his skin, then stood frozen to the spot. Torus lurched at him, and Frank slashed with the knife and cut Torus across the face. A supernatural howl emerged from Torus's chest, and he backhanded the knife out of Frank's grasp. It fell into the Pool of Remembrance.

Ripples crisscrossed the surface and destroyed the tranquillity. Frank bolted across the inch-deep pool. There was nowhere to run except up the steps into the monolith. He heard the panting and rasping breath of Torus behind him. Frank reached the top step. His eyes darted about. The shrine of the Eternal Flame burned in the corner. The walls reverberated with the echoes of his footsteps and breathing. *No way out.* He looked for a place to hide, and then realised that this place, right here, was where he would take his last breath, the life choked out of him by Torus's monstrous grip.

Torus was halfway up the steps. Frank stumbled on the top step and sprawled across the floor. He heard a clattering sound as his Scarlatti X3 skidded across the floor, dislodged from his sock. He snatched at it greedily, scrambled to his feet and crouched. He looked down over the balustrade and saw the statue of the sacrificial soldier, spreadeagled in a crucified pose on a shield and sword twenty feet below. A very lifelike sword. The soldier was naked and vulnerable. Frank gazed at it and then felt the sudden clutch of Torus's hands on his throat. Frank jerked and dislodged Torus's unprepared grip.

Behind him was the tiny alcove housing the Eternal Flame, and he darted towards it. *Trapped.* Frank's world turned into slow motion. He saw the little gas jets pushing out the flame with barely a flicker, barely a hiss, the rock wall behind it. He turned to face Torus, and his world spun around, and the walls shot past his vision.

His arm lifted like molasses, and the gun pointed at the chest of Torus. Frank's extended arm seemed to be sprouting out of a nothingness at his centre.

He aimed and fired.

At last!

The world went back to normal speed, and a little rip appeared in the centre of Torus's chest.

The sound of the shot from the Scarlatti reverberated wildly around the sacred chamber like a baleful sacrilege. Torus stopped and stumbled, wide-eyed, more in disbelief and rage than in pain.

How was that possible? The bullet had almost no effect. Torus smirked and snarled. Frank cursed himself for being so impulsive. He mustn't have hit any crucial organs or arteries. Only one bullet left. He ducked into the shelter of the alcove where the flame burned. He would need to take precise aim with his last bullet. He would need to let Torus get very close, so close that Frank might get choked. His neck throbbed and twitched at the thought.

He rested one hand on the stone table behind his back to keep himself steady, braced against the back wall. He lifted his knee up and rested his gun hand there. He was a good shot when he was relaxed. He aimed the gun at Torus's face and waited.

Torus stopped. Frank's arm was steady and secure. His heart lifted. It would be as easy as shooting in his back yard. Silence descended. He saw Torus's heaving chest but heard no sound. He saw a bird squawking past the entrance against the sky, but he heard no sound. The gun was aimed directly at the left eye of Torus. Frank had no idea what he would see after he shot. He had only ever shot at bottles and targets. The bottles shattered like crazy. Would there be a neat hole where his eye had been? Would his head shatter in blood and gore? They say there's not a lot of blood in the brain. Maybe there would be no blood at all.

What if he missed? If he missed, he was dead. Frank licked his lips. Torus stretched his grasp out towards Frank, wide-open and huge, ready to choke. There was the slightest quiver in the arm. *Another inch, and I'll shoot. C'mon a couple more centimetres.*

Frank's back was hard pressed against the wall, his left hand steadying himself on the stone bench. He thought of Thomas Traherne, the cat, and how he had been tempted to kill it for practice. He had never killed anything. Only the atrocity had changed that. No matter what, he could never kill in cold blood. And yet, here was Torus, only seconds away from strangling him.

Torus's eye came into focus. It had changed. It wasn't startled about the gun anymore. The eye knew. The eye was reading Frank's mind. Frank would not shoot, could not shoot. Torus grinned; his hand came closer and touched Frank's throat. A shiver went down Frank's arm holding the gun. Frank's view along the top of the gun barrel remained steady. His arm shivered. The image of Torus's eye began to shake a little, then more. His arm seemed rock steady, but the world at the end of the gun barrel flailed about crazily. He felt Torus's fingers squeeze his throat, right next to the shackle where he had been chained to Volf.

A clear part of Frank's mind thought, he's done this before. He knows exactly where to press. His head stopped throbbing. His arm felt monstrously heavy. His elbow folded up, and the gun pointed uselessly at the ceiling. The sound of Torus's rasping breath came back. The world darkened.

Frank dimly noticed that Torus's nose twitched. Then again. He felt Torus's iron grip loosen slightly. Torus was becoming distracted by something and looked down towards Frank's left hand sitting on the bench. Torus's eyes widened and jerked his hand away from Frank's throat.

Frank smelt smoke and the whiff of barbequed veal. A searing pain shot from his left hand, and he snatched it out of the Flame of Remembrance. His coat sleeve was on fire and the flames licked around his blackened hand. A small piece of melted flesh peeled off his left hand and fell to the floor. He stared at it in shock as if it was someone else's hand. The two men stared at Frank's burning hand as more pieces of peeling skin fell to the floor.

Frank screamed, the world stopped, and the gun exploded inside the small alcove. Frank's world came alive again with the reverberations of the bullet ricocheting around the marble roof, splintering deadly fragments in all directions. Frank felt dust particles in his eyes and saw in slow motion a large piece of marble tumble over and over and hit Torus straight on the top of his head. He was out cold, and his grip on Frank's throat loosened. Torus's face fell squarely into the still burning gas flame.

This was his chance. Frank rushed back to hold his face to the flame. Torus struggled, but Frank clambered up and stood on Torus's head, pushing him down, forcing Torus's face into the flame.

Die, you bastard, die!

Torus raged and howled, but Frank forced his face down harder. He was adamantine, and all his bottled-up rage joined in the force of keeping Torus's face on the flame. Frank was Theseus slaying the Minotaur. He was absorbing courage from Yo-Knee and the *Ritual of Atonement*. He heard the flesh bubbling and splattering and saw Torus's injured ear burning to a sizzle. Still, he pushed the face into the flame.

Torus was howling now and, with a mighty lurch, freed himself from Frank's grip. His face was a mask of blackened, burning flesh, but he would not stop. He barrelled ahead, had no bearings and so crashed into the wall. He spun around madly, not giving up, and Frank saw his eye sockets were bleeding and burnt, fused together to make him completely blind.

Torus lurched forward, arms flailing. Frank stared mutely, and Torus's thrashing hand banged into Frank's cheek. Torus clutched and grabbed Frank by the throat. He got his other hand round his throat and shook manically, howling like a wild animal, his blinded face dripping scorched flesh.

How can you still be alive?

Torus was a possessed demon up from the bowels of hell. Frank danced like a puppet at the end of Torus's powerful arms, his feet slipping on the burnt flesh on the floor. Frank's arm caught the balustrade, and he hung on. The demon from hell lost its balance, slipped and crashed to the floor, dragging Frank down. The fall dislodged its grip. Torus's head banged onto the floor, and the demonic energy possessing him plunged out like a deflating balloon. Torus staggered to his feet, howling in defeated rage. Frank backed off along the floor as Torus swayed about waving his arms, trying to find Frank.

But the monster was done. The blood streamed from its eyes. Frank crawled to the other side of the chamber, struggled to keep his breath quiet. Torus righted himself with one great effort and lurched towards where he thought Frank was. But it was the wrong direction. He hit the balustrade, toppled there for a second, and went straight over the edge.

He was gone. Frank stared in disbelief at the place where Torus had been, no longer there. All danger gone. Frank clanked his way to where Torus had gone over. He looked over the edge, and far below was the crumpled, bloodied torso of Torus, his head severed on the way down by the sacrificial sword.

A great bilge came up from Frank's stomach, and he vomited. He hardly felt the pain in his hand, just a small throbbing. The cuff of his coat was burnt off, and he stared at it, unblinking. I wonder why it doesn't hurt? His body started to shake. A wave of gooseflesh covered him from top to bottom. The gun dropped from his right hand and slid across the floor, through the balcony rails, and landed on the floor below. Frank slowly moved towards the balcony to look down and make sure it was real. The gun had landed next to Torus's severed head. Yes, he was certainly dead.

CHAPTER 39

Dawn was breaking as he ran from the building out into the park below and collapsed on a park bench. No more Torus. Normal life would beckon. He threw his head back. He thought of home and wife and family. He felt free. He felt power. He felt like the vanquisher. The thought of the dead Torus made him smile the smile of victory.

Duggy Harding stood by the Pool of Reflection. This time, Frank wasn't even surprised to see him there. He sat down next to Frank.

'Everyone will believe you now after they know about Torus,' he said. 'You have the only story now. You could say anything you want.'

Frank rose up to his full height and felt the pride of the victor. It was a strange feeling. His chest filled with air, shoulders back, like a soldier on parade.

'You could even make things up,' Harding went on. 'No one would be able to contradict you.'

Frank looked at him. He could tell that Harding was

playing him. His chest deflated.

'Except you, of course. You would know.'

Frank felt the guilt come back to him. Should he tell the truth about his own part in the atrocity? After all, he was the one who had pressed the button. He swept the guilt away. Why should he? Border Force would keep it quiet. Again, his chest filled with the feeling of victory.

He looked at Harding, turned and walked away towards the Archibald Fountain in the distance. Harding tagged along. They sat on the water's edge under the statue of Apollo, his right arm outstretched in a gesture of protection towards lovers of Beauty and Truth.

Frank looked at the statue of Theseus about to slay the Minotaur. He looked out over the park and pointed into the distance. Again, he had the strangest pleasant feeling that his arm was sprouting out of a nothingness where his head should be. He was as headless in his mind as Volf and Torus were in their bodies.

In the distance, Frank heard the police sirens and looked back towards the memorial.

Harding said, *'The profoundest delusion is that I am over here and you are over there.'*

Frank turned to Harding, but he wasn't there. Duggy Harding had disappeared back into the mists of Frank's imagination where he had come from.

'The Crucifixion of Civilisation' was placed on its rightful plinth on 24 November 2034 to commemorate the one hundredth anniversary of the opening of the ANZAC Peace Memorial.

A NOTE FROM THE AUTHOR

If you enjoyed this book, I would be very grateful if you could write a review and publish it at your point of purchase. Your review, even a brief one, will help other readers to decide whether they'll enjoy my work.

If you want to be notified of new releases from myself and other Alkira Publishing authors, please sign up to the Alkira Publishing email list. In return you'll get a free ebook of short stories and book excerpts by Alkira Publishing authors. You'll find the sign-up button on the right-hand side under the photo at www.alkirapublishing.com. Of course, your information will never be shared, and the publisher won't inundate you with emails, just let you know of new releases.

ACKNOWLEDGEMENTS

Thanks to The Writers' Studio in Bronte:

Roland Fishman
Kathleen Allen
Kelly Rigby

Also the readers who nudged me closer to the ideal:
Dave Morgan
Carol Staples
Radley Cramer
Kaye Greenleaf
Tamar Goldstein
Staphanie Smith
Phillip Parker
Louise Branson
Rachel Devlin
Danielle Solof